The Accusation

The Accusation
By Curt Finch

To Scott and Vickie

Curt Finch

The Accusation

Copyright © 2010 by Curt Finch

This is a work of fiction. Names, characters, places and incidents are the products of the author's imagination or are used fictitiously.

Any resemblance to actual events, locales, or persons, living or dead, is purely coincidental.

ISBN: 978-0-615-39574-6

Acknowledgments

A number of people were of tremendous help in getting this novel published. I thank my friends and co-workers who read early drafts and offered helpful feedback. I appreciate the work of Anthony Policastro who edited a substantial portion of the work, the assistance of Henry Hutton in his facilitating the publishing process, and also Elmore Hammes for print and cover setup. My family was very supportive including my daughter, Kelley, and granddaughter, Sierra, who both offered creative suggestions.

My wife, Debbie, deserves a special acknowledgement as she served as both my primary editor and the source of many of the ideas that became key elements in the story.

CHAPTER ONE

FRIDAY MORNING

The white piece of paper rests on the floor of my office as I enter, like a hotel bill slid under the door after a night's stay. Unfolding the page, I open a Pandora's Box of evil accusations aimed at me which fly straight into my unsuspecting mind like a guided projectile. The letter is not signed:

Reverend,

How can you stand before the church and pretend that you are a man of God? I know better. Your heart is perverse and arrogant. You are an abuser of children who has committed unspeakable and obscene sins. You think that no one will come forward to tell of what you have done. You are wrong; I will testify that you have satisfied your desires of the flesh with the young and innocent. You cannot hide your guilt forever as God will judge you for your transgressions. I remind you of what the Psalmist wrote, 'We have sinned with our fathers; we have committed iniquity; and we have behaved wickedly.' Your hands have fouled the purity of a child who will forever suffer from your evil touch. You will be cast into the unquenchable fire of hell. I give you until next Wednesday to resign as pastor of this church. If you want to avoid the full wrath of God's justice you will tender your resignation at the business conference. If you fail to do so you will face the consequences of your sinful actions, and the sordid details of your behavior will become public. I will be in worship on Sunday anticipating your admission of guilt. I pray God will have pity on you if you continue to pretend that you are a man called by Him to minister. I despise your pretense and your duplicity.

The words are neatly penned, and the letters are distinct as if each one has been painstakingly formed to add to the effect of the harsh judgment. There's a flow to the phrasing as though it were some eloquent sermon presented by one of those orators of past days who majored on the hellfire and brimstone style of preaching. This writer has been schooled in semantics and has honed the art of dissecting a prey with well-chosen words. I place the dreadful letter on my desk and wonder how so much anger could emanate from one single page.

As I stare at the white bond paper my questions about this person's motivations give way to a flow of puzzling emotions. My concern over their anger is transformed into a concern for my defense, an uneasiness over my vulnerability. These feelings are replaced by a flood of desire to arm myself with a psychological arsenal of weapons to parry any further attacks. A third mutation of my state of mind is to a sense of the unfairness of it all, how I should not be forced to expend any energy on a response to such a ridiculous array of words that have no substantive basis. Each of these internal reactions fights for attention as my mind seeks to organize a reasonable retort. I'm upset, hurt, but more intent on not letting one page of cruel words force me into a reply out of proportion to the provocation.

I've been the object of negative criticism before in my years as a minister, but never have I been the recipient of a malicious attack such as this. These words are so heinous that they far outweigh any criticisms of me in the past. There was the time in my previous church, I painfully remember, when I made a Solomonic decision which caused people on both sides of an issue to be angry at me.

The issue was whether or not the curtain over the baptistry window should be left open or closed when we were not performing a baptism. The opening was located behind the choir and the pulpit area, elevated as to afford a clear view for all who sat in the sanctuary. A painting covered the back wall of the opening over the pool with a bucolic scene of a tree lined river. The vegetation in the painting was not Middle Eastern in appearance, but looked more like a setting along the banks of a river in Virginia, not unlike ones near the church. The family of the individual who donated the curtain wanted it to remain closed, so the lovely red velvet drape would be the focus. The relatives of the one who painted the oak and pine tree lined Jordan wanted the curtain always opened. I ruled that it would be open half the time. Neither side was happy; in this, my first pastorate, I learned that pastors do not rule.

What a difference that rural church was from this congregation. I came here to First Baptist thankful that family squabbles within the fellowship would not be a major concern. Each church has its special challenges, but some are by nature more willing to let a pastor lead with his or her own style. In my five years here this letter is my first hint at any serious dissatisfaction with my service as senior minister. But, this is not about my leadership style or any decisions I've made. This is about character. Whoever printed these harsh words has chosen to attack me for some misplaced reason. I must find out who wrote this letter, who seeks to force me from my ministry here.

My immediate concern is how did this person get into the building to deliver this hate mail? It's seven-thirty, and I'm responsible this morning for opening up the buildings for today's activities. I volunteered to take on the task yesterday after the custodian told me he had a dental appointment this morning. This will give me a chance to see if any doors were left unlocked last night or if my accuser had a key to get in. Most of those who take turns securing the buildings after functions or opening before them choose to walk around the exterior of the church instead of traversing the maze of interior hallways. I decide to take this course now before anyone else arrives. This is a large church complex, and there are many doors.

I exit the education building by the side foyer where I entered and first proceed down the walk leading to the front of the sanctuary. The grass on the front lawn has been cut early this morning, and the tracks of the lawnmower are still evident on the moist surface. The smell of the freshly trimmed turf arouses my senses and provokes pleasant emotions, a welcome and uplifting aroma. The early morning Virginia air is beginning to heat up as the summer day promises to be humid and sticky.

Each of the six paneled front doors to the sanctuary is painted in a subdued red to match the Williamsburg architecture of the brick building. I pull on each latch and find them all to be locked tight before I put my key in to release the mechanisms. The front of the sanctuary is only about fifty feet from Church Street, named so because four churches stand within close proximity to each other. In my opinion our sanctuary is the most attractive of the ones on the street. The Methodist, Presbyterian, and Episcopal churches each have their own distinctive styles. I love the front entrance to our church with its wide columned porch and broad vestibule. The colonial architecture provides an elegant beauty to this award winning design. The sanctuary inside is octagonal with lovely stained glass windows on the sides and a soaring ceiling that reaches up to the inside of the cupola. One of the windows depicts Jesus holding a lamb in his arms. This hundred and twenty year old window was saved from the old sanctuary and is, I'm told, quite valuable. From inside the light penetrating this vitreous portrayal of the parable of the lost sheep is stunning when the sun hits it at a certain angle. From the outside this morning the stained glass is opaque, not unlike the murky message that greeted me just a few minutes ago.

There's one other set of doors facing the street which I find locked as well. The far side of the church borders an old frame house which our congregation has tried unsuccessfully to buy for years. This sounds crass, but we are waiting for the Episcopalian octogenarian who lives there to pass away, hoping her heirs will want to part with the property. No one is actually praying for her demise, but when her time comes it would be helpful if our congregation could buy the place. The passage between the house and the side of our oldest part of the church structure is only thirty feet wide. The grass is still slippery in this shaded area from the morning dew. The one door on this side is never used, but I pull on it, find it locked, and leave it that way.

Down a slope I pass by the beginning of a bank covered by kudzu. The green vines have overtaken the neighbor yard with tentacles that explore every avenue for growth. Mrs. Thompson, who owns the property, refuses to clear the lot of the expanding leguminous invader. This is another reason why it would be helpful for First Baptist to own the land; the kudzu would give way to a new church playground.

The furnace room door is located on this corner of our physical plant, and I check this door even though one cannot actually enter the rest of the complex from here. A few months ago, in the winter, we found that a homeless drifter had broken in through a window in this isolated area and slept for a few nights in the warmth. Someone saw him leave one morning and called the police. The overnight guest was questioned by the authorities, and our church helped him find appropriate temporary shelter.

There is a vestigial coal chute located behind the furnace room, still in place from the days when the black chunks were poured into the storage bin below. The empty coal storage cavern remains as a testimony to another time and ecology. This corner of the church is almost hidden from view and can give a person the creeps when visited after dark; it is not even that inviting in daylight. This is not a place where I choose to linger.

Life is full of places we would rather bypass, situations we choose to avoid, and experiences we wish were not in our path. But there are those doors we must go through, tasks that can't be evaded, and duties that can't be shirked. It is entirely possible that facing again the false accusations that await my return to the office will lead me into a labyrinth of challenges. Like the labyrinth in Greek mythology created by Daedalus, I may lose my way and stumble onto the lurking beast that waits. If only my other pastoral missions were as simple as unlocking these steel and wooden doors.

In the back of our education buildings, down a walkway from the parking lot, is an entry that opens into an area of the church which is used by a community helping agency called The Good Samaritan. There's a clothing closet as well as a food pantry in this downstairs wing. Many people in our town come here either to volunteer their time or take advantage of the services. These services include payments of utility and rent bills as well as food vouchers to be used to buy milk and bread. The churches in the area contribute resources to be used in helping those who are having financial difficulties.

This outside door isn't locked when I try it. Standing in the corridor, listening for sounds of movement, I become aware that I'm not alone in the building. The Good Samaritan is not supposed to be open this morning, yet someone is in the clothing closet about thirty feet to my right. Strangely, no light is visible through the window in the door to the large rectangular room filled with racks of used apparel.

I call out, "Hello."

For what must be thirty seconds there's no response, but the faint sound of someone moving about continues. There's only one choice for my next action; I must go in there and confront the early morning visitor. Flipping on the lights in the room, I again call out, "Who's in here?"

All sounds grow still as I move into the processing area where boxes and bags are stacked awaiting clients to secure the needed items. Then I hear someone sliding a wire hanger over a metal rod. This time I deepen my voice and loudly announce my presence again, "This is the pastor, who is here?"

From the far side of the jam packed space the movement ceases, and a male voice speaks, "It's only me."

There's no mistaking the southern drawl of Steve Ayers, the church's youth minister, who appears from between the long rows of hanging clothing. He's wearing a bathrobe as well as his oft displayed mischievous grin. "So, Ron, what do you think of my costume?"

"What're you doing in here?" I ask.

"I'm here for a wardrobe change. I needed to borrow something for my role as a biblical character today in the program. So, what do you think of my robe and sandals?"

"I think you look just like you stepped out of a two thousand year old department store," I say with a smile.

Steve offers his impish smirk again, "Amazing how little styles have changed. Why are you down here so early in the morning?"

"I'm opening the buildings for Joel."

"Playing the custodian role is a bit unusual for you," Steve says. "Do you get paid extra for this duty?"

"No, but it may be your turn next week. As you well know, sometimes we church employees have to wear many hats. Steve, have you seen anyone else in the buildings this morning?"

"No, I just came in by the back door. This is the only place I've been. Has there been an intruder?"

I'm not ready to tell him about my letter so I say, "Just thought maybe someone else came early. Was the outside door locked when you tried it?"

"Yes, so was the clothing closet. Sorry I gave you a start, Pastor. This place can be a little spooky when you're in here alone; there are so many hiding places."

Steve proceeds to gather up his borrowed clothing, and I notice he's not wearing his hearing device. Born almost deaf, he has compensated well with the assistance of technology and perseverance. He may be somewhat limited because of his audio deficiency, but his keen awareness of the needs of young people shows the way nature offsets one limitation with the enhancement of some other ability.

I leave Steve to his foraging for a suitable costume and continue my rounds, going back outside. I enter the buildings from the back downstairs door off the parking lot. After checking each outside exit and opening the doors needed for today, I return to the offices by way of the back stairwell. Our buildings have five stairwells, one elevator, twelve hallways, eight assembly areas, forty-three classrooms, a choir room, a library, a conference room, a fellowship hall, the community clothing closet and food pantry, eight offices, thirteen restrooms, baptismal dressing rooms, umpteen closets, a chapel, and the sanctuary. It offers the church great resources for meetings and tests the church's resolve to maintain. The doors were all locked overnight. Anyone entering this facility last night had to have a key which could be any number of people in our church family.

The wood paneled chapel is used for small meetings and for more intimate weddings. Standing alone inside, I reflect on the path that has brought me to this place of ministry. The church of my high school and college years in North Carolina was, at the time, located on the outskirts of Raleigh. It was the church of my father, grandfather, and great grandfather. It was there I decided to embark on my educational journey toward a ministry profession, and it was there I was ordained, thus validating my calling to the ministry. My role models were the two pastors who served during my years at this church, one a college religion professor, the other a young graduate fresh out of seminary. Both were men above reproach, mentors who instilled in me a desire to serve others.

I've never had close contact with a clergy person involved in any kind of scandal, though I know of a few who've had their problems. One pastor in a neighboring church was accused of inappropriate behavior with one of the young girls of the congregation. It was a nasty mess, his leaving his pastorate under a cloud of suspicion, and his wife and children suffering the humiliation of his alleged indiscretions. I never knew the full extent of the charges against him and have always wondered if he was guilty of the unseemly behavior or the victim of some exaggerated imagination on the part of the young girl. Can a pastor stay in his position even if the accusation isn't true? That's the question that haunts me now.

Back in the office after my tour of the exterior and turning on the lights for the areas to be used today, I read the few sentences of my mysterious letter over several more times and try to imagine who could compose such a vehement message, who could seek my ruination. I've been given by the correspondent until next Wednesday to resign as pastor of the church and am told to announce my resignation to the congregation at the church's quarterly business meeting on that evening. If I do not resign, my reputed guilt will be made public. It does not say how it will be revealed, but warns that my congregation will learn of "the sordid details". What details, I want to know? How can there be particulars when the charges are so absurd?

I type the word "blackmail" into my computer and go to Wikipedia for a definition. "Blackmail is the crime or threat to reveal substantially true information about a person to the public... The information is usually of an embarrassing and/or socially damaging nature." The letter I received can't really be called blackmail since the information is not true, and socially damaging is too mild an expression as to the outcome of any public disclosure of such an act. It doesn't matter what I call this threat. It may not matter that the allegation isn't true. An accusation made against a minister often has legs that carry it far beyond the original infraction or insinuation. Insidious insinuation is what this is. The person behind it likely knows the power of any suggestion of wrong doing committed by a clergy member.

I'm basically an optimistic person and always hope for the best. Well known theologian Elton Trueblood once wrote, "The honest facing of the darkness is one of the chief evidences of the brightness." I believe that Christians must be realistic in the face of negative situations such as this one and, at the same time, seek positive outcomes. I put the letter in a bottom drawer of my desk and vow to not let it totally dim my spirits today. Out of sight will not be out of mind, but out of view is at least some consolation.

This is the final day for our Vacation Bible School. VBS has always been one of the highlights of the year for our church. For a week in the summer, more than two hundred children flood into our buildings and for three hours each morning enjoy the creative Bible studies, games, and activities planned by an enthusiastic staff. I like the vibrancy of children propelling themselves from one part of the church to another with the occasional shoves and tugs of those recently freed from the more disciplined public school experience. These hallways and classrooms are meant to hold people excited about being here, and the joy of the students this week has been effusive. Today we will conclude the summer extravaganza, and four hundred of us will participate in the closing ceremony, including the faculty and the parents invited to the final hoorah of the week. We will all gather in the church's sanctuary, so the parents can experience a portion of the adventure that was the children's during the past few days.

* * *

It's ten-thirty and the sound of children echoes throughout the buildings. I step out into the hall to take in the excitement just as the

Apostle Paul passes by my door. It's actually a life-size cardboard cutout of what is supposed to be Paul carried by one of the VBS workers. I can tell it's the famous follower of Jesus because his name is printed at the base of the character. One of the teen helpers is carrying Paul to the sanctuary where he will likely take part in the closing program. The theme of the school this week has been Bible heroes, and these stiff Bible personages have been on display throughout the buildings.

I'm working on a sermon for Sunday centered on Paul's letter to the Philippians. In it Paul talked about the "supply of the Spirit of Jesus Christ." My plan is to address the need we often have of some extra strength just to make it through a day. Little did I know earlier in the week when I chose this message I would need something extra to handle the situation I find myself in today.

I'm especially intrigued by one word in Paul's letter, the word "supply" or "epichoregeo" in Greek. In Paul's day, the word literally meant "on behalf of the choir." In the ancient Greek world a large ensemble of actors would practice for a major theatrical performance, many of them choral members. But on occasion the money would run out, and the show would be cancelled. Then a wealthy contributor would make a gift "on behalf of the choir" to keep the troupe going. The financial support would supply what was needed, an abundance of help.

I could use an abundance of help today, an extra measure of spiritual guidance. It's challenge enough to pastor a church this size, but the accusation from my anonymous incriminator has stopped me in my tracks. I'm still not sure what to do about it. My message for Sunday morning has not yet been completed, and I'm tempted to borrow the Paul cutout for awhile for inspiration to complete my thoughts on the subject.

As I stand in the hall a group of children pass on their way to the sanctuary. My daughter, Sarah, a youth helper, leads them as they parade by me. She winks at me and then gives marching orders to her charges. It's hard for me to believe she's twelve now, almost thirteen, and over five feet tall. Sarah and her mother are very close, but I know she's proud to be my daughter, "first daughter" she says, meaning that in this congregation she is the child of the senior pastor.

Parents begin to come in for the finale to the Bible School week as I make my way to the sanctuary. My wife, Amy, meets me in the foyer as she has taken off from work to take in the celebration. Amy's almost as tall as I am, about five-ten, and her long blond hair sports ample curls this morning. A part-time social worker, she has some freedom in her schedule. She's five years younger than I, looks fifteen years younger.

"Did you just see Sarah?" Amy asks. "Can you believe that she's that tall and responsible for leading the younger ones? It was just a short while ago that she was one of the children being led."

"I was just thinking the same thing."

"Have you had a good morning so far?" Amy asks as she takes my hand.

I can't yet tell her about my letter for concern that she will be too upset. "Been an interesting one as most are."

Amy is intelligent in many ways, but she's not particularly perceptive. I can usually hide from her any fears, misgivings, doubts, or uncertainties without her discerning my emotions. There's no reason to cause her to be troubled over the anonymous epistle until I can determine who sent it and why. I don't think of this as being deceptive, instead it's simply trying to spare her any undue concern.

I can't help but remember when I told her those years ago now that there were some people in Grace Baptist who wanted me out as their pastor. Her immediate response was tears, and as I tried to comfort her the tears changed to anger.

"You work sixty hours a week trying to meet all of their needs," she said. "What thanks do you get for that – the ingratitude of those hypocrites. You help blow their noses when they have colds; you listen to their gripes about their spouses who are insensitive to the petty problems they magnify; and you sit with their shut-in grandmas while the senior ladies watch afternoon soap operas. They have no right to criticize you, especially considering the paltry pay you receive."

I remember her words well from that evening seven years ago. Afterwards she apologized and told me she actually liked most of the people in that church. She's a good pastor's wife, but there are times when she gets frustrated over some of the aspects of church work. I know she will not take my under-the-door letter well when she learns of it.

I lean close to Amy's ear. "Any glitches at your work today?"

"Do you mean in technology or personnel?"

"Either."

"The computers were virus free, but the staff is infected with summeritis."

"Don't ask me to swap co-workers with you. I have great people to work with."

"I know. You are luckier than most of us."

In the sanctuary the pulpit area has been turned into a set for a musical. The props are the Bible heroes and large artificial trees. Above and behind the stage setting is a huge banner that reads "God's Super Heroes." Superman and Wonder Woman will not be a part of this production, but the kids will draw the connection.

A teenager comes to the microphone and announces it's time to begin as the music from the purchased program CD starts. I recognize the tune from the musical of years past, "Jesus Christ, Super Star" which reverberates throughout the cavernous room. Dozens of children in navy tee shirts run up on the stage pumping fists in the air. The children are enthusiastic, and the program is very upbeat.

For a moment I think I see shock on the faces of the cardboard Bible characters as they stand in the middle of this lively performance, but realize this is just my personal upbringing coming to play as Bible School when I was a child was nothing like this. This is not your father's Oldsmobile, I think, and then remind myself that there are no more Oldsmobiles. There are also no more sedate and boring children's assemblies in the high tech world of church productions. The Bible heroes function as backup performers for a mass of children animated by the multimedia images flashing on screens behind them.

Amy whispers, "I don't know a few of these children or some of the adults here."

"A lot of these kids are visitors or children brought in on the church vans," I say.

"Are you sure this is our church?" Amy asks.

"No, I'm not even sure this is our world; things have changed so much."

As I sit here in this sanctuary that seats five hundred people and watch this major production involving some fifty persons, enhanced by a sophisticated sound system and professionally produced audio-visuals, I can't help but remember my first experience of Vacation Bible School. I was about seven years old and our family lived in the southern part of Ohio. The church was a converted dairy barn, and there were probably only a couple of dozen children enrolled in the VBS that summer.

One lesson stands out in my memory. There were maybe five of us in a small classroom, and the teacher used a flannel board to illustrate the Bible stories. This day we were focusing on the story of Zacchaeus, the tax collector, a small man in stature who climbed a tree in order to see and hear Jesus as he taught a crowd of listeners. On the felt board there was Jesus in his white robe, little Zacchaeus, and the tree. The teacher let me place the small man in the tree as the story unfolded. I imagine that I was very proud of my responsibility in assisting the teacher because I recall the day vividly, even now. I wonder if the children here today will be so affected by this multi-faceted production as I was from my rudimentary flannel board lesson.

Getting back to the present: I'm no longer that little boy who had such a simple understanding of life and of the church. That seven year old child had one basic assignment – put the flannel tax collector on the tree. Today, I pastor a fairly large congregation, and my responsibilities are many and complicated. Freud believed that religious people have a need for an all-powerful father figure, and other psychologists have picked up on this and theorized that church people often look to their pastor to embody this role. Thus ministers experience the congregation wishing them to be omniscient, loving, and protective; thus attributing to God's minister what they believe are the characteristics of God himself.

Some people expect their pastor to assume the role of providing a defense against the anxieties of life. When the pastor fails in that task, which is inevitable, they become disappointed and frustrated. There are those in the church who turn against ministers who don't meet their personal expectations. In several situations in my own ministry those I counseled were not satisfied with my guidance and became less supportive of me. When I was an associate pastor, one woman held it against me that I would not advise her husband to adopt her new charismatic view of faith and attend meetings where speaking in tongues was practiced. I told her that she must let him choose his own form of faith experience. After that she decided to leave our church and join a Free Will Baptist church. She also eventually left her husband.

I come to a startling revelation – there are more people in my ministry experience than I had first imagined who might have negative feelings about me. But who in this church has found fault in how I pastor? The menacing letter slinks its way back into my immediate consciousness despite all my efforts to store it in the recesses of my psyche. It seems to have the capability of escaping from its storage and penetrating my awareness with the ease of a snake slithering through a small crack in the defenses of a well built house. Is there no way to shield myself from these biting words?

The children on the stage are now singing a song about Old Testament heroes of the faith. Steve Ayers, in his clothing closet bathrobe, appears from behind the chorus in his role as Abraham, the first of the Hebrew super stars. I wonder if the first Abram, his original name, was as slender as the young man now portraying him and if he was endowed with any physical limitations such as hearing loss. A deep resonant voice from the sound system is heard over the music as the spotlight shines on the young man representing the "mighty father" from the second millennium B.C. The recorded voice echoes:

> **"I will make your name great,**
> **And you shall be a blessing,**
> **I will bless those who bless you**
> **And curse him that curses you;**
> **And all the families of the earth,**
> **Shall bless themselves by you."**

I think – what job security Abraham had with God protecting him. I also contemplate who would want such responsibility as he carried. But, every person who is endowed with special leadership skills also is charged with being responsible in using those skills. In the Old Testament blessings and curses are closely linked as if they were the on the flip side of each other. Abraham, however, owned a special dispensation – a sort of blessing card he carried in the pocket of his robe. The only negative for old Abram was that he served as God's point man, which is a lonely position. In a way all pastors who lead congregations are assigned this role but without any surety that God keeps them from all harm as this ancient Hebrew seemed to be protected.

There's a woman looking at me from across the sanctuary. She averts her attention when I look her way. I don't recognize her; she must be a visitor. Looking around the sanctuary, it seems there are several others glancing at me furtively until my focus is turned in their direction, some church members, others not. Perhaps they are trying to judge my reactions to the program on the stage, yet it's strange the way they all seem to quickly look away when I adjust my orientation toward them. Turning my deliberation back to the stage, but remaining aware of my surroundings, the surreptitious stares at me seem to be continuing.

After a couple of minutes it dawns on me that this could be my imagination. Is it possible that the critical letter in my office is making me paranoid? Is my subconscious mind worried that someone in this room could be my accuser? Is this the way it's going to be? Will I now constantly suspect everyone around me of being my plaintiff?

CHAPTER TWO

FRIDAY AFTERNOON

Near the end of the Bible School's closing program, I slip out in order to miss the traffic jam of the children leaving. It was a great morning for all involved, but I have some pastoral duties to attend to this afternoon. Home for a quick lunch and then to the hospital to check in on a few church members is my plan. The accusatory letter is still on my mind, but, for now, it shall be put on the back burner.

* * *

My car clock reads one-forty as I sit in the driver's seat at the hospital after my visits. My cell phone rings; the id says the call is from the church.

"Pastor, this is Kristen. One of the children is missing!"

It's hard to understand her as she's obviously very emotional. "What do you mean; one of what children?"

"Emma Wells, one of the van ministry children didn't get home. She may have been taken by someone," Kristen continues, her voice still trembling.

"Have you called the police?" I ask.

"Yes, they're here now."

"I'll be there in ten minutes."

It's hard to process the idea that a little girl who attended our Bible School went missing during the period of time since I left the church. At first, the call triggers the "what now" reaction which's natural when you are in a responsible position and are appraised of a problem. But, as I travel the few miles from the community hospital to Church Street, the import of the idea of a child possibly being abducted from our church transforms my attitude from that of how do I handle this to – has this child been hurt?

Back at the church now, there's a flurry of activity with police and congregation members all over the place moving with the frenzied pace of an ant colony that has discovered a pile of sugar. The scene is surreal, and I'm at a loss as to what to do next. Kristen, who called me with the news, and Debbie, a volunteer worker, are both sitting on a bench in the foyer holding each other. They are each crying and look up at me with expressions of disbelief and frustration, temporarily immobilized by the confusion.

One of the policemen comes up and asks if we can go to my office so he might touch base with me for a minute. It becomes clear immediately that by touch base he means question me. He's in his twenties, under thirty certainly, and dead serious in manner.

"Sir, where have you been for the last two hours?" the officer asks.

As I look at the young uniformed policeman, the only response that comes to mind is, "Why are you asking me that?"

"Reverend Fowler, we are just trying to figure out where everyone was when the little girl was last seen."

I tell the stiff and formal city law officer with a yellow note pad in one hand and a stubby golf pencil in the other of my lunch break and hospital visit.

"Did you leave before the program was over in the sanctuary?" he asks.

"Yes, I wanted to get out of the parking lot before everyone was ready to leave in order to avoid the jam."

"So, you were in a hurry to get away?"

As soon as those words come from his mouth I can tell that both he and I are uncomfortable over the phrasing of his question. "I wasn't in a hurry, just wanted to avoid the confusion as I needed to attend to other matters this afternoon."

"Well, sir, I guess all of our schedules have been interrupted now."

The young man asks a few more questions, thanks me for my time, and tells me that the lead detective will want to speak with me a little later.

One of the special ministries of our church is our van outreach where we are able to go out into the community and pick up children whose parents do not attend our services. This week we provided transportation for many children who could not have come to VBS without our fifteen passenger vans picking them up and taking them back. Emma Wells was picked up at her home this morning but did not arrive home this afternoon. Actually, she never got on the van for the return trip. The last time anyone saw her was during the closing celebration for the school. One of the other children said Emma went to the restroom right before the program was over. I don't think any of us at the church ever entertained the possibility that we could lose a child. But, Emma is missing, and there is the likelihood that someone took her from our church at noon today and has her now.

In the church office I find Janice Moore, our music minister. She's waiting to be interviewed by the police, she tells me. Janice is a quiet person who must, I think, have to ratchet up her personality to lead a fifty member choir as we have. The adult choir members are a difficult ensemble in that there are some who have overactive egos and are not particularly submissive to any leadership. I can see that she's uncomfortable as she waits for her turn with the detectives. She tells me that Karen Gravitt is in there now.

"Why are they questioning you and Karen?" I ask with concern in my voice.

"It seems they are interviewing everyone who was here today but was not at the closing program at the end."

"This is preposterous," I exclaim. "You and Karen had nothing to do with any of this."

"Ron, I don't know the little girl, but I'm so worried about her. Do you really think someone took her? How could anyone abduct a child from a church?"

"I just got back. I can't believe any of this. I don't know what happened to the child. I just know that they're wasting their time interrogating you, Karen, and me."

"You were questioned also?" Janice asks.

"Yes, briefly, but there may be more to come."

Janice explains why she is being questioned, "I went to the choir room before the children left the sanctuary today. I brought a sandwich and was trying to get some work done since VBS took some of my prep time. I didn't know any of this was going on until a policeman knocked on my door. They are suspicious of anyone not in the sanctuary at noon but somewhere in the building during that time."

The door to the conference room opens, and Karen comes out. Her eyes are moist, and she looks at me with an expression of incredulity. Karen is our church hostess, a mother of three, and loved by everyone in the congregation. A policewoman asks Janice to step in as Karen sits down on the reception area couch.

"Are you okay?" I ask Karen.

"I'll be fine," she says. "This is the first time in my life I've ever been asked a question by a policeman. I've never even had a traffic ticket. They were nice to me, but it was still disturbing. Ron, I just served refreshments to this little girl a few hours ago. I remember her because she hugged me and thanked me for the snacks we provided during the week. I know her mother at the bank."

Karen tells me she has learned Rachel Wells, Emma's mother, was at work today while her daughter was at our church, and Emma was to be dropped off at a neighbor's house until Rachel finished her day at the Bank of America branch on Logan Street.

"The neighbor called the bank at one to say that Emma had not arrived," Karen continues. "Rachel, in turn, called the church, and was told that all of the children left before twelve-thirty. She was given the number of the van driver, Roland Miller. Roland was reached at home and reported that the child was not on his vehicle for the last run but remembered picking her up in the morning. He was apologetic for not asking about her at noon but assumed one of the parents had given her a ride home."

A simple harmless assumption, I think, but one link in a chain of events which led to the disappearance of this little blond headed child.

Karen continues to fill me in, explaining that, when Rachel Wells, now distraught and in a panic, called the church the second time, it was Kristen, our children's minister, she talked with. Kristen, new on our staff, had just completed her first major undertaking as a staff member and was still euphoric over her accomplishment when she was hit with the news that Emma had not arrived home. In a matter of minutes the police were alerted.

This is all an amazing story. I can see that in the hour that followed the realization the child was missing our church was transformed from a place where children delight in unlocking the mysteries of the Bible to a potential crime scene where one child's disappearance becomes a mystery to be solved.

Karen leaves the office, and I check in with our secretary, Alice Stevens. Alice knows more about what is going on in our church and community than anyone else I know. For thirty years she has managed the church office with efficiency. She and Emma's mother are cousins she tells me.

"I just talked to Rachel a few minutes ago," Alice says. "She told me she had considered taking her lunch hour away from the bank to attend the closing program here at noon, but Fridays are especially hectic at her branch, payday for many hourly workers. She chose to work through her lunch break in order to cover for the tellers."

I've never met Rachel Wells, but feel for her now that hours have passed since Emma was last seen. She must certainly regret her decision to stay at work. In hindsight, we appraise our earlier determinations when something goes wrong and assume that the outcome would be far different if we had just made some simple kind of adjustment in what we did or did not do. We replay our choices in order to play out alternative scenarios and chide ourselves for not seeing in advance that our course of action held the possibility of a negative outcome. There are no words more painful than "if only". If we dwell in the "if only" it becomes a poisonous drug that incapacitates us and never lets us get beyond our questionable choices.

The police have searched the buildings and grounds thoroughly and have interviewed the staff and many of the volunteers who led the Bible School. Some two dozen officers and rescue workers have combed every corner of our property. The police even brought dogs in for the search. Somehow, the sight of the dogs impressed me as to the stark gravity of the whole situation. A church shouldn't be a place where dogs sniff for lost little girls.

There's nothing that touches the deepest emotions of a community more than when a young child goes missing. Even those who don't know the family of the child find themselves absorbed by the intense trauma of the situation. The complete attention of many in this town of thirty thousand people now is on the frantic search for eight year old Emma Wells, and I find myself at the center of a rapidly developing storm which is building into a full fledged whirlwind of yet to be seen complications. I'm in this uncommon position because I'm the pastor of the First Baptist Church, and this church is the last place Emma was seen.

Carl Brody, the police officer in charge of the search, is a no-nonsense veteran of twenty years on the force. He's a stocky man who wears a brown crumpled suit that looks like it may have come from the community clothing closet housed in the downstairs of our church. He's not a member of our church, but his brother is and I have met Carl before. He gets me aside and says, "This is the fifth case of a missing child this year in our town, Reverend."

"I never would have thought so many children could go missing in a town our size," I exclaim. "How many of them were found?"

Carl shifts his weight as he rests on the edge of an arm chair in my office. I can see in his eyes an intensity which is likely the product of many years of recalling the details of a myriad of criminal cases. He has a habit of cocking his head to one side when he speaks which I find lures me to do the same in order to square up with him.

"Three of the missing children were taken by estranged parents and eventually brought back. One ten year old boy is still absent after five months, we think taken by his mother who lost a bitter custody battle. Neither he nor his mother has been located, but we have reason to believe the kid is alright. If you ask me, the father in this case is a real ass. Pardon the choice of nouns, Reverend. You remember, of course, Michelle Preston whose body was found in the lake earlier this year. I authorized the Amber Alert at two today for the Wells girl. It will put other localities on the look out for the child," the detective adds. "Most child abductions involve family members or friends. I've spoken with the Wells and don't think that's the case here."

"Do you have a theory?" I ask.

"Not yet."

"Do you think someone from our church is involved?"

"Could be," Carl says.

He's a man of few words, I readily decide. He and his detectives have briefly interviewed over fifty people in the last two hours, all from those at church today, including me.

"Is there anyone from our church who looks suspicious?"

"All I can say is there are quite a few who had the opportunity to take her," Carl acknowledges.

"One of your officers asked me earlier about my whereabouts the last few hours."

"Yes, we're just trying to cover all of the bases, Pastor. I'm afraid that anyone who was in position to take the child must be considered a possible suspect. I'm sorry, but it has to be that way."

"I can tell you that no one on our church staff had anything to do with this terrible thing," I say with some force.

"That's probably true, but we can't rule anyone out at the present time," Carl says.

This isn't good, I decide. The implication is that there will be follow-up police interviews for many of us. Detective Brody tells me that the FBI has been notified and will likely send a team here to assist in the investigation.

The Michelle Preston case from February must be on the minds of many this afternoon. The nine year old girl was taken off the street in front of her house which caused an extensive search for six days. Her body was found in a wooded area at the edge of the lake by a jogger. The abducted child had been physically abused and beaten. It was determined by the coroner that she died from a head wound. I remember that Carl Brody was the lead investigator on that case as well. Three months later, twenty-four year old Denario Phillips was arrested and accused of the murder. Phillips is a drifter with a record of thefts but not of abuse. He now awaits trial. His face has been seen so often in the news that for many in our city his is the countenance of evil. His long sideburns, the scar over his left eye, the pierced lower lip, and his ever present scowl have made his physiognomy the representation of what we in this community think of when we imagine a child being harmed. I must admit his image is one of the first things that came to mind when I learned that Emma was missing. But, Denario Phillips is behind bars and not responsible for today's shock.

Our custodian, Joel Weaver, has been questioned for almost an hour now by two police detectives. Joel was in the building at the time the girl was last seen and on the same floor where the restroom is that Emma may have entered. The custodian told the police that he was arranging furniture in one of the classrooms about the time the program ended in the sanctuary and remembers hearing the noise of all the children set free. Joel's in his late fifties and lives alone in an apartment near the church. He's been on our staff for three years, a very private person who shies away from extended conversations with the others on the staff. He's a short man and has several tattoos on his arms, not unusual for a former military man. He was a marine, and I was in the army, so we have, on a couple of occasions, compared our military experiences. Not much of a comparison, really. I became an army officer through ROTC, while Joel enlisted in the marines when he was seventeen. He spent time in Nam while I never left the states. I was a chaplain for six years, he an infantry man in a rifle platoon where he lost several of his friends to enemy fire. I like Joel and have found him several times in the chapel alone on his knees praying. He grew up in a Catholic home up north with seven brothers and sisters and moved south to live near his cousin who has a place across town. He's been very reluctant to share any other details about his past, and I've tried to respect his privacy.

Joel often spends his lunch break in one of the classrooms down the hall from our offices. A few weeks ago I passed by and saw him sitting there reading a book. Stepping into the room to speak to him for a moment, I couldn't help but see what he was reading. It was a work by the Danish thinker, Soren Kierkegaard. I made no comment about his choice of reading at the time but later wondered what a custodian was doing reading the writings of an existentialist philosopher. In seminary I was introduced to Kierkegaard and have spent some time myself immersed in his theological thoughts. My favorite Kierkegaard quote is, "Life can only be understood backwards; but it must be lived forwards." The events of today, the letter, the missing child, will someday soon be looked back on and understood. Today, I must go forward without that valuable perspective.

* * *

It's now four in the afternoon and there have, as yet, been no solid leads as to what happened to this eight year old girl. The police have explored the possibility that someone came in from off the street and grabbed Emma. With the confusion of four hundred people moving around, this is entirely possible. Carl Brody and his people have been very considerate of our staff and church members and have treaded carefully in their interviews. This must be so frustrating for them since there were so many people at the church at noon today. I can't imagine anyone from this church involved in the disappearance of Emma Wells. I pray that my imagination is right.

I find Joel Weaver in the kitchen, a few minutes now after his police interview has concluded. He sits on a stool taking a break with a cup of coffee resting on the counter.

"I hear the police questioned you earlier," I say.

"Not a problem," Joel says calmly.

"They've questioned all of us on the staff. It's what they have to do, I guess."

"They have a job to do just like you and me," Joel says.

"This is surely the biggest mess I have ever been involved in as a pastor," I share with Joel.

"If anyone can handle it, you can, Padre."

Joel often calls me this, which I assume is from his days as a marine when he dealt with Catholic chaplains.

"I wish I'd seen the girl if she was on the hall near where I was working," Joel says as he picks up his coffee cup. "Maybe this would not have happened if I'd been at the right place."

"That goes for many of us here today," I say. "Evidently, I had just left the sanctuary before she did. It was almost impossible for her to not be seen by someone in those few minutes with all of the people that were here."

Joel agrees that timing was one of the contributors to her disappearance. "You know, all my life I've managed to miss opportunities to do something important. I always seem to be just a little too late, or a little too early. I'm not sure God trusts me enough with any big responsibility."

For a moment he looks at his coffee cup as if some response to this self deprecating assessment of his life might emerge from it.

I'm not sure what to say in response to his take on his life other than the weak bromide, "God finds ways to use us all in his work."

Leaving Joel to his break, I wonder how hard the police pressed this quiet fellow earlier. There was certainly some profiling taking place as my turn at questioning lasted less than half the time of Joel's. There is nothing threatening in his countenance or demeanor, but in his quiet self assurance a definite impression of strength makes him seem to have a latent power to be reckoned with when cornered.

There have been the representatives of the press here today also, as this is the kind of story which quickly dominates the news. I was interviewed on one of the local radio stations a few minutes ago and introduced on their lead-in as the pastor of the church which cannot account for why this child did not make it home safely. Without a direct charge, there is still the implication that we at First Baptist did not act responsibly. My concern is not for our reputation; it's for the safety of Emma Wells. That's not really the full truth. I'm far more concerned about finding the child safe than I am about how our church is seen but have to be realistic in accepting the fact that this isn't good publicity for a church. This should be a place where safety is a given, but in our society today there is no quarter off limits to those who are intent on mayhem.

* * *

It's now four-thirty, and I know what I must do. Ted and Rachel Wells live in a neighborhood of new homes about two miles from our church. Their house is bungalow style with a large columned front porch. The street in front of their home is already lined with press vehicles, and I have to run a gauntlet of those with microphones and note pads eager to interrupt my approach. One reporter recognizes me and walks up on the porch beside me. I tell her that I'll be available at the church later and need a few private minutes with this family. A pair of children's roller blades sits on a wicker chair, awaiting the return of the child who owns them.

I'm greeted at the door by a neighbor who is undoubtedly shielding the family from the profusion of well-wishers and story-seekers. A man and woman, the Wells I assume, come to the living room from the kitchen, leaving several others who have gathered. Both exhibit weary and sad expressions as the last few hours have certainly taken their toll. Ted, a slight man in his mid-thirties it appears, shakes my hand and musters up a faint smile as he welcomes me to their home. His grip is firm but tentative, and his words calm but measured. His wife nods at me with a courteous acknowledgement of my presence, in her hands a wad of tissues. She doesn't speak until I express my regret over the situation. Then she only manages a soft "thank you" as she takes her husband's hand. I'm somewhat surprised that this distraught mother is not sequestered in a bedroom and injected with medications to calm her fears.

The first couple of minutes are awkward as we've never met before. I'm accustomed to making visits to homes of prospects for our church, often unknown to me, but this is my first time in a home of strangers who have lost a child. The Wells, I sense, are also not sure of what to say as we each seek to bridge the gap of unfamiliarity. The normal pleasantries seem to be out of place as opening conversation. Social norms have not been prescribed for such an occasion as this. There's not the casual offer of tea or coffee, or the mundane comments about weather, traffic, or other common social ice breakers. This is a visit from a clergy person to a troubled family with both parties uncomfortable over the reason for the visit. I'm not invited to sit down but instead am guided over to the glass shielded fireplace on the left side of the room, a space which is obviously the central gathering area for the family.

The Wells show me pictures of Emma arranged on the wooden mantle, with awareness that I don't know their daughter. She's of average height for a girl her age. Her hair is blond and in a ponytail in most of the photos. In some shots she has this huge engaging smile that must belong to one who is truly happy. In a few of the frames there's a look of serious concentration that seems out of place on such a young face. The abundant stills trace the eight plus years of Emma's life from infancy to the present, her parents in about half of the familial snapshots of varying sizes.

"Emma's the center of our lives, as you can see, Dr. Fowler,"

Ted Wells says with an obvious build up of emotion.

"I can understand," I say. "My wife and I have one daughter also."

"This photo of her with the Bible was taken just a month ago after she came home from church," Rachel Wells says. "She was so proud that day of having her own Bible. It was presented to her by her Sunday school teacher. I've not had the chance to thank anyone yet."

Rachel is a slender woman with piercing blue eyes. She's clearly a professional person in dress, wearing a navy pantsuit with a crisp white blouse. She must be someone who is used to stress in her work, who can cope with most events capably. Today her poise has certainly been tested, and she appears to be numbed by the anxiety over what has happened to her little girl. "I should have picked her up today," Rachel says, bringing a tissue to her eyes.

"I could have gone as well," Ted says as he lightly touches his wife on the arm. "I was not that busy and even looked at my watch at around eleven, aware of her program."

"But, I was only a few blocks away," Rachel adds, her blue eyes pleading for some absolution of blame for her earlier choice. "And now our daughter's lost, and I'm afraid I will never see her again." She turns and walks a few steps toward the front door and stops in the middle of the room. "I'm sorry. I know that such talk is not helpful."

Ted cautiously moves the conversation in another direction. "I remember clearly, Dr. Fowler, the day that Mr. Miller came to our door and offered to take Emma to church on the van. Rachel and I were hesitant at first, but he looked a lot like my dad, and I instantly trusted him. Our daughter had been invited by a friend of hers from school who also rode the van. Rachel and I were just not ready to attend church yet, but Emma insisted we let her go. There are a lot of decisions you rethink on a day like this."

We're still standing in front of the fireplace with the array of photos of family memories on top. Rachel Wells picks up one of the pictures and holds the frame in both hands as if it were terribly fragile, slightly tilting it my way. It's a pose of the three of them in front of a large palm tree.

Rachel says, "This was taken on our family vacation to Disney

World at Christmas last year. Emma took the role of tour guide as she had gathered information off the Internet as to the best schedule for us on a two day visit. She's more comfortable on the computer than Ted and I, and we both use them daily at work."

Ted gently slips the frame from his wife's hands and takes a long look at it. "This was taken before we knew Emma was sick," he says, now looking at me. "Six weeks after getting home from Florida we learned she has... cancer. This is our last family photo before our lives were changed by the diagnosis that upended our normalcy."

The word cancer sits in the air for a moment before it begins to work its way into my awareness. "Emma has cancer?" I ask.

"Yes," Rachel answers, now sitting on the arm of a couch with her shoulders slumped. "It started with pain in her leg. When the pain would not go away, we took her to a doctor. Tests were run and we heard that awful word, cancer. For the next few months our precious daughter underwent radiation treatments."

Rachel begins to cry as Ted goes over to hold her. The two of them embrace for a minute or two as I watch from across the room. The photo is still in Ted's hands. My gaze moves back to the mantle as I look over the array of photographs. One I had not noticed before catches my eye; in it Emma is on roller blades, hot pink helmet on her head, pads on her knees. I think of all the precautions we parents take trying to insure the safety of our children, and of the unknown factors that catch us by surprise for which there is no real protection.

After Rachel calms herself some, Ted looks in my direction and says, "Pastor, we are still dealing with the shock of cancer attacking our daughter, now this."

I want to ask is the cancer curable but find that to be an uncomfortable question when we are here in this room because this little girl has likely been abducted a few hours ago. Instead, I ask the inane question, "Which leg?" This seems to be the safest direction to guide the conversation as any other question could lead to something more delicate and emotional.

Ted responds to my insipid question, "The right leg. At least that's where it started. She's to begin chemotherapy soon. She wanted to wait until school was out."

I want to ask about pain and prognosis, but again these are leading questions that call for responses that may be too burdensome on a mother and father who now have a worry even more grave.

"We considered coming to you with the news of cancer," Ted says. "We were afraid we might appear too angry at God and put you in a tough spot. We're not atheists or anything. Both Rachel and I grew up in the church. We just got away from religion and simply didn't feel the need for it before Emma's illness. I hope you can understand."

Before I can respond, Rachel stands up from her seat on the arm rest and speaks in a sob, "We should have come to you after the diagnosis. It would make this a lot easier now, but we appreciate your being here today and all you and your church have done for Emma. She's learned so much and loves every minute she spends at First Baptist. We thank you so much for your visit, Dr. Fowler."

I can tell that this is my cue to leave. There's but so much energy that Rachel Wells can invest in conversation right now. I ask if I can lead in a prayer before I go and do so with their consent.

"Father, you have been our dwelling place in all generations. You provide stability to the paths beneath our feet and assurance that we are never alone in our journey. You relieve the pain in our sorrows and stand by us in our bewilderment over the surprises in life. When our daily existence is turned upside down we are reminded of your mercy. We pray today for Ted, and Rachel, and Emma. May you return her unharmed to her parents. We take comfort in the incredible truth that we are all your children and you are a loving father who cares for each one of us. In Christ's name I pray, amen."

I leave the Wells house with a far deeper concern for this family than when I arrived. They are no longer people I have merely heard of. They're now my responsibility, a part of my congregation, even though they have not yet made a decision to be. They're my concern, the three of them. It's my duty as a pastor to invest myself into their lives, help them through this double misery they face. I now have a deep empathy for Ted and Rachel but realize that I cannot take their world into mine, for I've never been where they are today.

* * *

When I return to the church several television and newspaper reporters are eager for interviews. It's time for me to let them put a face on First Baptist Church, a face that will undoubtedly be seen as one representing a likely tragedy which revolves around a supposed place of good news. I can imagine the creative lead-ins to the many reports to come: no good news yet from First Baptist, or Emma Wells was last seen at church and is still lost, or the church is no sanctuary for child unaccounted for. I dread the thought of the media's insatiable appetite for sensationalism turning this into a mockery of our church, of religion, of faith.

"Do you know Emma?" I'm asked by one reporter for the evening news program.

"I recognize Emma when I see her, but I don't really know her well," I respond as I have several times in the last few hours to both the authorities and the press. I slipped once and said that I did remember her, using the past tense. As pastor, I'm called upon to speak in many settings, but this one is beyond my practice. I suppose funeral services are the closest thing to my experiences today as to this need for well chosen words. A pastor must select his or her verbal expressions so carefully when relating to the family of one deceased. Many times I've stood at the funeral home with a son or daughter trying to find the right condolences to utter in the loss of their parent. At one funeral I slipped and referred to the man in the coffin as a "diabolic" instead of a "diabetic", which certainly ranks up there in the top ten lists of funeral faux pas. There were some who assumed I meant it the way I said it since the man laying there was thought by many in the church and community to be wicked. Slip ups today will not only be unacceptable when spoken; they'll be on the record and replayed over and over again with all of this media coverage.

"Have you talked to the parents?" another newsperson asks. I've watched this local evening news field reporter many nights but never imagined I'd be the primary spokesperson for a lead story on child abduction on her broadcast.

"I have spoken with Ted and Rachel Wells. They are very afraid as any parents would be in such a situation as this."

"Did you pray with them?" the blond newswoman asks.

"Yes, I did. The Wells have not been attending our church, but they are people of faith and are willing to put their trust in God."

"Does that mean they think only God can save their daughter?" the newswoman asks, with what I determine is an attempt to add to the speculation of foul play and dramatize the fear even more.

"I cannot speak for the Wells. Like any parents they are hoping for the best which I'm sure you and everyone else in our community are doing as well," I say.

The reporter turns away from me and looks into the camera saying, "Dr. Fowler is the pastor of this church where Emma Wells was last seen over five hours ago now. This pastor, like many others in this town, is praying for her safe return."

My twenty minutes with the Wells earlier was as difficult as any few minutes in my ministry. They were not accusatory of our church, even thankful for all we've done for Emma in the past few months since she has ridden the van to our Sunday school and other programs. I'm not at liberty to divulge the information about the cancer. This will have to come from Ted and Rachel. I can understand why they may want to keep this private for now but know that there's little privacy when reporters are eager for details

I feel it's extremely important how I conduct myself this afternoon and evening. I must be careful of future legal ramifications for the church and of the example I set of civility in the midst of this trying time. I must be careful because I'm in a unique situation as a clergy person. Not only am I representing the church; I'm representing our faith as well. I remember the words of Thomas Moore as he spoke of psychology and religion not being totally sufficient in helping us understand the difficult periods of life. I go to my bookshelf and reacquaint myself with what he wrote: After first critiquing psychological advice he said, "Religion, too, often avoids the dark by hiding behind platitudes and false assurances. Nothing is more irrelevant than feeble religious piousness in the face of stark, life-threatening darkness." The Wells family will not benefit from avoidance of reality; neither will the public which agonizes with them. The way the church, that being to some degree myself in this case, communicates our faith is critical in offering helpful words when people face crises in life. There will be those critics who expect the church's response to be glib and trite bromides. There's only one legitimate comfort we can offer in a time such as this; I know from too much experience with life and death situations. The only thing of value to say is, "I'm sorry for your pain, I wish I could take some of the pain away, and let me support you in your sorrow."

We spend so much of our lives trying to avoid suffering. Sometimes we think that the role of religion is to protect us from suffering. The truth is religion's most vital asset is teaching us how to handle suffering, to learn from it. If our church is to help Ted and Rachel it will not come through denial of their pain. It will come through confronting their pain and allowing others to support them in it, and perhaps allowing God to touch their lives, our lives, with his spirit. One could argue that suffering is meant to teach us, indeed ordained by God for that purpose. This has been a long standing view of many who have studied the scriptures. I'm not comfortable with this analysis because the victims of suffering often die before they have any chance to learn from it.

CHAPTER THREE

FRIDAY EVENING

It's seven in the evening and Emma Wells has not been found. It's unlikely that she wandered off. It's more likely she was taken by someone. The police have been door to door in the immediate neighborhood for the last few hours asking if anyone saw anything. Any piece of information may be crucial in the search they say. Vacant lots and parks near the church have been gone over by volunteers, many of them from First Baptist. I'm proud of the people from our church family who have stepped up so well in this crisis. So often we watch and wait when a tragedy of this proportion unfolds, especially if it takes place in another city. The words from Shelley's *Adonais* come to mind, "Whence are we, and why are we? Of what scene – The actors or spectators?"

The church is quiet now as most everyone has gone home. My office is in one of our church's two education buildings. If I turn left coming out of the office suite and walk fifty feet down the tiled hall I enter the recently remodeled sanctuary. If I turn right at the door of the offices I'm on one of the main halls of the education building. Children's classrooms are on this corridor, including the one where Emma was a pupil in the Bible School just this morning. As I move down this hall, Moses, David, and Peter stand watch, propped against the wall on either side. Throughout the education buildings these painted sentries silently guard the passages as if they have stepped from the pages of the scriptures to observe how we moderns conduct our faith experiences. These flat panel heroes are likely the only witnesses to the last few minutes that Emma was here in this corridor. I don't believe God works this way, but in these circumstances I would not mind a little supernatural zapping to allow my hall companions a word or two of testimony as to what they know.

The women's restroom is the next to last door on the right. Across the door is a strip of yellow police tape, the customary indication of a crime scene. They've been over this room twice this afternoon, taking fingerprints. The tape is a warning to not enter, but there's this need on my part to go in and seek some insight into what happened today. I open the door, ducking under the tape, and enter this ladies' room which I don't think I've ever set foot in before. As the police reported earlier, there is no sign of any struggle here. The three gray stall doors offer privacy to the commodes, and the two sinks are clean white porcelain. Mirrors above the sinks hang as empty witnesses to images long gone. The paper in the waste containers has been removed for forensic study. The one large window is frosted and offers no easy escape as this is the second floor of the building due to the sloping parking lot. I suppose I've come in here to try and pick up some resonant psychic presence of what may have taken place earlier in this lavatory. I've never had a psychic encounter before, so I'm not surprised when all I sense is the blandness of the light green cinder block walls. My new need for supernatural and telepathic encounters surprises my rational self. I can't help but think that for over seventy years little girls have entered and exited this toilet with not a thought for their security. I hope this room does not become a memorial for the next seventy years to one little girl who found this place to not be secure.

The prevalent theory is that Emma left the building with someone by way of the stairwell beside the restroom. It makes its way upstairs to the third floor and downstairs to an exit to the back parking lot. The van loading and the parent pick up area this morning was the side exit closest to the sanctuary, some two hundred feet up a hill and around the corner from the back exit. I stand at the stairwell door wondering if Emma called out for help as she was being ushered out this way. The thought of this child, mouth covered by her abductor, eyes large with fright, squirming for release, suddenly takes over my consciousness. This is all supposition on my part for there is no tangible evidence as to how this child departed the building those few hours ago.

Ruth of Moab is propped beside the door to the stairwell, at least her cardboard self is. Her mouth is open as if she is speaking her famous line, "Whither thou goest, I will go." I've always had a fondness for Ruth and her amazing level of devotion. If only she could offer some faint hint as to the fate of young Emma Wells.

The stairwell steps have rubber treads to keep people from slipping as they make their way up and down. I proceed down the split steps noticing, for the first time, just how quiet it is in here and how the steel and concrete shudders slightly on my way to the bottom. Never before has the hollowness of the shaft been so dramatically impressive as today and the sense of hazard so possible. I open the fire door at the downstairs landing and stand at the back passage to the outside. There's a window in the door here, obviously placed to keep someone from opening this and hitting another as they are entering. So many safety features, and yet nothing to protect a little girl from being taken by a person she doesn't choose to go with.

The asphalt paved parking lot is lined to accommodate a hundred or more cars. This is one of three lots owned by the church. The vacant field of kudzu fills the view to the left, its vines traversing a slight incline. The creeping leafy plants have been pressed down by the feet of searchers who have attempted to comb the foliage for any trace of a missing child. The fast growing weeds appear to be a thick impenetrable jungle in the middle of a blacktop sea. They mock any idea that this will be an easy place to search for one who is lost.

I make my way up the steep drive to the right and enter the church through the porte cochere which spans the space between the sanctuary and the education building. This is the most used entrance to our physical plant, a wide covered porch that facilitates fellowship before and after our services. The prophet Jeremiah greets me at the hall entrance, flat and still, like his lifeless companions elsewhere in the buildings. When called by God, the young Hebrew argued that he was not ready for what he would be asked to do. I know the feeling, and am tempted to speak out loud to the vigilant comrade in faith. I want to say, "I know you Jeremiah of the Old Testament. You lived a life marked by great fluctuations in spirit, as I do. You did not mind questioning why God let things happen the way he did which I also do quite often. I loved it when you said, 'Lord, do you intend to disappoint me like a stream that goes dry in the summer?' Jeremiah, you knew that no one is the master of his own destiny, such wisdom for one so young in your day." I leave the prophet to stand his watch and head back to the office.

Several members of our church staff remain in the outer reception area awaiting any further word on Emma. I can tell by their faces the day has been taxing and the stress has weighed heavily upon them. Each has spent hours combing the neighborhood for clues to the location of Emma Wells. The police and the press have departed, leaving us to recap the events which have turned a morning of celebration and joy into an afternoon of depressing worry. The investigators haven't stated emphatically that some of us on the staff are persons of interest in the likely abduction, but the reporters have said repeatedly that "no one at the church today has been identified nor ruled out as a suspect." I've always been fascinated by statements from law officers who can say so little in their briefings, but imply so much with their guarded comments. Once in a while you will come across a police representative who likes the limelight and will let slip some sensitive fact, but for the most part they are very tight lipped, yet subtly suggestive of where the investigation may be headed. The most common words they speak are, "I'm not at liberty to comment on that at this time."

Kristen Davis is resting her head on the receptionist's desk, her short brown hair and squared off bangs revealing her youthfulness. She's brand new at the job and was, until a few hours ago, full of youthful enthusiasm and energy. As the children's minister and director of the VBS she has considerable responsibility. She's still wearing her yellow Bible heroes name tag like the ones issued to everyone at the school this week. I call Kristen the pied piper because she often has a few children in tow. She exudes charm and warmth which attracts the young ones to her. Several times this afternoon she has broken down when interviewed by the media. I'm sure there will be clips of her tearful responses to questions about this awful circumstance broadcast on news shows in order to tick up the ratings of this nail-biting story.

Steve Ayers is sitting on the floor with his back to the wall and knees up under his chin. He was the one in charge of the youth counselors who were, in turn, in charge of getting the children on and off the vans. Steve is gregarious and even sometimes wacky, traits which serve him well in his line of work with teenagers. He's also very focused on leading young people to a personal relationship with Jesus of the New Testament. Tall, with shoulder length hair, in his late twenties, Steve is a natural at relating to social misfits looking for a group to which to belong and has tremendous compassion for those who have some disability. There are plenty of young people who consider themselves estranged from society who gravitate to supportive groups like the one at our church. My wife says privately to me at times that Steve has developed his own congregation within the church which meets in the youth area of the old education building. I must admit his kids are devoted to him, and I'm somewhat intimidated when I must pay a visit to the "den" which is what the hangout is called.

Deanna Crowder, our education minister, is standing by a window looking out at the sun setting over the parking lot. In her mid-thirties and almost six feet tall, she's a by-the-book Christian education specialist who leaves no detail undone. Deanna hasn't said anything like this today, but I know she's bothered that we could mess up a factor as important as making sure a child returned home safely. She's counseled others in the church many times about the responsibility we have to provide a safe environment. She seems truly upset for the child's family, but it must deeply trouble her that we could have allowed such a lapse in discipline to have occurred. I can sense her frustration that she can't, in her take charge way, fix this whole mess.

Our church has a dozen staff members including the music minister, pianist, organist, hostess, two secretaries, the custodian, and the groundskeeper. I make number twelve. Each person was questioned by the police except the organist who was not here today. The custodian accompanied the law enforcement personnel on their searches of the properties with the keys needed to get into every crevice in our large plant. Each of the four of us here this evening provided assistance to the authorities this afternoon. In my opinion we couldn't have a better staff team, which makes today's disturbing events even more burdensome on me as I know the pain each of these three suffers as they assess their own position in the disappearance of Emma.

"This is my fault," Kristen volunteers, which breaks the silence as the four of us await news in the office. "I should've been more aware of the departure of each child."

"You were not responsible for the children getting on the vans," Steve reminds. "That was under my duties. I was to have one of our teens responsible for each group of six children. I missed the fact that Jeff Morgan had left for a family vacation this morning and would not be here to monitor his half dozen little ones. Emma was in his group."

I can't let this situation become an exercise in personal recriminations. "There are many other precautions we could have taken if we knew this could happen," I say. "It's true that we on the staff are ultimately responsible for the conduct of the school, but we never could have secured all of the children from all the dangers possible today."

Kristen has tears welling in her eyes as she counters my last statement. "If Emma is harmed I will quit my job. All I've wanted to be since I was in high school has been a children's minister. Now, in my first year on the job I blow it big time."

"There was nothing in your seminary training that equipped you to prevent such as this," I offer. "But, you were trained in ways to help people through difficult times. There are two hundred other children who will need a compassionate guide in the days ahead, and you're gifted in that area. They need you; we need you."

"I just want them to find the sicko who took Emma, and I refuse to believe it's someone in our church," Steve says.

The outrage in his voice is not what I'm used to hearing from Steve. Always upbeat and outgoing, he's a very hard fellow to dislike, even though many people have trouble deciphering his nonstop zaniness.

"Steve," I say, "we're all upset about the possibility that this child may be in the hands of someone who means to do her harm. I agree that it's inconceivable that one of our members is responsible. The police told me today that there are twenty-seven known sex offenders in our town. That's hard for me to believe. Never would've guessed the problem was that widespread. They're already in the process of contacting them for their alibis. One officer told me that there are three men living within eight blocks of our church who've been convicted of taking indecent liberties with children. He admitted that the system which keeps track of them is not adequate. They're having trouble finding some of them today."

"The problem is that any system is only as good as those who operate it," Deanna adds. "There are a dozen people who could've done one little thing differently and this would not have happened. That includes Emma's parents, our volunteer workers, those of us on the staff, perhaps even the authorities. Any one small change in what we did and Emma would be secure in her home this evening. Still, the attention here should be on what we do now, not on what we have or have not done earlier."

Steve and Deanna each decide the day has been long enough. They leave Kristen and me standing in the hall as we agree to lock up the offices for the evening. Kristen's eyes are puffy from an afternoon of tears, and her light brown hair is disheveled from her long day.

"Emma's one of my favorites," Kristen says as we walk out in the foyer.

"Why's that?" I ask.

"She reminds me of myself at that age. You know, my parents didn't take me to church either. My grandmother took me. She lived with us for a few years and took me to her church every Sunday."

"So you think Emma is going to grow up to be as gifted as you are in understanding children?"

"Oh, this girl's much brighter than I am. She could teach her Sunday school class right now if we let her. She not only knows how to find things in the Bible, she's a theologian as well. She has discovered insights in her few months at church that I didn't have a grasp on until seminary. I tell you, with a little prompting she could pass a test on the psychology of religion right now. I hope you get a chance to talk with her, Ron."

Kristen stops her discourse abruptly when it sinks in that I might not get a chance to talk with Emma. She stands there with new tears welling up. I touch her on the shoulder and say, "I look forward to learning from her and pray I'll have that opportunity." I wonder if this young minister knows of the cancer.

* * *

It's now ten in the evening and I'm finally sitting in the recliner in the den of our house. I've longed for hours to park myself in this chair, my favorite respite from the world of pastoral responsibilities. My wife and I have spent the last thirty minutes debriefing the day, and earlier I spent some time with my daughter when I first got home in order to see how all of this was affecting her.

"Dad," Sarah asked me earlier, "how do you tell good people from bad people?"

This caught me off guard. I've taught lessons on the problem of evil in theological terms, but never been asked this simple yet complicated question before.

Stumbling for an answer, I responded, "I don't think you can tell much about people's character unless you get to know them well."

"That's just it," Sarah says, "You never know when you first meet someone if they have a good heart or an evil heart. Sometimes I watch people at the mall and try to decide if they are terrorists or criminals. Some people just look creepy."

"Why are you trying to identify dangerous people at the mall?"

"Because...you see all of these shows on television where evil people are planning to do terrible things and you get so frustrated that those around them can't see how bad they are. Then you ask yourself if you were in their place would you be able to tell they were evil. Do you think Emma knew right away if the person who took her was bad?"

I didn't have a profound answer for my daughter and try imagining why Emma did not call out for help while being abducted. Did she know the person or trust the person and willingly go with them? Would my daughter ever allow someone to take her out of some lack of trepidation?

I turn on the television to the ten o'clock news on a local channel. The lead story, of course, is the disappearance of Emma Wells. The familiar face of reporter Mary Kutter appears on the screen:

"Earlier today eight year old Emma Wells attended the summer Bible School for children at the First Baptist Church downtown. At noon she disappeared from the church and has not been found. Emma was wearing a pink tee shirt with the words 'Life is Good' on it and white shorts. She is approximately four and a half feet tall and has blond hair. This is a recent photo of Emma provided by her mother and father, Ted and Rachel Wells, who live in the Sycamore section of town. Anyone with any information on the whereabouts of this child is asked to call the number on the screen.

Detective Carl Brody heads the investigation. Lieutenant Brody, what can you tell us?

We've conducted a thorough search of the church and the surrounding area. At this time we have no leads as to where the girl is, but we do think that she was abducted. We will keep you informed as we obtain new details. We welcome any assistance the public can offer and encourage your contacting our department at the number provided here.

Tomorrow morning a CARD team or Child Abduction Rapid Deployment team from the FBI will arrive to take over the investigation. This is a response unit with expertise in such matters. Our department will assist them in the search for Emma Wells. We have asked for their help because of the special circumstances of this case.

Thank you Lieutenant Brody. The police have issued an Amber Alert for the missing girl. Her parents have chosen to not speak to the press today but are cooperating with the police. They have told us that they will make public comments sometime tomorrow. Stay tuned for updates on the disappearnce of Emma Wells. We all hope that the

message on the shirt she wears today reflects the outcome of this story."

Rachel and Ted Wells only appear in video shots made from a distance. There will come a time when they'll have to speak to the public. At this point there's no mention of the cancer. That news most certainly will become public by tomorrow, I assume.

My dread for the next day mounts as I seek rest from this one. I know well the great debilitating power of worry, but how in the world do you not succumb to its hold when there's a situation like this one? One quote I keep posted above my desk is from Edward Hallowell who wrote, "Worry is like blood pressure: you need a certain level to live, but too much can kill you." The problem is there's no device one can wrap around the arm with a gauge that tells you there's too much worry.

This evening my prayers are with Ted and Rachel Wells. My daughter's safe in her bedroom right now; theirs is out there somewhere, likely afraid or in pain, possibly dead. My level of anxiety can't approach theirs. It's impossible for me to comprehend what they are going through this evening.

I've been reading one of Max Lucado's latest books, *Fearless*. One paragraph is marked because it stuck in my mind:

> *"The semitruck of parenting comes loaded with fears. We fear failing the child, forgetting the child. Will we have enough money? Enough answers? Enough diapers? Enough drawer space? Vaccinations. Educations. Homework. Homecoming. It's enough to keep a parent awake at night."*

I put the book down and close my eyes. Will I have enough of what it takes to be a father and minister tomorrow?

I've been so caught up in the search for Emma Wells that I've almost forgotten the letter that's in my desk drawer at the church. I open my eyes and go over the words that are well implanted in my mind and which indict me for past behavior. The missing child coupled with the accusatory letter will not let my mind rest tonight. I know that tomorrow will be a challenging day.

CHAPTER FOUR

SATURDAY MORNING

James Turner is a registered sex offender. He lives only two blocks from First Baptist Church. He can't be found and hasn't checked in with his probation officer in over a week. This is what Detective Carl Brody told me a few minutes ago when he called. The police have searched the place where Turner lives, a garage apartment behind an old house on Moore Street. There are no signs that Emma Wells has been there. She's still missing this morning.

The authorities did find in the small two rooms above the garage a voucher for food that came from the food pantry in the basement of our church. This means that James Turner has likely been in our church building before. A bulletin has been issued for authorities in the state to pick him up if seen, and the search is on. He doesn't have a driver's license or a car. Turner was convicted eight years ago for fondling a little girl visiting a playground. The child disappeared from the view of her mother who panicked and rallied several others to her side. In nearby woods Turner and the six year old were found together. The child told the police what happened, and Turner was convicted of molestation. He served seven years in prison and was released on parole six months ago, choosing our town as his new place of residence. He's listed as a person of interest in the disappearance of Emma.

I struggle as to what to think about predators. On the one hand I abhor the crimes they commit while on the other hand I wonder what has made them this way. I have a problem with those who do horrendous things to others and then claim that they did this because they were victims themselves. Since I have no experience with being a victim of child abuse or other extreme abusive treatment, it's hard for me to understand what that can do to a person. My natural take on the matter is that people commit crimes out of choice. This belief causes me to be skeptical of the "but I am a victim too" defense. Yet, it's our calling as Christians to treat others with a measure of compassion. Right now I doubt I will be able to have much compassion for the one who took Emma, and that concerns me.

* * *

It's now nine in the morning and I expect this day will be one of endless interviews and a renewed screening of the actions which led to Emma's disappearance. One of the national news media reporters has called to schedule a few minutes with me. Taken as a whole the situation is, I fear, more than my abilities can handle. The awful letter from yesterday rests in my desk drawer with its citation of my supposed sins perched like a bolder on a precipice waiting to start an avalanche of hardships that will bury me before the week is done. I can't help but wonder if the arrival of my letter and the girl missing on the same day are coincidental or intricately related. The Wells have spent what must have been an agonizing night with their daughter still not found.

There's a tap on my partially open office door and Stan Brantley sticks his head in. Stan is the Presbyterian pastor whose church is directly across the street from ours.

"How're you holding up?" he asks.

I answer with a shrug of the shoulder and a twist of the hand, the universal signals which mean the jury is still out on the matter.

Stan is a good friend and fellow traveler on the same road of pastoral bliss. He's simply more cynical than I about the pleasures along the way. A little overweight and with a receding hairline, he appears older than his forty years. With an intellect allowing him to hold his own in any situation, this pastor's acerbic wit is often intimidating.

"Listen, Ron, until yesterday I envied you and so wanted to be in your shoes. I mean I've coveted your church and your pastorate. You have more people, have nicer buildings, make more money, and don't have to deal with some of the crazies I do at my zoo across the street. But, today I wouldn't be in your shoes for all of the gentle parishioners in the world."

"I never knew you were jealous of me," I respond with the type of banter which is typical between us. "I always thought you loathed our Baptist theology and our low church worship style."

"I do. You guys are so liturgically incorrect, and so metaphysically lost. But, there is the higher salary matter, and I could do with some of your freedom from ruling elders. Seriously, Ron, what's the news this morning? Is there any word on the little girl? This is a gosh-awful predicament you're in."

"Predicament is not a strong enough word. I think of it more like a wretched nightmare that refuses to allow me to wake up and forget. There's no news of Emma Wells this morning."

"Her parents must be worried sick. I know I'd be if I lost one of my boys."

"They're holding up pretty well. It's difficult to imagine the anguish they feel this morning."

"If you ask me," Stan says, "some crazy person off the street came in and took this kid. Every week, it seems, we find some vagrant wandering our halls. That's why we lock the doors if one of our staff is in the building alone. You never know who might come in off the street like I just did."

"You make a good point by your presence here; no telling what kind of rascal might walk in," I say jokingly. "I shouldn't make fun of this, for you're right."

"You need to be more careful over here," Stan warns. "Even in a small city like ours there are plenty of people who see churches as easy prey."

"I guess we're going to have to reconsider our daytime open door policy in light of this situation."

"Listen, I know you have a lot on your plate today. Just want you to know that I'm available if needed. Don't expect me to sell you one of my sermons at a cut rate or anything like that; but just about anything else and I'm on call."

"You Scots are so cheap," I say with a common expression I use with Stan often. "Thanks for the offer. It's good to see a friendly face, even one as homely as yours."

"You'll regret that last remark," Stan says jokingly as he walks to the door. "The Lord will smite you for such as that."

I'm glad he dropped by for he's one of the few people with whom I share my professional pressures. I probably should have shown him the letter, but I've not had time to process it yet myself.

Most weeks I come by the church office on Saturday mornings for a couple of hours to complete my preparation for the next day. Stan, and any other preacher, will tell you that the pressure of the week builds as Sunday draws near. I, for one, never feel totally prepared, so this is why I value my time alone at the church on Saturdays. I often go into the sanctuary to rehearse my sermon. The time spent without interruptions is extremely prized. This morning has been far from typical. I've yet to work on any of what I'll say Sunday, and I'll have to change my message for tomorrow from what I had planned before the disappearance of Emma. There'll be a full house of those expecting me to provide words of comfort to all who have been touched by this horrendous situation. On the Sunday after 9/11, the need for the right homily wasn't as imposing on me as is this situation.

My first impulse this morning was to show the letter to the police. My next impulse was to give any such actions more thought. I'm already in the middle of the investigation of the whereabouts of little Emma simply because I'm the pastor of the church where she was last seen. This letter might make me the focus of the investigation.

I feel today like an oscillating fan. My thoughts turn back and forth from the accusatory letter to the missing child. I can't focus on either so long as the other beckons my attention. For a few minutes I'm absorbed by the image of someone dragging Emma from the building and forcing her into a car that's to transport her to an isolated spot as she struggles to free herself from her abductor. Then the letter demands I turn my focus to my own personal crisis which threatens to upend my well-being. I have always tried to live my life by prioritizing. I ask myself constantly – what really matters, what is the best use of my time in the next few hours? Of course there's a competition always taking place within as there are a number of things that really matter. The usual forces that tug on me are still very present today: sermon preparation, pastoral duties, family time, personal meditation, and those nagging administrative details. Today all of these have been relegated to a back compartment of my mind as the letter and the child pull me back and forth in their demand for my attention.

I hear people moving around in the hall outside my office, and I know that my privacy has been breached. The day of public scrutiny begins, and the sermon will have to be refined this evening. My clergy friends who talk of the stress of Saturdays for those who preach have no idea what real stress is. How fortunate I've been my previous twenty years of ministry to have been spared this kind of quandary.

The noise in the hall is the television crew. The reporter is one I recognize from CNN or MSNBC. I often get confused with the entire myriad of round-the-clock programs that cover every serious and every seemingly inane drama that arises. I watch them, like most people, in order to be up on what's happening. I never expected to be a part of the happenings. Watching coverage of a tragedy or scandal hooks many of us because we live such mundane lives and find our excitement in the escapades of those on the screen or in the paper. I would like nothing better today than the humdrum of my typical Saturday.

There are four people on this team with the camera and lighting assistants included. A few details are covered in the briefing before the overly friendly journalist holds a microphone in front of his face as the lights illumine the two of us.

"Reverend Fowler, have you had contact with the Wells family this morning?" the young man from Atlanta asks.

"No, not yet; I plan to call sometime later."

"Do you feel that anyone on your church staff acted irresponsibly yesterday?"

It's clear to me that this interviewer is primed for what the media like to call hardball questions. "Certainly not," is my natural answer issued with a quick defensive comeback.

"But, this child was under the care of your church," the reporter states what everyone already knows.

"Emma Wells was one of many children we cared for this week. Her welfare is on the hearts of our staff and our congregation," I say with an assured tone.

"Are you reluctant to speak with the Wells in that they may hold you personally responsible?"

This one takes me by surprise. I can't help but think of the accusatory letter in my desk which claims I am responsible for appalling acts. Back to the reporter's question, I realize that I've put off my next conversation with Ted and Rachel Wells because I'm not sure I have anything helpful to say to them.

"I simply want them to have some time this morning before I call them. I'm sure they have too many intrusions into their privacy already."

"You were at the church yesterday, Pastor?"

"Yes, I took part in the Bible School's closing program."

"What do you think happened to Emma Wells?" the newsman asks.

"I do not know."

"Do you believe that she is under God's protection?"

"I'm sure she is under God's care."

"If she's under God's protection, then why do you think God let her be abducted?" he asks. The overly friendly reporter has turned into a not so amiable critic of God's supposed inability or unwillingness to defeat evil.

"I know that there is a great frustration many feel when we try and grasp how evil seems to flourish in a world under God's control. I'm also baffled by this at times. All I can say is I trust God that his love will have the final word."

"The final word," the reporter says, "as in the resurrection after the death of Jesus on the cross? Does God's final word always come after someone has died?"

The reporter seems intent on putting my faith on trial.

I counter, "When Jesus was in the garden before his death, he spoke a word that we Christians believe is essential to handling whatever comes to us in this life. That word is 'nevertheless.' When evil strikes or death comes we speak that word – 'nevertheless' meaning that we have faith in what the final outcome will be."

"So, you have given up on finding Emma Wells alive?" the reporter presses.

"No, I have not given up. All of us continue to hope for the best."

The reporter chooses to have the last word, "Thank you, Dr. Fowler. We all hope your god is protecting Emma Wells."

The interview process lasts only ten minutes, enough time for a hit and run of shock sound bites. My decompression from it will likely last the entire day. I'll replay my words in order to determine if I put my foot in my mouth or embarrassed myself. I now know why politicians often say the dumbest things under the scrutiny of the camera. It's not easy being subjected to unexpected leading questions which can undercut any solid footing. I'm sure my wife will critique the interview later as she knows that my strength is well-practiced public speaking, not so much the off-the-cuff stuff.

Again, I find myself alone in the building after the television crew has left. The letter's in my desk drawer. I can't let it sit there and not tell anyone. This could be a clue to the whereabouts of Emma. It may also be a physical threat against me, not just simply a written diatribe. There's only one person I can think of to assist me. I make the call and am pleased to find that Ken is home and available to come over immediately.

Waiting for Ken to get here I recall that popular author, Rabbi Harold Kushner, has written that, "Friends have been defined as people who know you at your worst and like you anyway, people in whose company you can be yourself." Ken is such a friend and causes me to remember that Kushner also says, "There is a kind of holiness in true friendship." This is because friends are there for us when we can't handle life alone. I have been able to share with Ken some of my shortcomings in the past and know he has understood them, just as I have helped him with some of his. Today, I need someone to guide me through this thicket of prickly challenges and am sure I can trust his friendship.

* * *

Ken Matthews enters my office with his usual self confident stride. He's well over six feet tall and straight shouldered, very fit for a sixty-five year old man. "Formidable" is how I would describe the build of my golf buddy and good friend. Ken's a retired FBI special investigator and member of our congregation. He's on the teller committee of the church which counts the money after the services and delivers the offering to the bank's night deposit, a very appropriate job for one of his talents and experiences. No one would dare take on Ken for he exudes strength even at his age.

About a year after I became pastor here Ken's wife, Margaret, was diagnosed with breast cancer which was far along in its development. I spent many hours with them during her hospital stays and surgery. At the end of six agonizing months, Margaret passed away. After that I helped him through the adjustment of his loss, and we became very close. He took an early retirement to devote more time to his wife in those last few months. He doesn't regret those months by her side since much of his career he traveled extensively in his duties, and Margaret stayed home with their two children.

Ken was the first person I thought of earlier this morning when I searched my group of friends for someone to share the letter with. I like to handle my own problems, but this one is beyond my personal experiences. To have a former FBI agent in the congregation is certainly a plus in a situation like this.

"Thanks, Ken for coming right over," I say to my friend.

"I was off duty," Ken responds. "Then again, I'm always off duty unless you count housework and golfing as being on duty. So, let me see this letter."

He sits reading the letter in the wing chair across from me and makes no audible response to the few lines of accusations. I can't tell from his expressions what he's thinking as he takes his time in perusing the inflammatory words. I knew he would not be shocked at what he read, for his background has insulated him from the jolt others might at first feel upon reading such a dispatch.

Handing the single page back to me Ken asks, "What do you think prompted this?"

Spoken like an investigator. He assumes little and asks much in this one simple question.

"I have no idea."

"Somebody out there doesn't like you. Got any guesses as to who that might be?"

"No idea," I again answer.

"Then we have a pretty tough situation here."

I like his use of the pronoun "we". I have no doubt that Ken will help me, not simply because he may feel he owes me after my support during his wife's illness and death, but because he is the kind of person who does what he feels is the right thing to do. I know that I could not have a better ally in my cause and feel fortunate to know a person of his caliber.

"Do I go to the police with this?" I ask.

"We need to show this to the FBI CARD team when they arrive," Ken states.

"They arrived in town only an hour ago," I say, "and are scheduled to be here at the church in a few minutes. I received a call from Neal Heard who heads the team. Do you know him?"

"I don't think so," Ken answers.

"He told me he would like to go over a few things with me."

"Good, he will have another detail to discuss with both of us."

"Ken, I can't imagine why someone has chosen to attack me like this. I've never done anything close to what I'm accused of here."

"I'm sure you haven't, but the person who sent this letter knows the power of recrimination," Ken states assuredly. "It can be hard to defend yourself from this kind of charge if your prosecutor is determined to follow this course. You must become fully aware of how this kind of thing works."

"You know how it works?" I ask. "You've dealt with things like this in your work?"

"I have. At the FBI Academy I spent some time at the Behavioral Science Unit and National Center for the Analysis of Violent Crime. I was also affiliated with APSAC which is the American Professional Society on the Abuse of Children."

I'm glad that the one person I've reached out to just happens to be an expert in this area. For the first time since reading the letter yesterday and the news of the disappearance, I feel some relief.

"In my work I've been involved in profiling child abusers," Ken continues.

Trying to contain my enthusiasm I ask, "There's a way to narrow down who the person is that wrote this awful stuff through some of the techniques you have learned?"

Ken says apologetically, "There's no fool proof way to identify the type of person who blackmails others or who takes children. We've made great strides in profiling, but it's not as easy at it appears in the movies and on television."

"In general, though, what should I be looking for in this person who addressed these words to me?"

"I can tell you this – your accuser has likely had some experience with child abuse, either as a victim or as a perpetrator. They're probably a loner, or at least an introvert. The tone of the letter leads me to think that they've been seriously hurt in some way."

"Hurt by me?" I ask.

"That's certainly possible, without your knowing it, or maybe by some other clergy person. It could be they have a grudge against the church, or churches in general."

"Do they really think I've done something wrong to a child?"

"My guess is this is some kind of transference. They're getting their personal issues confused with you. These are all premature assumptions on my part, but from experience they're the best theories I have at this time."

"This is all becoming hard to comprehend. Will the FBI see it this way?"

"That depends on who is on the case and how astute they are in such matters. Most likely it will be clear to them that you are a victim here just as the Wells girl."

I've not thought of myself as a victim and the designation makes me very uncomfortable.

Ken leans forward and speaks with all seriousness, "Ron, I must warn you that the FBI will look into your past. This letter and the missing child both coming on the same day will force them to delve into your background. This will not be comfortable for you."

"What will they be looking for?" I ask.

"They'll ask questions of people who have known you. They'll check with people you have worked with and on your military record. Anything suspicious in all of this will lead them to look even deeper."

I swivel in my chair and look out the window so Ken will not see the full extent of my discomfort.

"But, you don't have to worry. Your record's clean. I would

know if you had any skeletons in your closet after the time we've spent together," Ken says.

I can't imagine anything that would interest the FBI in my background, but the thought of this tenacious law enforcement agency digging in my past is disconcerting. It is sobering to try and recall all of your past mistakes.

"Will they find out about my court appearance when I was in high school?"

"I don't think you ever told me about that," Ken says.

"I guess I haven't. I was pulled over one night by the Raleigh police, simply because it was one in the morning, I guess. They asked if they could search my car. I had nothing to hide so I said yes. They found a small amount of marijuana in a gym bag in the back seat. It belonged to my friend, Paul. We were heading to his house to spend the night. I didn't know he used the stuff and certainly didn't know it was in the bag. We were both charged with possession."

"Well, pastor, it seems you do have a tainted past, after all," Ken says with a big smile on his face. "You did two things wrong that evening. First, you chose a friend who was stupid. Second, you were stupid in agreeing to a search of your car without probable cause. So what happened?"

"Well, my friend said he didn't know how the stuff got into his bag. My dad hired an attorney who advised me to rat on Paul. I refused to do that, but the attorney did it for me. The judge lectured me on how I should be more responsible and made me take some classes on drug abuse. After I completed the classes the matter was expunged from my record."

"If it was expunged then it will not show up. However, the FBI could discover it through a court order. Don't wet your pants, Ron. If that's all that's in your past you don't have to fret. The FBI will want to, however, make sure this letter you received has no relation to anything in your past."

There's nothing in my past which has any relation to the accusations in the letter. Still, being investigated is not a prospect I look forward to. Hopefully, the authorities will readily recognize that I'm not a person who abuses children. But, there is no way to mitigate the power of the allegation leveled against me if someone chooses to believe the worst about me. There is much truth in the words of Publilius Syrus in his Maxims, "In times of calamity, any rumor is believed." I heard that on some law and order type show recently. I think the fellow quoted was a first century wisdom writer. The truth is crises cause the gullible to believe most anything.

Ken steps out to the restroom, and I wonder how he handles his more ordinary life after the excitement of being a federal law enforcement agent all those years. His days are now filled with morning coffee at Hardee's with his two retired state trooper buddies, usually followed by a round of golf with the "dandy duffers" which are three of our senior church members in their seventies. Once a week, if possible, he and I play eighteen with a couple of very competitive businessmen; their one goal is to beat the pastor/agent duo. So far we have their number.

One night, a few years ago, while we were at his wife's bedside during her last days, Ken shared with me his most difficult experience while he was with the bureau. A seventeen year old boy was hiding in a warehouse after fleeing from a robbery. Ken's partner turned the wrong corner in their search and was shot in the leg. Ken returned fire and killed the boy. For a year afterwards he could not sleep more than five hours a night, sometimes the replay of that day returning in vivid detail in his dreams. That evening, waiting for his wife's final breaths, his normal stolid guard was down, and he cried for almost thirty minutes. My guess is that an impending death provoked memories of a past death.

CHAPTER FIVE

SATURDAY AFTERNOON

Neal Heard and Denise Chevalier are the two federal agents who enter my office at noon. I introduce Ken and tell them about his background. I can see that the two agents are unsure of how to react to the former agent being there. Heard looks to be in his early forties and is dressed in a navy blue suit that fits his lean body well. His chin juts out extending further than the point of his nose which gives him an exaggerated look of ruggedness. Chevalier is dressed in black, a long skirt with jacket. She's much younger than her partner, probably under thirty, attractive and petite. They are certainly not an overtly compatible team at first introduction.

Ken shakes their hands and says, "Listen, I understand that you two are probably wary of any interference by a civilian like me. When I was at the bureau I would have had problems with some former agent sticking his nose in. But, the pastor here is my friend, and I do have some experience with these matters. I'm going be involved in some way or another. I hope you don't mind my working with you."

Ken can be intimidating, but Heard does not back away. "I know a little about your reputation, Mr. Matthews."

"A good reputation, I hope," says Ken.

"Well, not so good among the criminal element."

Agent Heard turns to me. "Pastor, we're part of a four person team assigned to this case. The FBI has been given jurisdiction over abduction cases since the so called Lindberg Law went into effect in nineteen thirty-two. We coordinate our work through the National Crime Information Center."

Agent Chevalier continues, "We just arrived in town and wanted to come as soon as possible to the church to see the place where the little girl was last seen. We also need to ask you some questions."

They waste no time in getting down to business, so I invite them to sit as my office now is overtaken by the Federal Bureau of Investigation.

"Sir, you are on a list of people the police have developed of those in the building yesterday when the Wells girl was last seen," Heard adds.

"I understand that," I say. "I was here until about noon."

I've seen in the movies and on television teams of investigators take turns in confronting witnesses and suspects. This is my first personal encounter with such, and the intensity of having two law enforcement officers use the tag team approach is threatening.

"Do you also understand that you'll be crucial to our investigation in that you are the leader of this congregation?" asks Neal Heard.

"Yes, I understand that as well."

"And you also realize," Heard continues, "that you're one of the people the police have identified who weren't seen during the crucial period the girl went missing."

"Yes, I was away from the church during that time."

"We will need to go over that time period with you later after we get our bearings here," Chevalier adds.

I interrupt their briefing, wanting to get to the point of why I asked Ken here and not hold back my letter any longer. "Agents, there's something I want you to see. It was under my office door yesterday morning when I arrived." I hand them the single page with the accusatory attack on it.

Neal Heard and Denise Chevalier look at the contents of the letter. When he finishes, Heard looks at me and speaks in a measured tone, "Reverend, do you have any idea who sent this?"

"None," I answer.

"Have you ever received anything like this before?" Chevalier asks.

"No, I haven't."

"Why did you not show this to the police yesterday?" Heard asks.

"At the time I was so caught up in the idea of the child missing that I didn't see the two as related."

"And when did it come to you that this could be important in light of the child's disappearance?" Chevalier asks.

"This morning when I came here and read it again," I answer in a subdued tone.

Ken, keenly aware of the pressure being applied to me, interjects, "I think that whoever wrote this letter could possibly be the same person who took this child. I think we have a very disturbed person on our hands, and that they've fixed their anger on the pastor. I also think that Ron has no experience in such matters and can't be expected to think like a law enforcement officer."

Agent Chevalier nods in agreement and turns to me, "Our first priority is finding this child. This letter may help us do that. If the abductor is the letter writer then we have a new aspect to our case."

"I hope you understand, Dr. Fowler," Neal Heard says, "we must still consider you to be a possible suspect while we follow this new lead. However, even though this paper would seem to cast suspicion on you, we'll not let it throw off the investigation of all the possibilities. The letter may not be from the abductor, but from someone who simply wants to attack you. Coming before the child went missing is a curious coincidence if not related to the likely abduction."

I'm uncomfortable that he uses the word "suspect" in reference to me, though I knew that was coming.

Chevalier picks up on my discomfort. "We've just arrived, Dr. Fowler, and there's much we need to look at. On the way here we went over the list of people the police questioned yesterday. You're on that list as one who wasn't seen by anyone at the time we think the girl was abducted. Now, we have this letter which accuses you of harming children. And, there is the Turner fellow who can't be found. There's much we have to do, and we like to keep all options open until we can get more information."

"Ron's a friend and my pastor," Ken interjects. "He's not a child abductor and hasn't done anything like what is described in the letter. You will also find that he, in no way, fits the profile you are going to develop as to who might have taken this child."

I feel left out of the discussion as the two law enforcement officers and Ken spend a few minutes comparing notes. It's agreed, that for now, the letter will remain between Ken, me, and the FBI investigative team. The agents do not want it to get out to the press and sensationalize the case any further. They also think that making the letter public may push the author to do something rash under the extra pressure. If Emma is still alive they don't want to do anything to force the abductor's hand. Heard and Chevalier decide to send the single piece of paper to one of the bureau's experts in handwriting analysis. We make copies of the original, and each of the four of us keeps one of the duplicates. The letter will also be tested for fingerprints even though several of us have already touched it. I noticed earlier how carefully the others handled it.

"One more thing, Reverend," Heard says. "You may be in danger here. This letter sounds very angry to me. I suggest you take precautions in your movements the next few days while this case is open and your family members as well."

I agree to be careful, and am uneasy by the prospect that I might be in physical peril. The FBI agents announce they will take a few minutes to become familiar with our church and return later today to take a longer look at the premises. I give them one of our spare door keys. At this time these two agents and the other two on their team are going to police headquarters to set up a command center. Ken tells me he'll lock the outside door when he leaves with his key.

The church's quiet again, and I sit at my desk pondering my situation, our situation when I include Ted and Rachel Wells, the FBI, Ken, and of course Emma. I'm a possible suspect and a possible target of violence. These are concepts I never thought I would hear. The suspect designation bothers me the most. That coupled with the accusatory letter is a lot to handle.

In this forced time of reflection I accept that I'm not a perfect person. I've managed, however, to not succumb to any of the temptations that would rank in the top echelon of grave sins for Baptist pastors. I do seek to live by Christian morals, but I'm not perfect. For the life of me, I can't look back on any past behavior that would prompt such wild accusations as the ones made in the letter. Even in my imagination I've never entered into the realm of these allegations. By most standards my life has been very boring. I have no dramatic conversion experience in which I gave up a wicked life and came to Jesus. My worst thoughts have never even come close to being acted upon, partly from wisdom, mostly from fear that I could not escape them. I suppose I could tell of my secret desires and muster up a testimony of some interest, but only the super pious would be negatively impressed by my darkest fantasies. Certainly, no one would be inspired by my confessions enough to believe that I have any tendencies toward lecherous behavior. I thought everyone who knows me is aware of how straight laced I am. Evidently, someone has another opinion of me or wants to change the opinions of those who do know me.

Malcolm Gladwell in his book, *The Tipping Point*, has a chapter on the power of context. When I first read this I wanted to shout "amen" as he explains that character is dependent at certain times on circumstance and perspective. He says that "behavior is a function of social context." So many people find themselves in situations which pressure them to make foolish decisions. As I think back, I've never been in such a place where the temptation was overwhelming. It doesn't take much of a change in one's situation to tip one over into a different behavior. Like many people, I believe I have the moral fortitude to withstand whatever enticement comes my way to act in a less principled manner. This is what we in the church usually teach, that people with high morals will not succumb to immoral lures. Gladwell's supposition that character is dependent on circumstance and context challenges traditional teachings on morality.

The copy of the letter is still in my desk, I realize. It seems to reek of an odor. I hope that Emma Wells will be found unharmed for her sake and now also for mine. The disappearance, the church's uneasy involvement as the setting for a crime, and the accusatory letter may all be a temporary episode in my life where all ends well. I'm always optimistic, but am also a realist and doubt this will all vanish in a beneficial turnaround.

This is too much to process now. As intriguing as it is, I don't have the freedom to dwell on my vulnerability. I'm the pastor of a church with hundreds of people counting on me to fulfill my responsibilities. There's a message of growing importance for me to deliver tomorrow. I'm forced by time constraints to pull out an old sermon preached a few years ago on the security we find in our faith. This, I decide, is what I'll rework for the morning sermon, now only a few hours away. Thank God for the barrel, as we pastors often call our files of old sermons that can be rerun if needed. I only go to it under special circumstances. This is as special as it gets.

There's a drink machine in a utility closet down the hall. I decide a Diet Coke and a pack of nabs will be my lunch today. Beside the door to the closet stands the Apostle Paul. I greet him with a polite, "Good day, sir." I can't help but think of Paul's time spent in prison when he was accused of crimes he didn't commit. I hope that I don't have to suffer his level of persecution before this is all over. I wish he was here in person, not in cardboard, to help me understand how God works for the good in all things as Paul once said. Where is the good in all of this?

* * *

It's now one-thirty, and the trustees have scheduled a meeting this afternoon with our church's attorney and me. There are four members of the trustees, chaired by Suellen Grayson. She's forty-something, extremely thin, and has short black hair. I couldn't have a better person in the position in these circumstances. She's deliberate and thorough, yet one of the most understanding persons in our church when it comes to handling interpersonal problems.

The trustees are charged with protecting the church in liability matters that could interfere with our mission to serve our people and our Lord. She was the one who pushed us to take out liability insurance for our staff in case there were complaints that arise from the counsel our clergy provide. Suellen is a high school guidance counselor and was once taken to court over what was alleged to be false advice to a boy who attempted suicide. The boy lived and was treated for his depression. Suellen was absolved of any blame.

Sam Haverty is a member of our church and the attorney we go to for handling legal documents such as land transfers and loan agreements. Sam's specialty is criminal defense and only assists the church in these contract matters because we have prevailed upon him to do so. I don't think I've ever seen him smile, but that's not so bad when you want a serious legal mind at your side. He's a short man and always wears a bow tie, fussy about his appearance, precise in his vocabulary. For a moment this morning I thought of calling Sam after I read the dreadful letter, but could not involve him in this yet. I can imagine the lecture he will hit me with if I later have to tell him.

Also present are Taylor Johnson, an insurance salesman, Carol Marks who is a CPA, and Greg Byers, a businessman. They each greet me warmly and express how awful this missing child crisis must be for me to have to handle.

Suellen begins the meeting with a prayer. She asks God to intercede on the part of the Wells family and for guidance for those of us in the church to find ways to help them. After the amen she looks around the conference table and calmly says, "This is certainly not a matter I ever expected our church to deal with. Our buildings have become a crime scene and our staff members have been questioned as possible suspects."

"Folks, we thoroughly screened all of our staff members before they were hired and ran background checks," Sam reminds us. "This includes everyone from the pastor to the custodian. There's no reason for anyone on our staff to be a suspect in this."

Sam's a careful man and has advised us on sensitive matters such as counseling those of the opposite gender without a third party in the room. He lays out what we're to do in order to take the proper precautions in this situation. He's also a practical attorney and has said more than once, "We do not have to be paranoid to be prepared." The man may not smile, but he does have plenty of common sense.

Greg Byers speaks up, "Sam, is there any possibility the church can be sued if something bad happens to this child?"

"There's always that possibility. This is one reason many churches do not have ministries where children are picked up at their homes. Churches have been sued over injuries in vehicle accidents. But, there must be proof of negligence on our part if we are to be sued."

"We must consider that prospect, but that is premature today," Suellen says.

Sam looks around the conference table and offers, "I advise that staff and church members should back away from press interviews, except for our pastor who must represent our church. We should give the police our full cooperation, but everyone should come to me with any information that may even hint at incrimination of any of our staff."

I sure have blown that last one, I acknowledge to myself with trepidation.

Suellen, who's also a deacon in the church, offers one other piece of advice, "Let's not let any cameras into our worship services so that our church does not become a spectacle on the shock television shows."

We all agree that our ushers will allow reporters into our services but no television or still cameras.

Taylor Johnson adds, "We should confiscate all cell phones at the door, including Walter Stone's which often plays that annoying ring tone in the middle of services."

Everyone laughs and the atmosphere seems to lighten up a bit.

I brief the trustees on what has transpired so far and how the circumstances yesterday led to the child's not getting on the van as planned.

Suellen makes a most esoteric final point, "We are meeting here in order to protect our church and our staff. This is what we should do. The more important issue, however, is what do we say to the parents of Emma Wells. If this ends up with a terrible outcome, all of the legal and defensive stands we take must be secondary to our concern for Ted and Rachel Wells."

This lady knows how to get to the gist of things. I assure them that our staff will minister to the Wells family. Suellen will brief the ushers for the Sunday service, and Sam plans to monitor the situation in order to offer legal advice to the staff as needed.

After everyone else leaves the conference room, Sam remains. "Reverend, if someone from our congregation did take this child we could be in a legal bind."

"What do you mean?" I ask.

"Well, our church's liability policy does not cover abductions. This means we may be obligated to pay any expenses incurred such as a reward if needed, psychiatric care for the child if found and traumatized or even for the parents if she is not found or found dead. We may be obligated to pay medical expenses and even funeral expenses, heaven forbid, if the latter is needed."

"Let's hope that none of this will be necessary," I say to our lawyer.

Sam puts a hand on my shoulder, "You do the hoping, Ron. I'll do the planning."

* * *

I remain at the church as the FBI team has asked me to facilitate their renewed search of the premises. Even though the police have gone over every inch of the property, Heard and his agents need to look for themselves. I'm introduced to agent Paul Rodriguez, a third member of the team. He and I trace the possible movements of Emma Wells on Friday from the sanctuary to the restroom and down the back stairs. He agrees that this is the likely path taken for her to exit the building without being seen. He and the other agents don't think she left on her own. Agent Chevalier at this time is engaged in a thorough look in the restroom for any trace evidence as to what happened. She tells me that with so many people using the space there is little likelihood of finding anything of significance. The police tape is removed so the facility can be used on Sunday.

Neal Heard asks me if he and I can talk. We sit in my office in two facing chairs. He tries to act casual, but I feel I'm in the room with a tiger about to lunge forward and press me to the floor with his teeth bared.

"Reverend, it's time you and I discuss the letter you received."

"Okay," I say.

"You see, Dr. Fowler, I must make sure there's not something in the accusation that reflects some improper behavior on your part."

"There's no behavior of any kind that would prompt such charges," I say with a measure of force.

He does not show any signs of my tone intimidating him. "You can see that I must entertain the possibility that something you have done has triggered this attack on you?"

"I suppose, if I were in your position, I might want to take a closer look."

"Good, then we are on the same page," says Heard. "I need to talk with your wife and daughter to make sure there are no domestic issues related to the accusations."

"Domestic issues! There are no such issues. Why do my wife and daughter have to be involved?"

"It's normal procedure," Heard says calmly.

I should have realized he would need to ask some questions about me but I'm caught off guard by the idea that he will go to my home. "We don't have any problems in our family related to the letter," I insist.

"I'm sure you don't," the agent replies with his unflinching coolness.

"I don't want them to be made aware of the letter yet. They already have enough worries with the missing child."

"It's admirable of you to want to protect them, but these are the two people who know you best. I'll just tell them it's routine that I talk with them since you're in the center of this. For now, I'll keep the letter out of it. We do need to keep it in a tight group."

"I would appreciate that," I say. "Please don't scare them."

"Dr. Fowler, I will be on my best behavior."

His best behavior is still that of a powerful animal who naturally gives off menacing vibes. He and Chevalier plan to go by my house in the next hour. I'm asked to call Amy to tell her to expect them. Chevalier advised me that they need to talk to my family without my being there. They leave the office to allow me privacy when I call home.

Amy answers and I tell her, "I just met with agents from the FBI. They are the team assigned to investigate the Emma Wells case. They want to talk to you and Sarah."

There's an extended silence until finally Amy speaks. "They want to speak to us, why?"

"They want to ask you some questions about me."

Another briefer silence and then Amy asks, "What kind of questions?"

"They say that I'm crucial to their investigation as pastor of the church, and I'm one of the people unaccounted for when Emma was likely taken. Because of this they need to know more about me."

"What if I refuse to talk with them?"

"I don't know. I think they will insist."

I can picture my wife pondering her options. "Okay, what should I expect?" she asks.

"Two agents will be coming over. One is the lead investigator, Neal Heard. The other is a young woman, Denise Chevalier. They are both professional and thorough. I'm so sorry you have to go through this."

"I'll be alright, but they better be careful with Sarah. I don't want her to have to handle any undue stress."

"I agree. Try and limit the time they have with her. I'm going by the Wells house and will be home as soon as I can."

I want to go home and be there when Heard and Chevalier arrive, but know I shouldn't. I have a few minutes before the Wells expect me. I decide to take the long route to their house using the drive that exits our church from the back parking lot onto Dwyer Street. It passes behind the kudzu lot next door to the church. It's evident that many feet have trampled the vines in the search for Emma. The area looks like a steamroller has been employed to press the plants into some kind of patterned mat. The drive then makes its way up a hill to the church's playground which is not actually adjacent to the other church property but a half block away. The playground has the usual equipment for children, swings and slides, also a picnic shelter for outdoor fellowships. There are no children playing here today as the community is still on a self imposed quarantine of public places in the wake of the abduction yesterday.

A car is parked on the side of the drive in front of the church's shelter. I recognize the car. It belongs to Joel, our custodian. I pull over in front of the light green Honda Civic and get out of my car. Taking a long look around, Joel is nowhere in sight. The playground is bordered on the far side by several houses facing another street. Not a soul is present in any of the yards or on the streets. A summer Saturday afternoon is never this quiet around here.

Joel lives about five blocks away so I wonder if something's wrong with his vehicle causing him to leave it here. Approaching the car with curiosity I can see the driver side window is down and inside spot the keys in the ignition. On the front seat is a copy of the local morning paper with the picture of Emma Wells on the cover. The headline reads: "Search Continues for Missing Child." I read this earlier and know the cover story is detailed and mentions my name as well as others from our church.

Surveying the scene in all directions there's no sign of Joel. His cell phone number is programmed on my phone. It rings inside of the parked car, and the paper on the seat moves slightly from the vibration. Leaving his keys and cell phone in the car is not what I would have expected from this ex-marine. Where is he?

Trying not to be alarmed, I assess the scene. Calling the police seems premature, and there's no one else I can think of who might know of Joel's whereabouts. Simply leaving and assuming he will return is not a choice. He could have left the Honda here and walked home, but would not have left the keys in the car with the window down. I imagine scenarios which would lead to this. Perhaps on another day my mind would not readily conjure up fears of some terrible misfortune befalling Joel. This day, however, my thought processes are swayed by the bold headline on the newspaper cover which testifies to the possibility of crime impacting our community.

A noise behind me in the playground causes me to turn abruptly. In the direction of the sound, I spot a flashlight on the ground which I'm sure was not there a minute ago when I surveyed the area. Suddenly the head of Joel Weaver appears rising up out of the earth beside the silver flashlight. In a few seconds his shoulders emerge from the hole, and eventually the church custodian is standing about twenty yards from me, his clothes soiled and his hands almost black.

"Padre, what're you doing here?" Joel asks as he brushes off a layer of dirt from his jeans and knit shirt.

Still dumbfounded by the scene, it takes me a moment to respond. "I was driving by and saw your car. What in the world are you doing?"

"I came by the church to check on things and remembered the culvert under the playground as I was driving out this way. Wasn't sure anyone knew about it. Thought maybe it had not been checked out in the search for the girl. It's not that easy to see when debris is washed or blown over it."

"It's big enough to crawl down in?"

"Oh, yea. The thing is almost five feet deep, three feet wide, and runs for about thirty feet under the street. Not so different from the tunnels I searched in Nam. A small person like me can easily fit in there. A lot of water runs off the lots which are higher than the playground. I guess this is why the thing is so big. The opening on the other end of the pipe is only about two feet by two feet and hard to see when the weeds cover it. This grate here was partially covered with leaves. Occasionally, I come over to sweep the shelter slab, and usually have to clear this drain cover as well. The grate was not that hard to remove which is not good news for a children's playground. It probably has not been searched in the last day with all that debris on top."

"Did you find anything in there?"

"Just small twigs, leaves, and dirt. I was praying that I would not find the child. I still feel a little responsible for her disappearance since I was so close when she was taken yesterday. You know, someone could have stashed the child in this culvert and kicked the leaves on top to hide the grate."

"I'm glad you thought of this, Joel. I wonder how many other such places the searchers have missed?"

"Don't know. My military training has always caused me to be more observant of hiding places. Too many ambushes I guess."

"Your military experience has served you well."

"Not well enough in civilian life, I'm afraid."

As I leave Joel continuing to brush off his clothes and replace the grate, the thought occurs to me that I simply took his word as to why he was there and what he found. I'm sure that the police or FBI would want to check it out for themselves. Perhaps my trust in Joel Weaver is not wise, but my instincts tell me to rely on his integrity.

* * *

It's now four-thirty, and I finally have a chance to check on the Wells. When I arrive at their house I'm greeted on the front porch by Kristen who is leaving.

"How are they?" I ask.

"I'm amazed at their composure," our children's minister says. "Earlier the FBI came by to talk with them. Ted says the interview took an hour as the agents asked many questions about the relationships in their family. He said that such an interview is necessary to rule out any family involvement in Emma's disappearance."

"That must have been difficult, but I would imagine this is how it typically goes," I say. "From what I see on TV, a family member is often involved in the abduction."

"I don't know how any of this goes," Kristen says with a sense of frustration. "This is my first church crisis, and what a way to start."

"You're doing just fine," I say to reassure her. "Your support of the Wells is a great service to them and to our church."

"I've never had to deal with any real problems in my whole life until today," Kristen confides. "I'm twenty-three years old and have never even been to a funeral of anyone close to me. My parents and grandparents are all living and relatively healthy. The closest thing to a crisis in my life was when a boyfriend broke up with me. I'm certainly a raw neophyte to pastoral ministry. There was nothing in my counseling classes at seminary about a situation such as this."

"This kind of ministry you don't learn about in seminary," I say. "To be helpful in a situation like this requires instinct and intuition. I knew when we hired you that you have what it takes to counsel with people. I think the personality profile with your resume was accurate when you were listed as sensitive and caring.

"I hope you're right, Pastor. I feel stretched today. I'll see you in the morning."

I spend only twenty minutes with the Wells. The house is full of family members, Ted and Rachel in the midst of well-meaning people who seem intent on keeping them busy. I've never been sure what is best in a crisis situation – lots of people and activity, or time alone to reflect. My guess is that some of both are needed.

In my brief time with him, Ted expressed great concern over the news about James Turner, the sex offender out on parole. I can understand his unease. Emma is still missing and a paroled predator living in our community can't be found. Turner's picture has been all over the news today. His looks, however, do not give any clue as to what kind of person he is. He appears to be just an average guy, certainly not sinister appearing in any way. What does a sexual offender typically look like, I wonder?

* * *

As I head home I think of Kristen Davis who has been thrust into the middle of this challenge so early in her ministry. From what I've seen this young children's minister indeed fits her Myers-Briggs personality type. This valuable tool in understanding personality traits is helpful. I'm thankful that I was introduced in school to the writings of C. G. Jung, his work on human behavior, and to the Myers-Briggs test based on Jung's work.

Kristen's type is prone to be very responsive to the needs of others and sympathetic to their feelings. She can read other people's needs with outstanding accuracy and in a caring and concerned way say just the right thing to help. The problem with having such a personality type is that one tends to unconsciously over-identify with others and take on their burdens. This can cause a person to become too emotionally involved in the struggles of those around them. I know this danger well, for I've tested out to be the same type as Kristen, but her feeling side is more exaggerated than mine. This makes her more susceptible to the pitfalls of extensive emotional involvement in the pain of others.

* * *

There are still a hundred or more people searching for Emma as dark approaches on this second day of her disappearance. I never knew that a search like this involves looking into culverts, dumpsters, and landfills. It's almost as if there is a gruesome assumption that the search will end in the discovery of a lifeless body. Police have canvassed far beyond the immediate neighborhood of our church and still have not found any signs of this little girl. I've wanted to be out there searching, but Carl Brody advised against it. His reasons were twofold: one was that I was still in the middle of the investigation; the second was that I needed to be other places such as in front of the press, assisting the FBI, and counseling with the Wells. It would be far simpler if I could just look for this child along with the others who have been deployed in the hunt. At least I might feel that I'm making some real contribution instead of standing on the sidelines.

On the way home I swing by the church to see if the FBI agents are still there. The parking lot is empty and the buildings sit quiet as the day gives way to the night. Sitting in my car in the parking lot I reflect on all that has happened these last two days.

I'm told there is a Presbyterian church in Jerusalem which rests on the side of the hill overlooking the valley called Gehenna. Gehenna was the name Jesus used to refer to hell since it was in this valley in his day where garbage was burned. That church became known as "the church on the brink of hell." My beautiful First Baptist looks so at peace on this eve before the day of worship. I wonder if it rests on a precarious precipice this evening. I guess more to the point is – do I totter on the brink of a deep fissure which opens to impending danger? I'm a novice to this kind of fear. The letter refuses to fade as if I have a temporary photographic memory, and the missing child tugs on my emotions like a pounding pulse of ominous trembling convulsions.

CHAPTER SIX

SATURDAY EVENING

My Saturday evening is spent at home with my family. Dinner is a private affair as my wife knows that there is no way she's going to let me out in public this night where my new celebrity status will certainly rob me of the little bit of anonymity I may have. It's rare that we can go anywhere without encountering church members. I'm never really bothered by the fish bowl pastors live in, but Amy gets tired of the lack of privacy on our evenings out. In normal circumstances a pastor's family ventures into public aware of the watchful eyes of those in the congregation who observe them and always try to be on their best behavior. Most church members are usually considerate of the need for our privacy in off duty outings, but some take advantage of opportunities to engage clergy families in settings away from the church. And, few of us would welcome being totally ignored by our parishioners in public places as if we were of some different species.

Neal Heard and Denise Chevalier's visit to our house earlier lasted only thirty minutes. Amy tells me Heard bluntly asked her if the two of us had any problems in our marriage. She could not understand why he would ask that question. He told her it was routine. She didn't buy that explanation.

"Ron, why is the FBI interested in our family life?" she asks me.

"Because I'm in the middle of this mess, and they must make sure I don't have any problems that are going to complicate their investigation," I explain.

"What kind of problems?" Amy continues.

"Heard wants to make sure I don't have any abusive behavior habits."

"Why would he suspect you of such behaviors?"

"Because, to him, everyone is under suspicion until all the facts

71

are in."

"That's ridiculous," Amy declares. "I don't like that man. He insisted on meeting Sarah and asked her if she and her father were close. She told him the two of you were best buddies, and I then asked her to leave us while we finished the interview. He said that he had another question for her and proceeded to ask if you had ever physically hurt her. I could not believe he posed such a question to a twelve year old without any warning to me. Sarah told him that you had never hurt her and that if he knew you at all he would know you were a good father. I then sent her upstairs."

"I'm glad you did that," I say. "The man presses too hard."

"Sarah's upset enough over what has happened to Emma Wells. I will not allow her to be subjected to any other pressures."

"I'll tell Heard that our daughter is off limits to his team," I say, assuring her.

"I made that clear to him today."

The resolve in her voice is bold. "Good for you," I tell her.

"I'm glad that agent Chevalier was with him. She seemed to be more understanding of the need to not frighten Sarah."

"Chevalier does offer a balance to Heard's harshness."

"Are there any leads on what happened to Emma Wells?" Amy asks.

"I'm afraid not. There are many people still looking."

"What about this convicted molester who can't be found?"

"They're using all their available resources in finding Turner."

"What about you? How're you doing?" Amy asks as she straightens a sprig of my curly brown hair.

"Me, I'm just great," I say. "This child has been taken from my church, and the FBI has questioned you, Sarah, and me. The media is salivating to blame the church, religion, and God for the whole thing. I couldn't have had a better day."

"Sarah and I will be fine," Amy says standing close and taking hold of both of my hands. "My concern is how much pressure you're under. You may look like a cool customer to others, but I know just how much you internalize everything. When you called earlier you said that Ken was with you. I'm glad that you have someone else's support in dealing with this. He's just the one you need right now."

While Amy finishes preparing dinner I sit down with Sarah for a few minutes. We're in her room where her summer reading books are scattered everywhere. I'm constantly on her about how messy she is. It's a continuing war of wills which I seem to be losing.

"I'm sorry you were asked those questions today by agent Heard," I say to her.

"Didn't bother me all that much," Sarah replies. "It's kinda cool to be interviewed by the FBI."

"Cool or not, I wish he had not been so crass."

"I don't think he goes to church," Sarah says. "If he did he would know that preachers are kind and don't hurt others. You're a super dad even though you need to lighten up on your rules."

"So, you're okay with what happened today?"

"Don't worry about me. They just need to find Emma."

"You know that there are people out there who are looking for children and young people to harm."

"Dad, I'm not stupid. How can I not know that as much as there is on TV about missing children. I just never thought it could happen at our church. It must've been some pervert who just sneaked in. Nobody from our church would do something like this. Do you think someone may take her to another state and lock her in a basement?"

"I don't know. Right now let's just hope for the best."

I leave my daughter's room wondering the same thing she is. There are all kinds of possibilities as to where Emma is. She may be somewhere close by or possibly taken out of town. We must all be prepared that she will not be found alive.

I came very close to telling Amy about the letter at my office during the conversation over the FBI visit to our house. I still could not bring myself to do it yet. I find that having to weigh my actions carefully is very difficult as I seek to protect my wife from any extra worry and yet share with her how the investigation is going.

Sarah asks as we are finishing dinner, "Dad, do you actually know Emma Wells?"

"Not really," I reply.

"When I saw her picture on television today, I couldn't remember seeing her at church," Sarah says. "Do you think there's something weird about that?"

"It's a big church and there were a lot of people in VBS this week. She's younger than you and in another class."

"I know that, but still, it's strange that a girl goes to our church, and I can't remember ever seeing her. Am I so self-centered I don't notice those around me? Is our church a place where people don't know each other? We need to get to know the kids who ride the vans."

Amy joins the discussion, "I don't remember paying any attention to her either. There are so many new faces."

"See," Sarah says. "That shouldn't be the way it is. Dad, you didn't tell me earlier if you think Emma is still alive?"

"I don't know," I say. "I hope so."

"What do the police think? You've talked with them a lot, haven't you?" Sarah asks.

"Yes, I have, and they don't know either."

"If she's found and is okay," Sarah says, "I'm going to get to know her. I need to know every kid in our church."

I agree that we've lost much of the personal touch in our church and should work on that. I'm surprised and amazed by my daughter's own sense of guilt over the inattention we give to some of our children brought by the vans.

Sarah leaves the table as Amy and I sit there a little longer. I can see that she has something she wants to ask me now that our daughter has gone to her room.

"What if this were Sarah?" Amy asks. "What if Sarah was missing and possibly hurt by someone?"

I anticipated this question from her. "That's what many parents must be asking this evening," I answer. "It's beyond my comprehension just how many children are abducted each year in this country. It's so easy to accept the statistics when they don't impact your own family. We're very fortunate to have a healthy daughter home with us this evening."

"In my social work I try and have empathy for my clients. I try and put myself in their position and feel for their difficulties; much of the time that's hard for me to do because they live such different lives from me. But, this missing child could just as easily be ours. I hurt for her parents, but I'm glad it's not us. And, I feel so guilty over my relief it's not us in their shoes."

"Me too."

"I see so many people in my work who suffer from difficulties that are more than they can handle," Amy says. "Some situations are almost impossible to overcome. How do people prepare for such as this?"

"You know my job is to promote faith as the means to deal with impossible difficulties. I do believe it helps. The problem is that I'm supposed to sell an argument which says that we must accept our pain as a part of God's plan. But, I've seen it go both ways. I've seen people with faith rise above their suffering and become stronger for it, but I also have seen people of faith crushed by their pain and curse God."

"I wonder which way the Wells will go if there is a bad ending to this?" Amy asks. "They've not had the advantage of a caring church family. I think I would blame God if this were my child missing tonight."

"I don't know how Ted and Rachel will handle all of this. Right now they are simply hoping for the best. The not knowing is hard, but it still allows for hope."

"I'm not sure," Amy says. "It may be more helpful to expect the worst. At least this better prepares you for negative outcomes. I think hope may be overrated."

"You can't believe that," I argue. "How can we live without hope?"

"We simply become realists. We recognize that life is full of pain. I know you can't preach such from the pulpit. You have to tell people that God will make things turn out well, but what trust can they put in you and other preachers when life falls apart. To those who face personal disaster the preacher then becomes a false prophet. You said yourself that sometimes people curse God when they are crushed by life."

"Yes, but that is because they can't yet see how God will help them grow stronger by keeping their faith through the difficult times."

"I, for one, do not want to grow stronger by losing my daughter, by her suffering with cancer and abducted by some stranger. I would rather remain weak if that is what it takes to grow stronger."

"I think I'd better go and work more on my sermon for tomorrow. I may have other people out there who think like you."

This is not the first time I've been in this type of debate. The most difficult of people to convince that God overcomes evil are those who are able to envision the worst of scenarios and make a logical case for such. The truth is that both the prophets of doom and the cheery optimists are presumptuous to think they know the future. I'm still in the camp of hope, however, foolish or not.

As we leave the dinner table, I think of the letter back in my office. I try this evening to get behind the motivations of my accuser. I can't, however, put myself in their shoes because I've no idea who they are and why they've written what they have. There have been times in my life when I've been able to perceive why someone is against me and in my imagination reverse the position. I've tried to look at myself through their eyes. This can be painful, but the technique has been very helpful in my making needed changes in my behavior. I've hoped at times that others would try and understand what it's like to be me.

* * *

At eight we turn on the television, I choose the national news show to which I gave the interview today. Why is it that some of us seek out situations which we know will not be best for us? You'd think that a person would shy away from unsettling encounters that can only foster painful moments. I know well that a news show can edit interviews in ways which make the one interviewed look bad. But, it's not easy to miss the only time in your life when you might be seen on national television, even if you have reason to believe your performance may be less than desired. It turns out to be not only less than desired but simply less, or near nothing. I've one line in the unfolding drama, **"Emma Wells was one of the many children we cared for this week."** It was taken out of context and makes me look like a person oblivious to the seriousness of this heartbreaking story.

The network anchor for the evening interjects into the report that the name Emma in English means "universal". He makes the point that this little girl stands for all children who suffer, and goes on to illustrate the many ways children today are harmed in our country and around the world.

Rachel Wells appears on the screen next with her husband at her side and shares what I anticipated would need to come out, **"Please, whoever you are who has our daughter let her come home. Emma has cancer and needs her pain medication. Do not let her suffer. Do not let our little girl go through another night away from us in her condition."** Rachel's anguish is evident in her trembling voice.

Ted Wells then speaks, **"Our daughter needs to be home with her family. Please return her to us. She is only eight years old and has already been through enough pain."** His voice is steady and pleading.

Another layer is added to this mounting drama. The world is now aware that Emma has cancer. What other dispatch of trepidation can come next, many must wonder.

I make a brief phone call to the Wells household and offer my additional concern over their continuing emotional trial. Ted Wells thanks me and asks if I'll come over tomorrow afternoon as they have something to show me. I agree to come by and am curious as to what other aspect of this case is yet unseen.

If there has ever been a day to test my faith, this is it. It's so easy to be confident in your faith in the sane and normal days, but in the insane and abnormal days the confidence can erode.

I'm reminded of the words of C.S. Lewis from his book, *A Grief Observed:*

> *"You never know how much you really believe anything until its truth or falsehood becomes a matter of life and death to you. It is easy to say you believe a rope to be strong and sound as long as you are merely using it to cord a box. But suppose you had to hang by that rope over a precipice. Wouldn't you then first discover how much you really trusted it?"*

My connection to God is being tested today. I'm not sure how much I trust it. Lewis was referring to trust of another person in this passage, and this is on my mind. Trusting Ken with the letter seems to have been the right thing to do, and we had no choice but to let the FBI see it. Sharing this with anyone else now does not seem wise. I have some training in counseling as most pastors do. In that training I've learned that many people have a built-in tendency to not want to be privy to the pain of others. We don't like the responsibility of giving a genuine response to another who discloses some special secret to us. Who is there who truly wants to hear of my dilemma? By sharing my situation I will force that other person to listen and respond, to have to help solve my problem. Can I put that pressure on anyone else?

The phone rings and interrupts my thoughts. It's Carl Brody from the police station.

"Reverend, there's some news," Carl reports. "We have found the name badge that Emma Wells was wearing yesterday at your church."

I picture the yellow Bible heroes name sticker each person involved in VBS wore. "Where, Carl?" I ask.

"We found it near the church in a ditch. One of the volunteer searchers picked it up. It was folded and looked like any other piece of trash. Our best guess is that it blew across the parking lot and landed in the ditch on Friday. It supports our theory that she left the church by way of the back door of the education building."

"What do you think this means?"

"It means either the girl or her abductor may have taken it off on Friday," the detective states dryly. "It could have been pulled off of her during a struggle."

"Do the Wells know about this?" I ask.

"I just called them. Ted Wells asked me the same question you just asked. He thanked me for the call, but I could tell by his voice that he was shaken by the news."

"I just saw them on television. What a rough day for this family."

"This is neither good nor bad news, Pastor," Carl says. "We still don't have any idea where she was taken."

"Which ditch? Where exactly did you find the badge?"

"It was over by that kudzu lot on the edge of the church property."

I thank Carl for the update. When this comes out there will certainly be many parents who will look for the name badges their children wore this week and be thankful their child is at home as well as the badge. The Wells now have this puzzling clue to deal with tonight as to what happened to Emma.

Sitting on the couch in our den, I begin to doze off. A morbid image pops into my tired mind. I see a little blond headed girl's body in a tangle of green vines, her pink tee shirt covered in mud which blots out the message on the front so that only one word is clear, "life". The name tag is still attached, and I think it's good the yellow id is there to help identify her. My stupor is broken by the provocation of this semi-dream. I don't know how this gruesome image comes to me. With all my heart I hope it in no way is a premonition of reality.

I read a while back a book on the inner dummy we all have at work inside of us which is why normal people often have such crazy ideas. I think the author was named Weiner. Pastors must read extensively if we are to make our sermons informative. In this book there was a section on "emotional memory". The theory is that certain memories bypass our rationality and come from the limbic system of our brains. We cannot help this, but images or actions can arise that make no sense. I suppose that I have seen too many crime shows on television where bodies are found, and my limbic brain produced the image of the dead child with her name tag visible. Such irrational thoughts can't be helped according to the theory of the book.

This might explain other instances when irrational thoughts or behaviors have taken control of me. I may have been limbically captured, as this book calls certain experiences. There was the day on the golf course recently, for example, when something came over me and, for a few minutes, I couldn't hit a golf ball in any direction but in a seventy degree angle to my right. I'm not a very good golfer, but usually can drive the ball down the fairway. On this day I stood on the tee and hit six straight shots into the woods in the exact same location about fifty yards almost due right. After the first three, I tried to gather myself and think of what I was doing. On the fourth try I went through all of the disciplines a golfer is to use including: keep your head down, come back slowly on your swing, and keep your arm close to your body. I did all of these and the very same thing happened as on the previous three attempts. I then remembered when I was young and first started playing; I had trouble hitting a straight drive. It was at the time an embarrassment for me and made me shy away from the sport for years. With the knowledge that I was reverting to that old intimidation, I teed up for attempt number five. Once again the ball went into the woods at the same angle. After shot six, I quit and moved on to the green. On the next hole I was back to my better form. It was a strange experience. I've had a few other encounters with this type of emotional hijacking of my rational self. The mind can do some pretty strange things. I don't welcome any further images of dead girls this evening.

I take a couple of mild sleeping pills before I go to bed. There must be a few hours of rest for me this night if I'm to function tomorrow. As I lay down, the letter hidden in my desk at the office battles the sleeping pills as I struggle to clear my head. I'm sure I'll have one of my frequent anxiety dreams where I'm not prepared for the worship service when the time comes. I will not be able to find my necktie, or perhaps my sermon notes will be misplaced. I've talked with other pastors who have told me they have similar dreams. There's the one when you are still in your pajamas, but at the church, and it's time for the worship service to start. Some ministers find themselves driving but can't find their way to their church. Others are lost in the church buildings. I only hope my thoughts in deep sleep are those of such mild burdens as lost sermon notes and wardrobe errors, not dreadful images of dead children.

CHAPTER SEVEN

SUNDAY MORNING

The truth is that I'm preoccupied with one thought this morning – who here wants to destroy me. There are over five hundred people sitting out there on the burgundy padded pews waiting for the worship service to start, most anticipating what the pastor is going to say in defense of a god who lets a little girl disappear from church. One person out there is here for another reason entirely, to slander me. My job is to help people get through this difficult time for our community and church. I know well what is expected of me; the congregation is looking for reassurance and hope. My adversary, however, is looking for me to crack under the pressure of their attack.

Another morning comes with little Emma still missing. People across the country are following the story of the abduction. Her parents have become more desperate each hour, and our church family has searched and prayed for two days and nights. And here I am today with this other matter on my mind as I still worry over what has happened to this bright eight year old girl.

I look out from my vantage point on the platform, scanning the crowd, trying to pick up any hint as to who it might be that dislikes me so terribly that they would resort to the awful letter which is in my office only fifty feet away. Some offer smiles as they notice my passing glances. Others are not looking my way, likely preoccupied with their own personal dramas, oblivious to my hidden anxiety. Is my accuser one of those smiling at me while covering their malicious deceit or one of those seemingly lost in their own personal concerns? Whoever sent the shocking missive Friday is here for a far different purpose than anyone else in this gathering.

Louise Bracken is reverently producing magnificent winded notes on the pipe organ as she performs her prelude rendition of

"Nearer My God to Thee." It's her thirtieth year on that bench, and her obvious musical gifts have won many admirers. In my sixth year as pastor of this church I've not yet earned the kind of tenure she enjoys, but I think I'm on my way to gaining the respect of the majority of those who called me to be their spiritual leader. To my knowledge, I've not made any atrocious blunders in my pastoral duties. There have been many other Sundays when I've felt uneasy up here on this dais as I studied the faces of those gathered for worship. Some weeks I've been burdened with thoughts of inadequacy when I realized that there were those in the pew who needed a pastoral visit and I failed to respond through some time constraint or possibly misuse of my time. There were the counseling sessions in which I couldn't muster the wisdom to assist one with deeply rooted personal problems. Then there were the weeks when I found myself in some disagreement with one of the church's lay leaders and worried about the consequences of the minor confrontation for the church and for my position as pastor. But, for the most part, I would judge my performance as well above average.

But my restiveness this morning is not because of any fear that I'm not a good pastor. It's possible that my failures to give attention where needed, or my limited skills as a counselor, or my stance on certain issues is behind this attack on my personhood, but I can't trace the intensity of the impeaching communication I received to any of these typical shortcomings that we clergy often are guilty of or are accused of. No, this is beyond the scope of those matters. The fusillade of wrath in this accusation is far beyond anything ordinary. The language and tone of the letter I received exudes a severe dislike, no, a terrible hatred.

In another minute I'll have to stand up and welcome the worshipers with a warmth and enthusiasm that's a requirement of my profession. This is not fakery on my part, for I do care about this church and do enjoy my work among these people. But, only I, and two other persons here this morning, know how extra difficult it will be for me to turn on some internal switch and function in this already tense worship hour. Is he or she looking for signs that I can't muster up the courage to do my duty? Some pair of eyes out there is watching for an alteration of my voice modulation or for a modification in my posture. Are they hoping that the pressure will manifest itself in some even more dramatic way?

My wife is in the third row on the left with our daughter snuggling close to her as they whisper intimacies, private thoughts of a mother and daughter who are close. Neither of them is privy to my letter, as I can't share the horror of my accuser's scheme with them until I can sort out the reason for the design of his or her initiative. My wife doesn't receive well any criticism toward me as such is seen as a threat to what she believes to be a precarious position as best. This threat not only puts in jeopardy my job but my reputation as well, possibly even my freedom if it were to ever be believed. In no way do I think that my wife would suspect there is any truth to the indictments in the letter, but what spouse would not wonder briefly if there is some onerous smidgen of fact that is behind the scurrilous insinuations. I stop that thought and correct my assumption for my wife would never give any credit to these accusations. Right now she's pulling for me to adequately address the power of faith in meeting crises in life.

The prelude has stopped, and as I approach the pulpit to greet the five hundred who have gathered my steps are, to me, surprisingly steady. My voice seems to be strong and my delivery fairly normal. I've done this so many times over my twenty years in the ministry that it's routine. I wonder if perhaps there should not be some occasional pressure to examine the routine in order to not bore the faithful who considerately give their attention each week to the same formula. My nemesis must be disappointed that I have not yet overtly succumbed to the pressure. I know this person is out there for they said in the letter they would be here today. They have their prey in their sights like a sniper camouflaged in the jungle, only in this setting they're disguised by their Sunday-go-to-meeting outfit. I refuse to humor their illusion that I'm easy to rattle.

The congregation rises to sing the opening hymn of praise, "All Creatures of our God and King." I know the song by heart and, therefore, my eyes are free to survey the congregation as we sing. My detractors are out there as on every other Sunday. I know who some of them are. You can't suit every person in a congregation of nine hundred plus individuals. Rupert Rogers is seated on the aisle about midway down. He thinks that I don't preach the Bible and can't accept that I don't read from the King James Version each week. He's an ornery old cuss and has visited my office many times with his objections to my style. He's hard to take, but he's not the writer of letters. He prefers to confront face to face. Rupert would never choose anonymity to intimidate. Whoever is out there with their false intimations prefers to accuse from behind a veil.

The hundreds of voices carol the words of the second verse of the great hymn attributed to Saint Francis. I continue to look over the congregation and search the faces for either subdued animosity or for those obviously supportive in demeanor. George Shields is visible in the very back of the church. He's an usher today and will soon come to the front and say a prayer before the offering is taken. George is my most ardent supporter on the diaconate and a person with much influence in the congregation. I thought about calling George after I received the letter to seek his counsel but decided to give my situation more thought before bringing him into my predicament. I fancy myself a problem solver and take pride in my ability to handle difficulties on my own. Still, it's a lonely feeling standing up here as one under attack without others to help deflect the missiles aimed at me. Ken Matthews sits on the very back row, the one soldier present in my tiny defense force.

I choose to offer this morning a prayer once delivered by Peter Marshall, chaplain to the United States Senate in the mid nineteen hundreds:

> **You know, Father, the things of which we are afraid – the terror by night, the arrow by day that takes us unaware and often finds us without a vital, ready faith.**
>
> **We know that you have not promised to surround us with immunity from all the ills to which flesh is heir. We only pray that when they come, if come they must, they shall find us unafraid and with adequate resources to meet them.**
>
> **Give us constant faith and steady courage that we may neither whimper nor, in peevish petulance, complain before you.**

We thank you that you still rule over the world that you have made. Kings and emperors come and depart. All the shouting and the tumult, the screaming hurricanes of time have not deviated you from your path.

Help us to remember, O Christ, that you are victorious – victor – reigning over all; that in due time, in your own good time, you will work all things together for good to them that love you, who are called according to your purpose.

May we find our refuge in that regnant faith, and so face the future without fear. Give to us your peace, through Jesus Christ, our Lord, Amen.

Joan Riebert comes to the pulpit to present the special music, "His Eye Is on the Sparrow." The selection of the song was made well before the events of this Friday, and I just now pay attention to the choice. The emotional edge in the congregation is running high, and I shutter to think of what this tender and moving anthem will do to those who are burdened by the plight of Emma Wells. I'm not sure if I can avoid a soul-stirring response myself that will hamper my ability to stand up and preach after Joan finishes. Joan often is called upon to sing for our congregation, not only in worship services but at weddings and funerals as well. I have heard her present this particular song on several occasions before and know the power of her dynamic contralto voice. She's the soloist of choice for many in our church. Joan works at the county library and is the daughter of one of the former pastors of this congregation, Stephen Riebert, who is now deceased.

As usual Joan begins in a muted tone which, I know, will soon rise to a crescendo. With great feeling she sings the words of comfort:

Why should I feel discouraged, why should the shadows come,
Why should my heart be lonely, and long for heaven and home,
When Jesus is my portion? My constant friend is He:
His eye is on the sparrow, and I know He watches me;
His eye is on the sparrow, and I know He watches me.

There's an astounding quiet in this crowd of five hundred people as she reaches the refrain:

> **I sing because I'm happy,**
> **I sing because I'm free.**
> **For His eye is on the sparrow,**
> **And I know He watches me.**

As Joan finishes and turns to go back to her seat in the choir, the incredible hush slowly mutates into applause as the overwhelming sentimentality of the words and melody folds into a roar of ovation and appreciation. For at least a minute I remain bonded to my chair by the explosion of applause. As the clapping recedes, I stand to walk the four paces to the pulpit which is, I sense, still trembling from the vibrations of the vigorous anthem. It takes a moment for me to reorient my mind to the task at hand. The expectations of my performance have now been elevated to a level that is almost unimaginable.

I can't concentrate now on the people out there who might not like me or even the one who put a venomous letter under my office door. My responsibility is to speak to the many that trust me to offer ideas that will, in some way, provide hope in the midst of uneasiness. How paradoxical is it that on the day when I'm most called upon to focus on the needs of others, I have to be so absorbed with my own well being. I want so much to alleviate some anguish with this sermon. I begin with a humorous story to take away some of the tension:

> **There was a man who was afraid to fly but had to make a required trip by air. It would be over the ocean and when he boarded the plane a storm was threatening. As he sat in his seat a voice came over the cabin intercom saying, "Ladies and gentlemen, this is your captain. We will be flying overseas, nonstop to Germany. Our flight speed will be about six hundred and fifty miles per hour; our**

altitude will be thirty-five thousand feet. As you can see the weather is not good. We will be taking off as soon as I get up enough nerve." The already frightened passenger began to pray.

It takes a moment for the people in the pews to take in this story, and slowly many begin to smile and chuckle. The seriousness of the day is given a brief reprieve, and a calming transition is created as a bridge from the heart grasping solo to the message which is to follow. I now continue and have set the stage for what I want to say to my listeners.

I feel like the pilot of that plane this morning. There is a storm which has settled over our community today. It is a storm of anxiety, insecurity, uncertainty, and fear. I do not feel adequate to face this storm and offer some hope of deliverance, but it is my assigned task to bring words from our faith which we all know are available because we have a loving God.

We all crave some measure of security. It is humanly natural to do so. Theologian Paul Tillich wrote, "To be finite is to be insecure." He said that man's anxiety is expressed, "in anxious attempts to provide a secure place for himself, physically and socially." We cherish security even though our world is not a very secure place. During the time it takes to preach this sermon there are, in our country, over three hundred and fifty thefts, one hundred and fifty break-ins, and sixty-some violent crimes. There are other threats to our security such as issues of health, economics, and relationships. And, of course, there is that which is no longer a threat but a reality – a little girl is missing.

The picture of Emma Wells on the mantle in the living room of her home pops into my consciousness. I don't want it there for fear of becoming too emotional and not able to finish the sermon. I must clear it away from the forefront of my brain, so I pause for a brief moment to collect myself.

> **In the book of Acts in the New Testament there is this account of Paul on a ship which is soon to set sail for another port. Soon after they leave the port of Fair Haven a powerful storm develops and lasts for days. It is dark and dangerous, and those on board huddle together, anxious, fearful, waiting for the ship to capsize. At the height of the impending doom, Paul stands up and says, "Be of good cheer!" He announces that he has a message from God that all will be saved.**

I tell the congregation that I do not have any such message today. I have no promise that everything will work out as we hope. I tell them that I have not heard any direct word from God that Emma Wells will be found safe and sound. There's no specific good news on her whereabouts, I say with regret in my tone. All I can do is tell my listeners what I believe, that God will help us in these days of our uncertainty. There's a hushed silence in the room, and it seems the entire contingent is in a deep trance.

> **The Psalmist in the Old Testament promises us that we will be able to rest in the shadow of the almighty, that rest is a gift from God. In addition to rest our God offers to us stability. The winds still blow, but our faith helps us stand. God's stability is like the wings of the parent eagle that supports the shaky flight of the young eagle. God's presence helps us stay upright when our troubles attempt to knock us over. Our heavenly father offers to us spiritual walkers somewhat like the physical ones senior adults use in nursing homes to help when their legs are wobbly. In the roughest storms of life, God is by our side to keep us**

upright.

Jesus demonstrated a great sensitivity for the plight of those who were victimized in his day. He said things like:

If anyone strikes you on the cheek...
If someone forces you to go a mile...
If someone takes you to court...
If your brother has something against you...

Our Lord had then and has today compassion for those who are wounded, hurt, lost, and victim of the evil others do. We come here this morning not knowing what fate has befallen Emma Wells. We come here hoping that her disappearance is only temporary. But, we come here this morning also with dread that the situation will not end well. That is natural, even practical. Hope and dread are the opposite sides of the coin we hold in our hands today. We pray for her life and health. We also pray for the strength to handle the unthinkable. There is only one thing we can be sure of this morning – our God, our Christ, both care for Emma as they care for all of us. Her security and our security are in the hands of a loving God. There is not much I am sure of today, but that does not apply to the care of God for his children. Let us pray today for all of God's children, the one or ones who know where Emma is, Emma herself, her family, and for those of us who are so concerned for her and her family.

The congregation stands to sing the closing hymn, and I sense there is much more emotion in the voices than at the end of other services. Five hundred people sing, "Just a Closer Walk with Thee." There's a bond in this fellowship as if each person is on the same page of a script waiting to discover the ending. The commonality of purpose pervades the body as each one is hoping for a positive conclusion to the drama that unites us.

The benediction is given and I proceed down the aisle to the foyer where my duty is to greet those who have worshipped with us today. As I walk past the congregants two questions capture my thoughts: did I offer ample support in my message, and is my accuser standing there as I pass?

I stand at the front door as a parade of people pass by me. Most extend a hand, and I take the hands as I hear their parting comments. To a person, they express their concern for the Wells family. I think I can likely eliminate those who shake my hand as the author of my letter. My mind works hard to log the faces of those who pass through this line. I'll make a list later in the day, a list of those who exited the church through this passage as a way of ruling out suspects. But, can I be sure they would not look me in the eye and speak some inane phrase in order to throw me off track? What nerve that would take. I will not make a list after all. I will not resign my pulpit as he or she has demanded. I will not let them destroy my career, my ministry, my family.

CHAPTER EIGHT

SUNDAY AFTERNOON

After I have shaken everyone out at the church's front door it hits me that there are no members of the press waiting outside. On the way back to the office, passing through the main foyer, I glance out the side door and notice no reporters to interview me or others from our church. This is strange. I thought they would be here in droves pouncing upon us like crows on a carcass. Ken is waiting for me at my office, and I ask him if this is not peculiar.

"Ron, the reporters are all at the lake. While we were in worship the police received a call that someone found a shoe like the one Emma was wearing on Friday in the edge of the water at the state park beach. The blue croc is fairly common but the possibility that it belonged to the Wells child could not be ignored since Ted has confirmed it's the same color and size Emma was wearing at VBS. They have boats out there now with divers in the cove and people searching the woods nearby."

The news takes my breath away. "Do you think the child is in the lake?"

"Can't say. All kinds of false leads turn up in missing child cases. There are also plenty of kooks out there who like to plant items in order to watch the police waste their time. The inventory of Emma's clothing has been in the papers."

"Come on, nobody would deliberately put a shoe there to cause such a stir."

"I've seen it happen. But, this could be the real thing. We have to be prepared they will find her body in the lake or somewhere close by."

"Is anyone with Ted and Rachel?"

"Denise Chevalier is at their house. Ted Wells wanted to go to the lake but was advised it would not be best for everyone involved.

91

They have family and friends with them, and Kristen just left to go over there on my suggestion."

"What should I do?"

"You should go home and have lunch with your family. It will be all over the news as to what is happening, and I will keep you informed as to what the FBI knows. I'm going down to the command center."

Amy and Sarah have already gone home. The three mile drive to my house alone is a period of role confusion. Is my time best served as a family member, counselor to the Wells, or detective monitoring the search? Ken is probably right in that I should go home but as I pass the turn off to our neighborhood my foot stays on the gas pedal. It's only seven miles from my house to the state park where the shoe was found. On several occasions Amy, Sarah, and I have been there to spend an afternoon enjoying the water and the park's natural beauty.

The four lane stretch of highway crosses the end of the cove and as I slow down it's easy to see the array of police, rescue, and press vehicles in the parking lot to my left. There's a pull off often used by fishermen beside the bridge. I decide to stop here away from the crowd which is a hundred yards away. From this perspective I can make out three boats in the water and a man in a diving mask hanging on the side of a seventeen foot skiff. From my visits here I know the lake is only about fifteen feet deep in this area at the most. The water is a dark green and the surface is calm other than the tiny wakes left by the trolling motors.

On the cordoned off man-made beach there are a dozen or so people, most in uniform. I pull out the small set of binoculars I keep in the glove compartment of my car for sporting events and focus on the shore. Neal Heard and Carl Brody rest atop a picnic table watching the progress of those in the water. Across the cove two state patrolmen in wading boots are on the opposite bank making their way through the thick scrub bushes. They are using their billy clubs to part the branches and probably for protection against the water moccasins which claim these shores as habitat.

Another diver surfaces as the first one slips below the top of the murky lake, his fins protruding from the slick olive colored water as he makes his vertical descent. The man who just came up shakes his head sideways to indicate that his effort was fruitless. I find my own head shaking no to insure he did not spot the water-logged remains of the missing youngster. A part of me craves closure while another part prefers the search for the child continue if a dreadful end is delayed. It's like reading the obituaries in the morning paper where you hope to not find any names listed of persons you know, yet in some sick way you still wish you recognized some listing so as to not make your search a waste of time.

My phone is ringing. I know the caller must be Amy wondering where I am. My home number appears on the display.

"Yes, I know I'm supposed to be home. I'll be there shortly."

"Where are you?" Amy asks with what I know is her concerned slash aggravated tone.

"I'm at the lake watching the police search."

"Why are they searching at the lake?"

"There is the possibility Emma was here on Friday."

"Oh, my God! Not like the Preston girl earlier this year."

It was not far from here where they found Michelle Preston in February, I remember. "Yes, pretty close to where she was found."

"Tell me they haven't found anything."

"They have not, but they're still looking."

"Ron, please come home. Sarah and I need some time with you. It's not your responsibility to find this child. If they do find her there Sarah and I will need your support."

"Okay, I'll be home in fifteen minutes."

The search in the distance is still being conducted. This cove is not very wide but it connects to a larger body of this sprawling lake system which spans the border of Virginia and North Carolina. I'm no expert on the currents but assume a body in the water must move in some direction. A body in the water – I used that term like an unemotional observer. This is not just a body they are looking for but one belonging to an eight year old child who was enjoying a morning at our church with other children only two days ago. I've been to her home and met her parents. A shiver runs down my spine as I let it sink in that they may pull the lifeless form of Emma Wells from that lake. I really don't want to be here when that happens. I crank the engine and sharply turn my Malibu in the direction of home.

My phone is still on the seat where I laid it after Amy's call. My daughter just recently downloaded a new ring tone for me. It's the song "Upside Down" by Jack Johnson which she says comes from the Curious George movie. She printed out some of the words for me and put them on the console by my seat:

> *Who's to say I can't do everything.*
> *Well, I can try.*
> *And, as I roll along I begin to find*
> *things aren't always what they seem.*
> *I want to turn the whole thing upside down.*
> *I'll find the things they say just can't be found.*

There is wisdom in places where we don't expect it.

* * *

The three of us sit at the lunch table. We each pick at our food as our appetites have been stolen by an anxious dread that Emma Wells may be pulled out of the lake. The anticipation of a phone call with news of unbelievable tragedy is our common concern. Sarah steals looks at me occasionally, perhaps to see if I'm watching her. Amy is moving a red bliss potato around on her plate in circles that outline the piece of roast beef in the center, oblivious that her motions are frivolous in light of the seriousness of the atmosphere in the room.

The phone in the kitchen rings. Ken's voice does not give away any portent of his message. I turn to look as Sarah and Amy have both put their utensils down and are poised to decipher my end of the conversation.

"A few minutes ago," Ken says, "Two teenage boys were brought into the police station. Yesterday, they bought a pair of size three blue crocs at the local Belk store. When the clerk saw the news of the discovery at the lake on television she called to speak to the FBI agents. The boys had used a debit card for the purchase which helped the authorities learn who they are. They were found at one of their homes watching the story unfold on channel seven."

"You mean they deliberately placed the shoe at the lake to create all of this mess?" I ask.

"They have confessed to taking the shoe to the lake at dawn this morning, roughing it up in the dirt, and placing it on a short reed at the water's edge. Who knows what they were thinking when they did this. I know what they are thinking right now – we're in a crap load of trouble. Cleaned that up a bit for you, pastor."

"Thanks, Ken, for the news. This is a great relief."

"It is for everyone," Ken replies. "By the way, special agent Fowler, next time you ask my advice on what you should do with your time, take it. Going to the lake was not wise."

"I get the point."

My wife, daughter, and I all hug in our kitchen. After this I call the Wells. Ted comes to the phone and tells me that Rachel was mildly sedated an hour ago and is asleep. I'm sure they have both been through the wringer. I offer to cancel our appointment later so they can have a chance to breathe after the turmoil of the last few hours. Ted asks me to please come as we had planned. More than ever, he says, they need to share something with me. It's one-thirty and thank goodness Emma Wells has not been found, in the lake at least.

* * *

It's three-thirty in the afternoon and I keep my appointment with Ted and Rachel Wells. What is it they want me to see? It occurred to me this morning that they may have received something from my accuser. I approach their door nervous as to what to expect, my hands shaky as I press the door bell button. I anticipate them both to be totally worn out from the latest addition to their ordeal. Three press trucks are lined up on their street and a tent has been erected on their front lawn to shield reporters from the sun. Two policemen are stationed on the walk to assure the family their privacy.

Rachel opens the door and appears eager for me to come into their house. I'm surprised by her alertness after her being sedated only a few hours earlier. She hugs me for a moment, then motions for me to follow her. The living room, I notice, is spotless as we pass through it. Perhaps there's a need to have some aspect of their lives in order. I'm led into the dine-in kitchen where the counters are loaded with a variety of covered dishes, perhaps thirty in number. Ted is seated at the kitchen table.

"We can't believe the outpouring of food that has come in the last two days," Rachel says. "Much of what you see here has come from people in your church, Dr. Fowler."

Ted adds as he rises to greet me, "Rachel and I have never attended a service at First Baptist, and look at this spread of food. I don't know what to say or think about this outpouring of help."

"Our people think of you as a part of our congregation and want to find some way to assist. Bringing food is an uncomplicated way to express concern and care," I say.

They motion for me to sit with them at the round pedestal table. I take a seat in a ladder back chair. Ted and Rachel each sit on opposite sides of me. On the table are a laptop computer and a box of tissues. Rachel offers a glass of tea, and I accept.

I share words of concern for their struggle, and they both nod in acceptance. I don't mention the search at the lake. We all know the fear the found shoe brought, and the relief over the false alarm. I'm sure they wonder like I do as to how many more hours of agony are ahead and how many other cases of misdirection.

Ted's wearing a sweatshirt with a Virginia Tech logo on it. There are purplish bags under his eyes which are the consequences, I suppose, of sleepless nights. Rachel has the same puffiness, but is attentive. Her hand is not steady, however, as she places the tea glass before me. Her eyes are moist and her hair is brushed with evidence of limited effort at precision. Her khaki skirt and sleeveless blouse are wrinkled. I'm amazed by the resilience of this couple.

"We want you to see something, Pastor, which may help you better understand the extent of our sorrow," Ted says. "We haven't shown this to the police or the press."

He motions to the computer on the table.

I don't know what to say as I have no idea what this could be that I'm to see.

Ted turns the laptop on and rotates it so that I can see the screen. The whirr of the disc drive breaks the silence and Emma

Wells' face appears on the fifteen inch visual; she begins to speak. I've seen videos of her on television over the last two days, but have never heard her voice. She's dressed in a light green knit top and has a matching ribbon in her hair as she begins to address the camera.

> **My name is Emma. I am eight and a half years old and live with my mother and father. I have the best parents in the world. I like to play with my friends and my favorite activity is roller blading. This is my disc diary. I have cancer.**

Ted pushes the pause button and explains that the video was made over the last few months. I marvel at how this little girl's blue eyes match those of her mother. Her voice is that of a child, but her composure is so mature. Again Ted starts the recording.

> **They think this kind of cancer starts when we're babies and only shows up later. More boys get it than do girls. I'm somewhat of a tomboy, so that could be why I got it. There's a good chance it can be cured. That's good news for my parents who are so sad that I have it.**
>
> **My parents do not know that I'm making this DVD. I only want them to see it later when I'm well or when I die. They are pretty strong, but this could make them sadder at this time. This is my private diary which I hope will help everyone know what it's like to be me. Mom and Dad, I don't like keeping secrets from you, but this is what I must do.**
>
> **I just want everyone to know that I have faith in God. I've been going to church for a while now and have learned about how God cares for all of his children. Most people probably don't think about this very often. I think about it every day now. I would like to tell Miss Kristen at the church I'm sick, but have decided she does not need to worry about me right now. She's so nice, and I'm afraid**

she will cry and not be as happy as she needs to be.

My mother and father do not go to church, but they believe in God. I think they will need to go to church if something bad happens to me. It'll help them, knowing that God is so good. It has sure helped me. I heard my dad say that God should not let children have cancer. I wish he would not be angry with God. I'm not. Dad, when you see this, I hope you and God are friends.

I've seen Pastor Ron a few times at church and wish I could talk with him. He probably knows why God does what he does. I think I could help him know what it's like to be sick like I am so he could better help others. The pain has been bad for about two months now, and I have found that reading my Bible is a good thing to do when the medicine does not stop it very much. Pastor Ron needs to know that, so he can tell others who have pain to read their Bibles.

I hope that my mother and father and Miss Kristen and my pastor all can see this video sometime. I'll hide it in my room until I get better or worse.

I know that I'm just a child, but there are some things I feel now that may even help grownups be better at sadness. I hope to be able to grow up and do important things. My doctors tell me that I'm brave. They are good at knowing about cancer, but they don't know about how I feel inside. I'm very tired now – will do more later.

Ted Wells stops the recording. I look at him and his wife as they both have their faces turned toward the window, obviously seeking to contain their emotional pain. I don't know where to look or what to say as the lump in my throat causes me to swallow hard. These two people must be overwhelmed with all they are facing. The press is outside their door eager to cover the story of a missing child with no idea that the child is so brave. Emma Wells is not the universal child they have described. Emma Wells is special. She's an inspiration.

Rachel extracts the disc from the computer and hands it to me. "Pastor, this is a copy we made yesterday after we found it. We want you to have it. There is more on the DVD. Please do not let it get out to the press at this time. We want you to get to know our daughter better."

Ted says, "Emma's been tested at school and we are told her IQ is very high. She's gifted in several areas, but what has amazed us the most is how intuitive she is concerning the needs of others. We're not sure how to act as parents for she's often wiser than we are in understanding why people act the way they do. If her abductor has not harmed her then she's finding a way right now to figure out their motivations."

"Look at the rest of the video and you'll see what we mean," Rachel adds.

"Thank you," I say. "I don't think I've ever been so touched by the words of a child. Emma's an amazing girl and deserves to live and grow up. I've found that there is usually more to all personal stories than is evident on the surface."

"You can understand our desperate concern for our daughter," Ted says. "She needs her pain medication. She was to start chemotherapy last week, but asked us to wait until after Bible School. She may be out there somewhere hurting and getting sicker. This is why we put out a plea on TV yesterday, begging her captor to release her or, at least, help her with her pain. We were hoping not to make the cancer public just yet, but had no choice but tell the police. This is one reason they were so sure she did not wander off yesterday as she needs her pain medication."

"We're trying to remain hopeful," Rachel says with a resolution in her voice that surprises me. "We understand it's very possible Emma will not come home alive. How do rational people hope when the odds are against them, Pastor?"

I share with them some of what I said in the service this morning and try to assure them God has a way of changing the odds. The next few minutes are spent trying to find a way to alleviate some of their concern, but I find I can only stumble through expressions of sympathy. As I leave the Wells house, my anger takes over as I think of the possibility of Emma held captive somewhere and suffering. A part of my anger is at God for this double tragedy which is beyond the scope of any reason. Another part of my anger is toward this monster who could take a little girl, one already facing pain and possible death. I'm an agnostic on the subject of there being a hell, but if there is, then this child taker should suffer the full measure of pain possible in an eternal pit. This thought is not for public consumption, just between me and my God.

On the way home from my kitchen table session with Ted and Rachel the car CD player is on. Usually I pay little notice to what is playing as the volume's set low, and my mind is preoccupied with pressing matters. But, the song on now catches my attention. My wife gave me this recording of Josh Groban's music at Christmas. The selection playing is "You Raise Me Up," which is one of my favorites. The words haunt me as I think of the Wells family and all of their troubles. As I pull into the driveway of my home tears form, and an emotional wave overtakes me while I sit in the parked car trying to hold back the overflow of sentiment. It takes a couple of minutes for me to collect myself before going into the house.

Amy and Sarah are not home to see my moist eyes which is a relief. Not that I'm embarrassed to have let my feelings progress to tears but that I feel the need to be steady in the face of this terrible ordeal and not let emotion crowd out rational responses. I can't help others if my own responses are not stable and composed. It's my responsibility to live in such a way as to testify what Paul of the New Testament taught – God supplies us with adequate inner resources to face the most difficult of times.

* * *

My day isn't done yet. The FBI has asked that, Kristen, Steve, Deanna, and I meet with them at the church. We are to go through the list of the people who were at First Baptist on Friday at noon and help them with further screening. I can't imagine a worse task than that of pointing out possible suspects in a child's abduction from my own congregation. The conference room table is covered with pages separated from our church's pictorial directory. We are to circle with a red pen everyone who was at church at that crucial hour on Friday and a place a check mark beside the ones not remembered as being present as the school ended. Our church directory has become a mug book for us to peruse. I've been through the directory many times in order to match names and faces. This exercise will be far different in purpose.

Steve refuses to oblige. He says this violates his constitutional rights and puts his hands out for the cuffs he believes will be his reward for not cooperating.

"Steve, we all want the same thing here, to find Emma Wells," says agent Chevalier. "Our job is to cover every base. This is one of the bases. I know you would rather not do anything to incriminate your church people, but we can't rule out the possibility that someone pictured in this book took Emma."

Steve looks the agent in the eye and says, "You want us to tell you what we know about these people. We clergy have the trust of those who come to us for help that we will not disclose what they tell us. So, I go through the directory and come upon one of the families whose teenager has told me something in confidence about his or her parents. I'm to tell you what I know so you can put them on a list of suspects?"

"Has one of your teens told you something that might be pertinent to this investigation?" Neal Heard asks.

"That is what you are after isn't it?" Steve says. "You already have a list of who was at church Friday. This is an attempt to get us to share any secrets we have."

"Steve, I doubt they are asking for us to divulge confidences," I interject. "I think the point is for us to help with eliminating those who we know were not in position to leave with the child."

"Pastor, you're right, but so is your youth minister," Heard says. "We need any information we can get. You folks may know things about these people that will enable us to put our focus where it should be."

Kristen, who has been standing by the door, says, "I'm with Steve. I can't share with you anything I've heard in private."

Deanna and I nod in agreement with what Kristen just said.

"I didn't think you Baptists had confessional booths," Heard says with some attempt at levity.

"We don't," I follow. "We hear our confessions in our offices, in the church kitchen, on the playground, in homes, and at restaurants."

"Just about anywhere people feel comfortable opening up to us," Deanna adds.

"Alright," says Chevalier. "You will not divulge any private testimonies. Just look at the pictures and help us with who was and was not there when Emma disappeared."

With the ground rules agreed upon we collectively go through the directory, giving the agents information, but nothing held confidentially. We point out who had cars at church, and who took groups of children home. We put x marks beside the names of those who stayed at church to help clean up and, therefore, who could not have left early with Emma Wells. We're all surprised at how many people we're able to eliminate as suspects.

My three staff members handle themselves admirably. I watch them cope with this unpleasant task with determined resolve, especially Steve who's cooperating under stated protest. He has a way of hearing what is not said, picking up on innuendos and deciphering body language with an adeptness not matched by many. His hearing loss has forced him to adapt to the world around him in such a way as to more than compensate for his limited audible senses. He once told me he was made fun of as a child because of his slow speech. Now I look at this super capable youth minister and marvel at how he relates so well to all the teenagers, the popular ones and the loners.

How is it that some people are so messed up by troubled childhoods and others overcome their challenges to become strong and contributing adults? My guess is that difficult childhoods often form strong adulthoods, not always of course, but frequently. Peter Gomes, of Harvard University, in a sermon on strength from turmoil, points out that when infants are baptized in the Greek Orthodox tradition the priest takes a large cross and strikes the child on the breast with some force so that it often leaves a mark. It's meant to be a reminder to the parents that there will be pain in life which must be overcome. Through faith and resolve many are able to get beyond their early pains.

After an hour long process, we've made check marks beside nine people who were at church Friday and whom we can't account for during the crucial time between twelve and twelve-thirty. We add to this list three people whose pictures are not in the directory. Here are a dozen possible suspects in the disappearance of Emma Wells. The list includes four staff members: Janice Moore, our music minister; Karen Gravitt, our church hostess; Joel, the custodian; and me. Janice was in the choir room alone during the period after the final program on Friday. Karen was in the church kitchen cleaning up, and Joel somewhere in the education building. I left right at twelve to go to the hospital for a visit but stopped at home for lunch for a few minutes. My wife and daughter were not there at the time. As far as we know there is no one who can vouch for any of us four staff members being where we said we were during those few minutes. The FBI will need to interview again the dozen people we have identified, myself included.

* * *

Steve comes to my office after we finish with the identification process.

"Ron, I need to ask you something."

"Sure, Steve, what's on your mind?"

"This evening the youth of the church are going to meet over at the den as is customary. I thought it would be better if we didn't cancel our regular youth group meeting. Some of them have been involved in the search today and are very caught up in this matter. I want your opinion on something."

"By all means."

"Well," Steve continues, "I would like for us to spend our time tonight debriefing what has happened these last two days. I think it would be therapeutic for us to explore our feelings about this."

"That sounds like a good idea to me," I offer.

"Here's the issue," Steve says with caution in his voice. "I'm not sure I know how to deal with the anger that some of them are feeling. There's a lot of rage brewing in their adolescent minds. I don't want this to be a rally which expands those feelings. Do you think this could be a dangerous discussion, possibly harmful to their spiritual growth?"

"Whew, that's a tough one. I can understand your concern."

"This is especially hard for me," Steve continues. "As you know I'm a pacifist and am against all types of violence, including war. Many of these kids, however, do not feel as I do. They tend to go along with most I teach them, but we've had some lively discussions on this subject. I want us tonight to look at what Jesus said about loving your enemies. I think that would be helpful."

"So, you're worried about the kids being too riled up to accept such a teaching?"

"No, that's not the real problem." Steve puts his head down on my desk, and then raises back up. "The real problem is that I have so much anger in me today. I've never felt this level of hostile emotions before. I'm afraid I could feed their angers."

"As you well know, you have to deal with your emotions first," I caution. "But, you're a person too, and have the right to share the struggles you're dealing with today. I think if you share your inner turmoil with them they'll learn much about the tug between love and hate that we all have to manage within ourselves when we are close to a great injustice such as this."

"So, you think I should open that can of worms with them?"

"Yes, it's both honest and revealing. They already know your views on war and the death penalty. Now, they'll see that you are not impassionate in regard to life and death situations. This is a valuable opportunity for you to lead them in examining their own responses to sensitive issues."

"I think I can do that," Steve says. "I've been trying to teach them that Christianity is an ideal that is very hard to attain."

Steve leaves with a little more confidence than when he came in. I really did nothing more than serve as his sounding board on this matter. He was going to come up with what he should do on his own. I can't help but remember the dynamic words of G. K. Chesterton, "It is not that Christianity has been tried and found wanting. It is that it has never been tried." This evening we in this church have been presented an opportunity to think and live on a new level. I wonder what would happen if a new generation could truly live out the Christian experiment.

CHAPTER NINE

SUNDAY EVENING

When I finally arrive at home, my wife greets me with a hug. She asks me how the time with the FBI went. I inform her that I'm on the suspect list along with others on our staff and tell her about the dozen possible abductors.

"Janet and Karen are suspects also?" she asks.

"That's right."

"I can't believe this. Will you all be questioned again?"

"Yes," I say nonchalantly.

Amy is clearly very upset over this news. I want to tell her how concerned I really am and about the letter as well. I just can't bring myself to cause her more anguish at this time.

"Who else is on the list?"

"Well, there are Lee Williams and Marge Abernathy," I say. She knows that Lee was one of the teenagers helping with Bible School, and Marge was a nursery worker. Lee's an Eagle Scout and honor student while Marge is a seventy-two year old grandmother who often volunteers for child care duty.

"This is the most ridiculous mess I've ever heard of," Amy says. "They should put all their time and resources into finding James Turner, not investigating church people."

"I'm sure they will quickly find each person on the list had nothing to do with the abduction. It was likely someone other than a church member who came in during the confusion and took Emma. There's something I want to show you."

I take her hand and lead her into my study. An extra chair is pulled up to my desk and I ask Amy to sit down beside me. I put the disc into the computer. Emma Wells appears, and I watch Amy's face as she takes in what I saw earlier. I pause the playback at the point where it was stopped for me at the Wells' house.

Amy looks at me with astonishment, "Poor Ted and Rachel Wells. How can they bear all of this?"

"I don't know. I don't think I could."

"If this were my daughter, I'd be a basket case right now," Amy says.

"They're brave people."

"I want to meet them."

Amy is a very caring person. This is one reason she chose social work as a career. She concentrates on domestic violence and has worked with many women at the city's shelter for those who need a place of refuge. The Wells might benefit from her support.

"We can go over there together tomorrow evening," I say.

I start the DVD, this time at a part I've not seen as Emma appears again.

> I have been looking in my Bible to try and find someone who had cancer. I guess people did not know about it back then. A lot of sick people came to Jesus for help. Maybe some of them had Ewing's Sarcoma but didn't know what it was. I asked Mrs. Stone, my Sunday school teacher, if Jesus heals people today. She said she was not sure, but she knows he wants to. My mother told me we cannot know all of God's ways, but we can still trust him. I think she learned that in church when she was young. I know she used to go with her mother and father. I think my mother and father will go with me soon. They're just taking their time in deciding.
>
> Mom and Dad, if you are seeing this now and I'm very sick, I want you to know that I believe that God can help you even if you do not go to church.
>
> We've been learning memory verses at Sunday School. I like doing this, but sometimes I think the teachers don't think we can learn the hard ones. I've found a verse that I like very much and have memorized it. It comes from Romans and goes

like this – "I am convinced that neither death nor life, neither angels nor demons, neither the present nor the future, nor any powers, neither height nor depth, nor anything in all of creation, will be able to separate us from the love of God that is in Christ Jesus our Lord."

I don't really know what it all means, but I like the idea that nothing can separate us from God. I hope angels are real and demons are not. I like to think that I have an angel that is watching me. I think I'm gonna need some help when I start my chemo treatments. An angel there would be nice.

Amy reaches over and hits the stop button.

"Ron, I don't think I can watch anymore tonight. This hurts too much. How can one little girl go through all of this? I hope she's alive, and if she is, I imagine she's so afraid right now. I'm so afraid for her."

Amy's crying and reaches for my hand. I move closer to her and put my arm around her shoulder.

"I know," I say. "We must find her soon. I refuse to believe she's dead. She's too special to not survive this."

"Ron, do you remember that passage you pointed out to me a few months ago in one of Henri Nouwen's books, the one on children being gifts?"

After a moment it comes to me. "Yes, I do remember it."

"It has been on my mind today," Amy says. "Would you find the quote for me? I left a bookmark in the page."

I pull the book from the nearby shelf and locate the passage:

"They are given to us so that we can offer them a safe, loving place to grow to inner and outer freedom. They are like strangers who ask for hospitality, become good friends, and then leave again to continue their journey. They bring immense joy and immense sorrow precisely because they are gifts."

Amy then hugs me and I hold her tight. We both know that our

Sarah is such a gift and that Emma is just as special for the Wells. The two of us continue to embrace for a few minutes without speaking.

* * *

Sundays are draining for most pastors. The energy spent leading the worship service and in preaching is exhausting. A pastor must be both personable and responsive as he or she greets people on Sunday mornings. Some ministers lead multiple services on Sundays. I'm fortunate in that there is only one morning service at First Baptist. Periodically we have Sunday evening programs, but this evening I'm off duty, at least as off duty as a pastor gets. In my first church in rural Virginia we had an evening worship service every Sunday to which a dedicated handful of people would come. I can't imagine how I did that for those years, gearing back up for that second service and another sermon.

Sarah calls out to me from her room, "Dad, get on the Internet, there's something on the news you need to see."

At the desk in my office I open my laptop and go to my home computer page. There are several news stories highlighted on MSNBC, but I quickly see what Sarah is talking about:

> **"Emma Wells, the missing eight year old, may have been spotted this evening at a service station/convenient mart in Richmond, Virginia. A person pumping gas reported they saw the blond headed child in a light blue Toyota van. She was wearing the pink top with the words "Life is Good" on it. The van was being driven by a man with a beard, and there was another passenger in the front, a large woman with dark hair. The woman, who called the police to report the sighting, failed to get the license number of the van though she said it had Virginia tags. The State Police are reviewing the surveillance tapes now. The van left the station and headed south towards Petersburg, according to the witness."**

I turn on the television just as Amy comes into the office. There's nothing on the local news channels yet.

"What's going on?" Amy asks, noticing the concern on my face.

I tell her about the reported sighting.

"Do you think it's really her?"

"I don't know. The sighting was twenty-two minutes ago."

I change TV channels to look for any updates while Amy tries to find our portable radio. Sarah comes into the office. The three of us frantically seek any updates, Sarah on the Internet, I surfing the television channels, and Amy tuning into local radio stations on the portable found in a kitchen drawer.

The phone rings. It's Ken Matthews, my friend and former FBI agent. "Have you seen the news?" he asks.

"Yes, briefly," I say. "I just saw a snippet on the Internet."

"Same here," says Ken. "One of my neighbors alerted me. Hang on while I try to get in touch with Neal Heard."

Finally, there's a break in network programming for a TV special report:

"Several law enforcement agencies are looking for a light blue Toyota van south of Richmond, Virginia which may be transporting Emma Wells, the child missing from a church in a nearby town last Friday. The van was spotted thirty minutes ago at a gas station by another motorist. We go to Jim Ahorn in Richmond."

"I'm here with Missy Clark who believes she saw Emma Wells a few minutes ago. Can you tell us what you saw?"

"Yes, I was putting my credit card into the payment slot when I looked over into the van on the other side of the pump. A little girl was in the middle row of seats next to the window. She was trying to get out of her seat belt, and as she leaned over I saw her shirt with the logo on it. It said 'Life is Good'. The child seemed to be trying to escape

from the vehicle. The man in the front reached back and grabbed the child, keeping her from undoing the belt. He then started the vehicle and pulled out. He put the van in reverse, I think so I could not see the plates, and did not go forward until he was at the street. I could not get a clear view of the plates other than I'm sure they were Virginia tags."

"Mrs. Clark, what makes you think it was Emma Wells?"

"I've seen the child's picture on the television several times and am pretty sure this was her. She was trying to get out of the van."

"You said there was a woman in the front passenger seat. What was she doing?"

"She just sat there as the man grabbed the child and pushed her back against the seat."

"Thank you Mrs. Clark. This is Jim Ahorn in Richmond, Virginia."

The phone rings and again it's Ken. "Ron, Neal Heard just learned of the reported sighting when we did a few minutes ago. He says that the FBI in the Richmond area is working with the local authorities in trying to find the van. He says we must not get too excited, for such sightings are routine in missing child cases and often turn out to be false."

"But, what if it is her?" I ask.

"Then they'll find her. There are a lot of resources out there employed in this kind of operation."

"What about Ted and Rachel Wells?"

"Denise Chavalier is on her way to their house now," Ken says. "She will stay with them until there is some news on the van. This is standard operating procedure. I will call you if I hear anything."

Sarah is glued to the computer. She has her fingers crossed and can't keep her legs still. Amy and I sit on the couch in front of the small television I have on a credenza on the other side of the room. Sarah's BlackBerry is on the desk beside her. I have my office phone on the arm of the couch, the remote in my right hand. Amy has both the radio and her cell phone in her lap. We're linked to the world. Sarah receives a text.

"Just Marisa asking if I know any more than what's on the news," Sarah says.

Another twenty minutes pass without any new reports, just announcements running on the bottom of the TV screen with the earlier report. The three of us say little to each other as we await the next update. This reminds me of the time we all sat together two years ago as a hurricane was threatening our town. That was a long night of anticipation that ended with only minor damage to property.

I'm not very good at waiting, especially if I can't do something in the meantime. My options for action are very limited this evening, actually nonexistent. There are no calls I can make, reading seems out of the question, television programs are a distraction. Amy and Sarah are not interested in any conversation as there is nothing to be said about the possible sighting that will help in any way, and any other discussion is inconceivable. It's now been almost an hour since any further information has been broadcast. I remember an old German proverb which says, "Long is not forever." I appreciate that wisdom which implies that there will be an end to every period of waiting. The proverb, I think, needs a caveat which says, "Long can seem like forever, however."

The phone rings.

"Ron, they have found the van in a subdivision of Richmond," Ken says. "The child was not Emma. It was a family out for the evening. The little girl did have blond hair and was wearing one of those tee shirts which are so popular. The father says she was having trouble with her seat belt which she had unfastened after they stopped for gas. When they got home they saw the reports on television and called the police." I thank Ken and tell my two girls the news. The disappointment is pervasive in the room as we all hoped Emma was going to be found alive tonight. Like us, many others were connected to their information sources, hoping and praying for a positive breakthrough in this sad story. Sarah goes back to her room, Amy back to the den, and I stay in the office. All I can think of is Ted and Rachel who must have been on edge like we were.

My home study is a room filled with books. This room is a refuge from the pressures of the world, and the books provide a peace of mind in that they are the place I go to find sustenance for my mind and spirit. There are numerous translations of the Bible, and I read from them in preparation for sermons and devotional periods. When I need the help of others outside of the Bible, but don't want to seek the advice of my wife or friends, I go to my books. This evening I think that I've lost any control I have over my fate. There is something I read recently on this subject, and I search my memory as to where. My reading is often random, and I don't have the discipline to take notes like I should.

I look at the pile nearest my reading chair and am drawn to a title that is close to the top, *Scarred by Struggle, Transformed by Hope*. My suspicion is that this is where I can go to find help after this challenging day. Joan Chittister is a gifted mystic who presents hope like few others I've read. She writes:

> *"Powerlessness strips away all pretenses and renders us human…Powerlessness is such a burden to modern existence because it cleaves like a barnacle to the myth of control."*

This is my problem this evening – I feel powerless. I can't help Emma Wells. I don't know who my accuser is. I can't really help Ted and Rachel. I can't even share with my wife all that has happened on this day. I can't find sufficient trust in God to seek his guidance. Joan Chittister says powerlessness leads to surrender, surrender to God. But I don't want to surrender yet. Perhaps that'll come in the days ahead. Tonight I feel like fighting, and excuse me, God, but if you want to help me – help me fight. I will only raise the white flag when I absolutely have to.

CHAPTER TEN

MONDAY MORNING

Another night has passed, and Emma has not been found. Carl called this morning from the police station and said that the search is stalled until some new lead comes about. One main focus of his department is on finding James Turner. Two four-person police teams are working full time on trying to locate him. He's the only registered child abuser in the town still not accounted for. His photo has been constantly seen on television for two days now.

In the phone call earlier Carl asked if I would come down to the police station at nine-thirty this morning. There are, he said, some questions they needed to ask. "Will I be coming as a suspect?" I asked. His answer was evasive as he simply said again that there were some questions.

This is my first time in the law enforcement center for our city. I've had no reason before to visit the building. My only encounter with the police since moving here was a speeding ticket three years ago which was extremely embarrassing as the officer who pulled me over was the son of one of our church members. I had a pretty good excuse, saying I did not notice the change from forty-five to thirty-five. The young policeman was cordial as he handed me the yellow form with fifty-two mph on it. It was handled at the old magistrate's office by paying the cost of court.

This complex is only two years old now, and the expansive main lobby is as inviting as our church's foyer. A young uniformed woman sits behind a large reception desk, and I ask her where Detective Brody's office is. She asks if he's expecting me, and I answer yes as if I were visiting in a corporate headquarters.

Another officer is summoned to take me back to the detective's office. Carl's space is a small private room down a long hall. On the way there I look into a selection of cubicles where uniformed officers are all working on computers or moving papers across their desks. It appears to be a busy place, and I wonder how many of these people are working on the Emma Wells case. When I stand at the open door of Carl's compartment, the detective rises to meet me and motions for me to accompany him to a conference room. He's wearing the same brown suit he had on the last time I saw him.

The conference room has one large table with seats for at least eight people. There are three people seated at the mahogany table: Neal Heard, Denise Chevalier, and an African-American man, probably in his thirties. He's introduced as agent Paul Thomas, another member of the FBI team. Carl stays in the room; he and I sit on the side of the table nearest the door. The walls are all glass offering a panoptic of a passive pastor on display for the whole department to see.

Heard reaches over the table, extends his hand, and says, "Thank you for coming down, Dr. Fowler. Pastor, we don't believe you had anything to do with the disappearance of Emma Wells. Your reputation in this community is a very positive one, and you are very much respected from what we've learned. I feel foolish even asking you to come down here, but there are certain procedures we must honor. You certainly understand our need to be thorough in this matter."

I sense that agent Heard is a man who is used to steering all such interviews to his purposes, is accustomed to being manipulative, and I can tell that he's all business.

"I can appreciate your need to do your job as you see fit," I say.

"We thank you, Dr. Fowler, for your cooperation," Heard says with a smile that's obviously calculated and practiced through years of such interviews.

"Reverend," Heard begins, "you left the church Friday right before the closing program in the sanctuary and went home for lunch, correct?"

"Yes," I say, waiting for what will come next.

"And you were there about forty minutes?" Heard continues. "You got to the hospital at about ten after one?"

"Yes, I think that's right."

"There was no one at your house, you said. I also recall that you visited a patient in the hospital who was coming out of minor surgery," the agent states while looking at his notes.

"That's correct. A member of our church had a skin growth removed."

"And no one was at your home the whole time you were there," the lead agent reiterates.

"My wife was at work, and my daughter went home with a friend," I say.

At the end of the table I see agent Thomas typing into a laptop, notes of the interview, I assume.

"Pastor, let me be frank with you," Heard says, as he leans toward me across the table, pointing a pen in my direction. "Because of the letter you received with the accusations, we must be careful that our information is as accurate as possible. We all think the letter was written by a disturbed person, and the allegations are not true. But, we're required by our rules of investigation to cover all the bases."

"I thank you for doing your job well," I say, realizing immediately that this sounds insincere.

Denise Chevalier, seated across the table to my right, then asks, "Where was your car parked when you left the church on Friday?"

"It was at the side entrance to the church in my reserved spot."

"Did you tell anyone you were leaving?" she asks.

I turn facing her directly and say, "I stuck my head in the secretary's office and told her I would be back later."

"When you left was there anyone else in the hall or foyer?" Chevalier queries.

"They were both empty as there were a few minutes left before the program in the sanctuary was over."

"And you left by the side door?" she asks.

"Yes."

"When you left the sanctuary to go to the office did you see anyone then?" Neal Heard asks as he resumes his questioning role.

"No."

"So you didn't see the custodian, Joel Weaver, at any time while you were leaving?" the lead agent asks.

"I didn't see Joel until later in the day after the police came."

"Let me move to another area," Heard says. "Tell me about your parents."

This turn in the questioning causes me to tense. Looking around the room, it's evident that all eyes are on me.

"I don't understand why you are asking about them," I say, confused over the change in subject.

"This is all just a part of background," Chevalier replies. "Where did you live as a child?"

"I grew up in Raleigh, North Carolina."

"What kind of work did your parents do?" Heard asks.

"My father was an electrical contractor. My mother ran a daycare center for young children."

"They are no longer engaged in these careers?" Heard follows.

"My father died of lung cancer three years ago, and my mother is retired."

This was such a heart wrenching time for our family. The cancer was a draining ordeal for us that lasted over a year. My mother was a wonderful care giver as she was going through her own trials. My brothers and I watched as both parents suffered.

Sitting back in his chair with his hands behind his head, Heard continues the questioning. "When did your mother retire?"

Realizing now where this is headed, I lean forward and look at all three of the agents, finally resting my gaze on Heard. "No doubt, you know that she sold her business four years ago. I'm sure you also know that her daycare was under investigation two years earlier after a parent accused one of the workers of taking indecent liberties with one of the children. You also have in your files there on the table that the accusation was dismissed because the investigation could not substantiate the charge."

Heard leans forward and shuffles a few pages in the folder before him. "Yes, that's all here. Sometimes, however, these files are not as thorough as they could be."

I can see that Heard enjoys his use of innuendo. I speak forcefully, "My mother ran an excellent business which cared for many children. She spent a number of months upset over the accusation which proved to be baseless. It's not easy facing all of the questions that come at you even when the charges are unfounded."

"I am sure that was hard for her. One other question," Heard says. "Why did you leave your previous church to come here to First

Baptist?"

This question stuns me. I have to collect myself before I can answer. "I came here because it was a great opportunity to minister."

"So, there was no other reason why you left the former church?" Heard asks.

I start to say that this makes two questions but decide that a smart comeback will not be helpful in this situation. "There are always a number of factors when a pastor accepts another call. It's a complicated process leaving one church as pastor and going to another to start a new pastorate."

"Did you leave Grace Baptist in good standing with the members?" Heard asks.

Now I realize that the persistent agent has already taken it upon himself to make inquiries at Grace where I served before coming here. "Agent Heard, my guess is that you already know something about my situation there. I'm not sure who you talked with, but there were some problems at Grace Baptist."

"How would you describe those problems?" he persists.

I notice that the others are sitting back letting their superior handle all of this. I get the feeling that Carl Brody is not comfortable with the way this is going as he fidgets in his chair.

"I was caught in the middle of a battle between two warring families in the church. My diplomacy skills were not up to the task of mediating between them. They both turned against me when I would not take sides."

"So, there were not any personal issues you had which caused you to leave there?" Heard asks.

"Are you asking if I was involved in child abuse? If you have talked with someone over there you would know there were no such issues."

"It just wasn't clear to me why you left. My source over there simply said that you left under duress," Heard continues as he spins his pen on the table before him.

I wonder who his source is. Duress is an interesting term. It signifies pressure or coercion. The truth is that any compulsion to leave came from inside myself. Yes, there were a few who wanted me gone, but they were covert in their workings.

"Agent Heard, as the tension rose in the church over how I handled some of the disagreements, it became clear that our problems needed attention. One evening the deacons met with me for two hours and we laid out all of the issues that were dividing the church. I was asked to leave the room while these nine men proceeded to a vote of confidence on my pastorate. The vote was six to support my continued service to the church while three voted against me. The three were tied to the contending families. After some thought, I decided that I didn't want to pastor a divided church, so I put my name out to try and find another pastorate. Six months later First Baptist called me here."

"So First Baptist is your second pastorate. Have you had problems in other churches?" Heard presses me while looking over at Carl who is playing nervously with his wrist watch.

"I was an associate pastor in two churches. In both of those I left with good recommendations. Before that I was an Army chaplain and received excellent reports from my superiors."

Heard nods his head as though he approves of my answer. "I was in the army as well, an MP."

"I might have guessed that was your job or MOS," I say with an edge in my voice.

"It was good experience before joining the bureau," Heard says. "The letter you received accused you of some pretty awful things. Do pastors often receive such hate mail?"

"I have never received such before."

"Not even when you crossed some of the people in your first pastorate?" Heard asks.

"No, not even then. The person who wrote this letter is either very twisted, or they are thinking of someone else when they list the supposed transgressions."

"That's the way I see it too," Heard concedes. "I just have to make sure we are on the same page. By the way, were you ever at Ft. Bragg?"

"Yes, I was there for ROTC training in college and was stationed there as a chaplain later," I reply.

"You didn't happen to be at Bragg in 1991?" Heard asks.

"Yes, I was there for much of that year. That's where I met my wife."

"Do you remember there was a missing child on the base that July?"

I had forgotten that story, but now recall that a daughter of one the enlisted men and his wife was abducted that summer. She was found dead two weeks later, and to my knowledge the case was never closed. The child's family was not in my unit, but I had to counsel several families who were traumatized by the situation.

"Yes, I remember it well," I answer. "You know I was there. Am I a suspect in that case too?"

"No, Reverend, of course not. I just wondered if you remembered. I was at Bragg then as a captain in the military police. That was the first abduction case I worked, and now here we both are again in a town where a child has been taken."

"I think it's time for me to go. I have church work to do," I say as I stand up.

Agent Chevalier speaks, "Dr. Fowler, I know it's not easy to sit in a room like this and be grilled. We consider you a part of our team in finding Emma Wells. You have helped us tremendously."

I suppose that she's the good cop today. On another day she probably can be just as tough as Heard was.

Heard gets up and leads me to the door. He pats me on the shoulder and says politely, "Dr. Fowler, again, we thank you for coming down. By the way, do you know Louise Carter well?"

I think for a minute and then ask, "Do you mean my neighbor, Louise Carter?"

"Yes, the lady who lives next door to you on the right," Heard replies. "Well, she was home on Friday and saw you leave your home around twelve-forty-five. She did not see you come home at twelve-ten as you said you did, but Mrs. Carter has verified you were at your house some of that period."

"You mean you put me through all of these questions and you have someone who verified I went home Friday?"

"Yes, that's correct," Heard answers. "This helps support your timeline."

"When did you find this out?"

"Yesterday afternoon."

I give the agent a hard look and turn away. This guy's a piece of work, I think. I choose to not say anything else as any further conversation might not benefit agent Heard or myself.

Carl Brody sees me out and apologizes for the way Heard pressed. I thank him and leave the law enforcement center angry and yet satisfied; angry at the questions about my former church, and satisfied that I refused to take more of what Heard dished out. I'm particularly angry at his not telling me earlier about Louise Carter and his delving into my mother's situation at her daycare.

As I get in my car I begin to reflect on the influence that one letter can have and how easy it is for a pastor to be the target of slanderous accusations. My almost three years at Grace Baptist were a challenge as the church was divided even before I arrived there. I wasn't the only pastor in recent years to leave under some pressure. There are just some churches that are difficult to serve. Many ministers run into one or more of those over the course of their careers. I'm fortunate to be in a church now that does not seem to have any major internal issues.

My time as a chaplain was both rewarding and frustrating. I saw so many families in distress under the pressure of the military life and the many separations as soldiers were deployed. There was an abundance of counseling, some of it related to spousal abuse. I wonder if Neal Heard and I passed each other on the base that year. It's a sprawling place and the odds are not high that we crossed paths. The one good thing about my year at Ft. Bragg was meeting Amy, who was just beginning her social work career. We actually met at a conference on abused women. A year later, Amy and I married. She only spent one year as an army wife as I completed my service and moved on to become an associate minister at a church.

We cherished those honeymoon years before Sarah was born. I remember the night I surprised Amy with a new puppy. I had been to a committee meeting in a church member's home. Their family had a litter of Maltese puppies ready for new homes, and this one tiny white female was so adorable I could not resist. It was pouring rain when I arrived at our townhouse and decided to not use my key but ring the doorbell. Amy opened the door and there I stood, puppy in one hand, umbrella in the other. It took my wife a moment to take in the scene and then she squealed with delight and hugged us both. Over the years we have mentioned occasionally how special that night was to us. So many momentous events have impacted our lives in our nineteen years of marriage, including the birth of our daughter, Sarah. But, the memory of that rainy evening is still fondly recalled.

* * *

Ken Matthews is waiting for me when I arrive back at the church office. He pulls one of the wing chairs up close to my desk and looks at me with what I sense is going to be some kind of frank advice. "Ron, have you told your wife about the letter you received?"

"Not yet," I reply.

"Well, you need to tell her today."

"I've not wanted to upset her any more than she already is."

"Amy can handle it," Ken says. "What she will not be able to handle is your keeping this from her. I just wanted to tell you this before we get to anything else. I'm your friend and I have experience with this kind of matter. The best time to share bad news with your spouse is sooner, not later. This does not come from an FBI agent, but from a husband who learned his lessons the hard way. The longer you wait the harder it will be."

"That's for sure. I'm afraid I've waited too long already."

I agree that I'll tell Amy this evening, wondering what Ken experienced in his marriage. Then I tell him about my visit to the police station earlier.

"Neal Heard is a professional," Ken says. "He's doing what a good interrogator must do. It's better that all this stuff about your involvement in the abduction be cleared away up front. If he persists in hounding you, I'll have a talk with him. His withholding the partial verification of your alibi was not very professional, I admit."

"It was a bit intimidating for me being grilled by the guy playing the bad cop role."

"Oh, that was not as tough as it can get. Now what they didn't yet know when you were down at the station was that we got a report back on your letter just an hour ago. Agents worked over the weekend in studying the letter. There was one set of fingerprints on the paper other than yours, Heard's, Chevalier's and mine. There's no match for the extra prints in the FBI database, however."

"So, the person who sent it has no record of any kind?"

"That's right, and they were never in the military nor had any job that required government clearance. We could fingerprint everyone in the congregation to see if we can determine who the prints belong to but that would be a little extreme. The person has not actually committed a crime if they did not take Emma Wells."

"Then, we don't have anything new to help us determine who wrote the letter?"

"Not exactly; the bureau's handwriting analyst believes it was more likely a woman who did the writing, and a psychologist working with them concurs based on the language of the letter, especially the references to a man of God. Combining their expertise they think it is a ninety percent likelihood the writer is a female. One other thing – the person is probably left-handed. This is determined because of some faint smears in the ink at the top of the letter. Many lefthanders write with their hand upside down, crabclaw as it's often called. This can cause smudges where the hand passes over the still damp ink. Handwriting analysis is not a pure science but does produce educated guesses. The psychologist also believes there is a likelihood the author has had experience themselves with abuse, possibly abused as a child."

"All of that should narrow our search down," I say.

"Mind you, we can't be a hundred percent sure that it was a woman, nor a left-handed one," Ken says. "But, here's what best fits the evidence so far: the letter writer was a left-handed female who has had no reason to be fingerprinted, and probably is a loner who may have been a victim of abuse. The writer may have been molested themselves as a child. Let me ask you – have you ever counseled someone involved in an abusive relationship?"

I think for a few seconds. "Not in reference to child abuse. I've counseled several wives who claimed abuse by their husbands."

"Are they in this congregation?" Ken asks.

"Two of them are."

"Without giving me the names at this point, do you think they might be angry as to how you handled the situation?"

I ponder this and say, "I don't think so."

Ken studies me for a moment and says, "Sometimes, pastors can be naive. You have a tendency to believe the best of people. We in law enforcement tend to see the worst in people."

"That's too bad," I say. "I still don't think my counseling techniques have caused people to be angry at me to this degree."

"Right now, I want us to put together a list of people in the congregation who fit our profile."

"There were about five hundred people out there Sunday," I remind Ken. "I only know a handful that have been critical of me in my years here. How do we find out who wrote the letter with what we have to go on?"

"I know it's a difficult task, but we can eliminate many of the worshippers last week, young children especially."

"I've run this through my mind since the service and tried to remember as many faces as I could from looking out over the group. There were probably seventy children and youth under sixteen in the sanctuary yesterday."

"Great, that only leaves four hundred and thirty suspects," Ken drolly says. "There's something else we must consider, that the person was not actually there. They may have said they would be there to throw you off. Still, we must put together a list."

"Okay."

"Let me work on this today, and I'll touch base with Heard about what he's come up with. Right now the team is keeping me in the loop. It so happens that Heard's boss and I worked together for a couple of years. He and I became good friends, and he's told Heard that I could be of assistance in their work here. The FBI team does not think your letter writer should be their main focus, however. This means I'm going to have to follow this trail on my own for now."

"Why is that?"

"Heard does not think the letter and the abduction are necessarily related. His team is much more concerned with finding James Turner and following up on people who were known to have been around the church on Friday."

"Thanks for all of your help," I tell my good friend. "I'm fortunate to have by my side someone who knows me so well, and whom I can trust."

After Ken leaves I try to process our conversation. This person may have been abused. They may have been hurt by me or another clergy person. They may not have really been out there Sunday. So many things to think about, and yet, I'm thankful for the services of my experienced private investigator and friend.

I wish Neal Heard could see that my accuser could be the one who has Emma.

There are a few other matters on my plate today, so I can't give my personal problems my full attention. Nor can I fully concentrate on the Wells family, though they are constantly on my mind. Later today I'll take Amy with me to see them. I now have two days until I am to be exposed as a villain, a person who harms children, a monster disguised as a minister. I almost wish that the accusation against me was for something that I had truly done wrong so I could at least go the route of seeking repentance for my deeds, something not this terrible, however. For some less deplorable sin, I might could beg the plaintiff's forgiveness and enter into some therapeutic relationship in order to restore trust. You can't have a relationship with an anonymous adversary who falsely accuses you of the worst of deeds. I can't imagine this person being able to sway any in our congregation of my supposed atrocities. If this person took Emma, then we desperately need to know who he or she is, and soon.

* * *

I spend the late morning at the hospital visiting three of our church members. Two are in for tests, the other recovering from surgery. Only one of the three was in church Sunday. How strange, I consider, that as I go about my pastoral duties I'm also in the role of sleuth trying to gather evidence. Pastors must wear many hats: preacher, teacher, counselor, spiritual advisor, and administrator to name a few. My new hat of detective does not have a comfortable fit, yet the challenge has energized me in a peculiar way.

There's one other visit I must make this morning. I promised Ed Dickinson that I would visit his mother in the assisted living home behind the hospital. Doris Dickinson has Alzheimer's and is in a secure dementia area of the home. There's a security system on the outside of the main entrance where visitors must enter a coded number in order to gain access. I enter it on the numerical pad beside the door and press the star symbol. The door opens, and I sign the guest register in the foyer. The same code operates the elevator so it can stop on the second floor where the dementia residents are housed. This is not my first time here, and I know well the procedure. I also know that the second floor is home to about sixty residents who all have some form of severe memory loss. As I step off the elevator, I'm confronted by a tall woman who scolds me for not wiping my feet as I enter the floor. Looking down I see no extra rug, but proceed to wipe my feet on the carpet and apologize to the lady. She accepts my apology and warns me to not let it happen again. I vow I will not, making a mental note to steer clear of her for she may be confused but does not appear to be frail, actually very powerful for one her age.

I find Mrs. Dickinson in a wheelchair in the hall across from the nurses' station with her head bent down. The attendant tells me I should not worry about waking her, that she will welcome a visit. There is a slight smell of urine in the place, but it is masked by some form of air spray, lilac possibly. The building is in the shape of a cross with four hallways, each meeting at the crossroad where I stand now.

"Doris," I say as I kneel down beside her. She slowly lifts her head and stares at me for a few seconds. "This is Reverend Fowler from the church. Your son, Ed, asked me to come see you."

Doris Dickinson nods her head and weakly says, "Ed."

"Yes, I saw him at church yesterday. How are you doing, Mrs. Dickinson?"

"Ed," Doris says again.

"No, this is your pastor. Your son Ed is not here today."

She smiles and motions for me to sit.

I sit beside her in a vacant chair and look up and down the hall. My lady from the elevator door is pacing the floor, probably watching out for other violators of her rules to discipline. A short man wearing jogging pants and tennis shoes is standing a few feet away listening to my conversation with Mrs. Dickinson, if you could call it a conversation. He does not speak nor move, just stares and smiles. Several workers are busy handing out snacks and leading residents up and down the halls. A large uniformed attendant sits at a desk in the office, a lady who appears to be physically capable of handling any unruly residents. Another aide is looking at a computer screen on a rolling cart which I can see has profiles of the residents. I assume this is used in dispensing medications.

Again I attempt to engage Doris in conversation, "Your hair looks nice today."

She puts her right hand on the top of her head and pats it a few times. I tell her about talking with her son and daughter-in-law recently, and she looks at me with a pleasant smile as though such reports interest her. I ask her what she had for breakfast, and she looks around as though there will be a prompt to help her remember, but she only shrugs her shoulders in futility. I can tell this is going to be a brief visit for there is not much awareness on the part of my memory-loss congregant.

"We keep you on our prayer list at church, Doris," I say trying to find a way to engage her. She again nods and smiles.

A diminutive lady wearing bedroom slippers passes by carrying a baby doll and mumbling some words in the ear of the pretend child. I make a few other attempts at getting some response from my wheelchair bound church member. She stares off at a blank wall, and I can't help but wonder is she is at all cognizant of her situation.

As I stand to leave, Doris grabs my hand with surprising strength for someone so frail and appears to want to speak. I bend over so as to be able to hear what she says as she continues to hold my hand.

"The little girl is not here," Doris says.

I'm stunned by her words and ask her what she said. She does not speak again, lets go of my hand, and bends her head back down. I know I heard her correctly. Was this just some expression that surfaced from past memories or did it refer to Emma Wells? Could she have heard about the disappearance? It's clear that her short term memory is only a few minutes or less in duration. For a brief while I sit beside her and study this elderly lady who now lives in a world unknown to me. I have read some on dementia and know that the illness is still puzzling even to experts who study it for a living.

I stand in front of the elevator door and again punch in the code numbers and star. As the door opens, the smiling man in the jogging pants attempts to get on with me, but one of the ladies in uniform holds him back. Perhaps he's not so out of it that he knows escape is preferable to another day locked in with his fellow oblivious patients.

I can't get what Doris said out of my mind as I drive back to the church. I'm sure that Emma Wells is not in Doris's small world, though I wish she were there to delight the residents with her charm and wonder.

CHAPTER ELEVEN

MONDAY AFTERNOON

It's one-thirty in the afternoon and I'm back in my office after a lunch break. Carl Brody calls. "Reverend, I just want to give you an update. We have concluded our interviews with all of the church people. Of the dozen persons from your church we know were in the building last Friday but had no corroboration of their whereabouts from twelve to twelve-thirty, we have ruled out seven for one reason or another at this time. This leaves only five church people whom we cannot close the files on. You are now not a main focus because of your neighbor having seen you at home last Friday."

"That's good," I say. "Can't you just give me and our other church members who you're still looking at lie detector tests?"

"Agent Heard does not trust polygraphs. He told me yesterday that since the Supreme Court in nineteen ninety-eight ruled them not totally reliable he has shied away from using them. I wish we could use a shortcut to rule you and others out as suspects."

I know that Heard will not take me off his list totally. I think he's naturally suspicious of ministers. There have certainly been plenty of clergy persons who have transgressed over the years, and there is wariness among many of those ministers who seem to be too good to be true. I can understand this because I also have trouble with those preachers who harp all the time on moral righteousness and then are caught with their pants down or their hand in the till. They make it more difficult for all of us who seek to lead others through our calling as pastors.

"One other thing, Dr. Fowler," Carl says. "We'll need to search the residences of these five people in your church in order to make sure there's no physical evidence. I thought you might want to be aware of that in case any of them call you."

"Who are the five people?" I ask.

"Well, there's your custodian, Joel Weaver; the music leader, Janice Moore; one of the young people, Lee Williams; a man named Dyson Walters; and a woman named Janet Corello."

This list amazes me, certainly not the faces you expect to see on wanted posters in the post office. "I'm sure you will find that none of these five had anything to do with this," I say. "I know them all well. It's ridiculous they're considered suspects."

"I understand your feelings, but sometimes the least likely of people turn out to be the ones guilty."

When we are off the phone, I go over these five individuals in my mind. Janice Moore is a very gifted musician. She's been on our staff for five years and is very easy to work with. She's a divorcee who went through a rough time after learning her husband was having an affair. She was thirty-seven at the time and their one son was a senior in high school. After her divorce she took the position here and moved from the city where she lived to start a new life. Her son is now in graduate school. Janice is a perfectionist and is able to draw out the talents of those in the choir. She has not remarried and gives the church more time than is expected. On Friday she led the music in the opening part of the closing program and left early to work on her other duties. She was in the choir room from twelve to one.

Lee Williams is a rising high school senior, an Eagle Scout, and a member of the honor club. His parents are very active in our church and are on a two week extended vacation. Lee chose to remain here because he is on the local American Legion Baseball team. He was one of the worship leaders in the Bible School and handled the sound system for the programs, but left on Friday early to go home and get ready for ball practice.

Dyson Walters is a retired maintenance worker at a textile plant and one of our most ardent volunteers wherever he is needed. His wife is presently away helping their daughter who just had a baby two weeks ago. In his late sixties, he's one of those people who can fix anything. He was in the church building on Friday repairing some tables over in the senior adult department.

Janet Corello is a single young woman in her late twenties. She has a learning disability and works part time through one of the agencies in town which helps persons with lower skill levels try and make their own way. She lives in a group home a few blocks from the church and is the daughter of one of our deacons. Janet helped out in Bible School all last week but left early on Friday because she was going to walk back to the group home for lunch.

And then there's Joel. Of course, Joel must be at the top of the list. He's a natural suspect, living alone and quiet by nature. I'm sure he's not capable of hurting a child. Joel was in the buildings on Friday handling his normal duties and was close to the restroom which Emma is believed to have used. This puts him square in the sights of Heard and Chevalier.

I realize that I'm probably naive in my judgments of other people. I don't have the experiences of law officers like Carl Brody or Neal Heard which certainly must sour one's outlook on humanity. The Apostle Paul in his letter to the Corinthians wrote that love is "eager to believe the best." I've always been fond of that verse and basically that has been my approach to life. Of course, I've been burned by such an overly optimistic view of humanity at times. But, I still believe that we must not judge others too quickly. And yet, there's still the need for judgment. There is evil in this world. Someone did take Emma Wells, and someone did write the awful letter that's in my desk.

* * *

It's now three-fifteen and I've taken care of the administrative tasks that demanded my attention today. I told my wife I would pick up our daughter from the library where she is volunteering three days a week this summer. At twelve years of age we're still not comfortable with her staying home by herself, so a variety of activities have been planned when Amy and I are at work. Amy works part time, and we try to coordinate our schedules. In light of what happened last Friday we are thankful that we have made sure one of us is responsible for Sarah.

I open the door of my Chevy Malibu, put my briefcase on the passenger seat and proceed to start the car, turning the air conditioner up high on this sweltering June day. Something catches my eye before I put the car in gear. On the floor on the passenger side there's a white piece of paper. I reach over to pick it up, and as soon as I touch it I know what it is. There's nothing on the outside of the page just as before. I don't want to unfold the paper, don't want to know what's inside. That's not possible, of course, and so I carefully open it with my hands touching just the outside edge of the page:

> Reverend,
>
> Transgression speaks to the wicked deep in their hearts; there is no fear of God before their eyes; for they flatter themselves in their own eyes that their iniquity cannot be found out and hated. Your sins will be found out, and the pain you have inflicted on a child will not go unpunished. You are a vile molester of the innocent and must resign your position as pastor this Wednesday evening at the business conference. You dared to use humor in your sermon Sunday when so many are suffering. You have provoked the Lord to anger with your doings. You have put God to the test by your disregard for the suffering of others. The Lord says that no man who practices deceit shall dwell in my house. You men do not know how to repent of your evil ways. May you receive your just reward for your offenses.

There is no specific mention of Emma Wells, but again there is the accusation that I've harmed a child. The copy of the original letter is tucked away securely in a section of my briefcase, so I add this one to the expanding collection and wonder how many more there will be before judgment day this Wednesday. Even though the letter is now out of sight it burns through my mind like acid poured from a bottle. There is little doubt now that my accuser was in church on Sunday. As ludicrous as the charges are, I find myself questioning my words from the pulpit yesterday. Was I indeed insensitive to the suffering of my congregation through something I said?

I call Ken Matthews and inform him of this latest correspondence. He tells me to show it to Amy and he will come by our house this evening to look at it. I am now more apprehensive than before as to what this will do to Amy when I let her read the letters. I'm nervous at the thought of her displeasure over my withholding this issue from her.

As I leave the church it hits me that I'm not as threatened by this letter as I was by the first one. For some reason I only feel sadness, sadness that there's someone in my congregation who is this disturbed. It's likely a woman, and she was there in the service on Sunday. At an intersection now the light turns red; my thoughts turn back to Emma Wells. Is it possible that it was someone from our church family who took her, someone who is doing all of this to get at me for some reason?

Sarah's waiting inside the library front door when I pull up, and I see her face pressed against the vertical window light. Upon seeing me she bolts out of the door, bounces down the steps, and approaches the car with her normal sweeping wave of the left hand while her right hand holds a stack of reading matter. I can't help but take pride in my daughter who has the same light brown hair of her mother. The only features of hers that gives her away as my offspring are her hazel eyes and small mouth. Her pointed nose and thin eyelashes are an exact copy of her mother as are her perfect and dainty ears. She loves to read as I do, and devours books with an appetite that would make her obese if she took in food the same way she does literature.

In the car, Sarah asks me if there is any news on Emma Wells, and I tell her that the eight year old is still missing. She looks out the passenger side window for a few seconds and finally says, "Well, this sucks."

I respond with added volume to my words, "You know I don't like you using that word."

"Well there's no other way to put it," she says.

"I understand your frustration. This is a horrible situation, and I'm so upset for her parents."

"What about Emma? If she's still alive she must be like – so terrified. I'd like to kick the butt of the monster who took her. I know, don't say it – another of your little forbidden popular expressions. Dad, there are times when using such language best describes my feelings."

"Okay, I agree that no one should have to go through this and I'm willing in certain circumstances to resort to declarative slang."

"Right, you may even resort to something as drastic as 'darn' if you get angry enough. I don't think a pk has to be as careful with her words as the pd does, pd being you, preacher dad."

"Another subject, what are you reading?" I ask.

Concealing the pile of books from my view Sarah says, "You know the usual stuff: *War and Peace*, *The Grapes of Wrath*, and *Rebecca of Sunnybrook Farm*."

I take my eyes off the road to glance over at her book selections. "I doubt that. What did you really check out of the library?"

"If you must know, I have the third book of the *Twilight* series, a *Maximum Ride* novel, and the latest by Sarah Dessen; yes, Sarah Dessen because she is a good writer and has a wonderful first name."

"Those sound like they are too mature for you."

"Dad, I'm practically thirteen. That's a teenager. You can't expect me to read *Nancy Drew* books forever."

"I don't see why not," I joke.

When we arrive home Sarah makes haste to get to her bedroom where she spends much of her time absorbed in her recreational reading. Under her mother's insistence she is also tackling a few books from her school's summer reading list. I try not to censor her choices as her enthusiasm for literature is admirable at her age.

I'm nervous over telling Amy about my letters. I'm afraid that she will be thrown into a tizzy of insecurity and that she will be furious with me for keeping this from her. Right now I go to my study to make a call to Carl Brody.

"Hey, I'm glad you called," Carl announces. "There's some news. We've visited all of the residences of your five church people and have not found anything solid to link them to Emma Wells. There are some questions raised about what we found at Weaver's apartment. The janitor guy is a strange bird. His place was loaded with books. I never would have figured him for the intellectual type. The man has a whole shelf on philosophy, Aristotle and Plato, and guys like that. Other than the books the place is almost empty. There're no beers or booze, and not even a television. Chevalier wants to pursue the man's choice of reading matter, but no physical evidence is there to point to the Wells girl."

"I was sure you wouldn't find anything that tied him to the missing child," I say.

"Yeah, but you didn't tell me he was a monk living in a room filled with books. Isn't that something, a monk with tattoos? Whatever you say, Reverend, the man's strange. He may not bother little girls, but he's a weirdo."

"And the other four?" I ask. "I'm sure that they are all just regular folks who would never harm a child."

"I wouldn't use the word regular. In my line of work there's no such thing as regular. Everybody has their own quirks. Everybody's into something that's just not normal. Pastor, sometimes I think I'm the only normal person on the planet. You would not believe what I see when I search people's homes. The Walters guy is something else, too. Did you see that movie with Clint Eastwood where he had these foreign neighbors?"

"Yes," I say. "It was called *Gran Torino*."

"Well, the Walters guy has twice as many tools as Eastwood did in the movie, you know in his garage. I've never seen such a collection of tools. It looks like a Sears and Roebuck warehouse in his basement, except they're not in any order. I think he's Eastwood and Fred Sanford combined, a total slob. And in the house, whoa, is this guy's wife gonna throw a fit when she gets home if he doesn't clean the place up. We still couldn't find a thing to connect him to the lost girl."

Carl goes on with his report, "The Eagle Scout kid is okay, but a little too perfect for me. He sure ain't like my son. My son's an average boy, this Williams kid is a superstar. His room is full of trophies and awards, I mean dozens of them. Did you know his batting average in legion ball is over four hundred?"

"I didn't, but I knew he was a good athlete."

"The only thing is," Carl adds, "He was late for ball practice on

Friday. He says he left the church at eleven-thirty so he could go to the practice field, but he didn't arrive until one."

"That's not a crime," I counter.

"No, but it is suspicious. Then there's the girl with the disability," Carl continues. "She's a real sweetheart. How in the world can someone with her problems be so nice? There's no chance she could ever hurt anybody. I think we can rule her out because we will likely find someone who saw her walking home on Friday. The problem is – it took her an hour to walk ten blocks, as she did not get to her group home until one."

"She probably lost concentration and took some detours," I suggest.

"Now, Reverend, your music lady is a puzzle. Why is a woman her age, and with her looks, not remarried? The only thing I see to keep a guy away would be her cats. She has three of them and these animals are treated like royalty. You ever been to her place?"

I must admit that I've never been to Janice's house. She's been to ours for staff functions, but I've never even been to her door. My wife has gone by on a few occasions as she and Janice have become friends. Amy told me about the cats, so I have a little knowledge of how she lives.

"Did you know that Mrs. Morris was seen talking with Emma Wells earlier in the day on Friday?" Carl asks. "She told us today that the child asked her about joining the children's choir, and she told her that she would talk with her parents. That's a pretty big matter for her to not have told the police on Friday."

"But, still a trivial encounter," I argue. "Janice is not your abductor."

When Carl finishes his detailed rundown of the home searches, I tell him about my second letter.

"Damn, I guessed there might be more," he says. "A person with that much anger just has to vent it. What concerns me is why this is all coming out now. It sure makes me suspicious that this letter writer could be the one who took the child. However, I'm not sure this second letter will convince Neal Heard we should follow up on this more closely. Make sure you keep it safe, perhaps in a file folder. We'll come by your office in the morning."

I'm relieved that the police and bureau haven't found anything incriminating in the homes of our church people. But this leaves them nowhere in the search for Emma Wells. They will continue to look more closely at Janice and Joel, but that will not turn out to lead them to Emma.

I decide it's time for me to look at more of her DVD. I wanted to wait and view it with Amy, but I feel I must learn more about her now. Putting the disc in my office computer, I become aware that each time I see and hear Emma on the recordings I become more attached to her, and more disturbed at her disappearance.

I've learned a lot about cancer in these last few weeks. I already knew that my body is made up of many cells, but I didn't know that cells divide to repair injuries. Doctor Medlin told me that cancer cells divide when they are not supposed to and then you have too many cells. So the treatments try to keep the cells from dividing. I like to know the facts. They don't scare me. I don't mind talking about death either. One thing I would say to people in talking about death, don't call it sleep. This could make a child afraid to go to sleep, like they might not wake up. My grandmother died in her sleep, but I'm not afraid to go to sleep. I would rather die while awake, so I can say goodbye to my Mom and Dad.

Sometimes when we go to the cemetery to visit grandmother's grave I see the tears in your eyes, Mom. You walk away, pretending to be looking at other tombstones, but I know that you are trying to stop the tears. I won't mind if people cry when they see my grave. On my grandmother's stone there's a Bible verse which says, "So we are always confident; even though we know that while we are at home in the body we are away from the Lord." Under it is says Second Corinthians 5:6. One time I looked for that verse in my Bible. I just don't get it. I would like to find out what it means, but my guess is that my grandmother picked it out as one of her favorites because she wasn't afraid to die.

Today is Sunday and I went to church this morning. Mom and Dad, you should've been there. We didn't go to children's church until they had a baptism in the big church. Our teacher later told us what baptism is all about.

I think I want to be baptized after I lose my hair like the doctor said I will. It would be so much easier to not have to dry my hair when I get out of the pool. My friend, Charles, at school, said he was baptized at his church, but he only had water poured on the top of his head. I want to have mine done in the pool. I know that you shouldn't get baptized unless you believe in Jesus. I talk to Jesus a lot in my room, and I think he would approve of my being dunked soon.

There's one more thing I need to say. If I die from this cancer I want to be buried in that place we pass on the way to school, the one with the statue of Jesus near the pond. It's not too far from our house and it's so pretty there. I never noticed it much until I was told that I'm sick. Now, every time we pass I look to see if there are any new tents up. I know a tent means that someone has died. But, I haven't given up yet and hope to live long enough to go to college. I hear they have big libraries at college. I'll stop for now.

This is the most emotional thing I've ever experienced, which says a lot since I've seen my daughter born, and my father die. Both of those were deeply touching times in my life, but this is a tug on the heart that causes both deep joy and hurt at the same time. What a remarkable little girl. If there is any possibility that she's still alive, I will want to be with her as she faces her cancer and I want to baptize her.

Emma's facing the possibility of death head on. Not many adults are able to do that. We live in a culture that often faces death with denial. I can't help but recall what Russian novelist Tolstoy wrote about this dishonesty in the face of death in *The Death of Ivan Ilyich*. My copy is here somewhere so I look through my library and finally search through the novel for the passage I've dog eared:

> *"What tormented Ivan Ilyich most was the pretense, the lie, which for some reason they all kept up, that he was merely ill and not dying, and that he only need to stay quiet and carry out the doctor's orders, and some great change for the better would result. But he knew that whatever they might do nothing would come of it except still more agonizing suffering and death… The awful, terrible cry of dying was, he saw, reduced by those around him to the level of a fortuitous, disagreeable and rather indecent incident…This falsity around and within him did more than anything else to poison Ivan Ilyich's last days."*

The honesty of this eight year old girl is a testimony of both her faith and her understanding of reality. Where does this come from in one so young?

* * *

Amy's home from work and calls out to see if we're both here. I step out of the office and ask her to come to where I am. In a minute or two she stands in the doorway.

"Did Sarah have a good day?" she asks.

"She brought home more books and not a one of them was *Doctor Zhivago*."

Amy says, "You'd better give up on that. What are you doing?"

"I just looked at more of the Emma DVD."

"Did you see the part about her grandmother?" Amy asks. "I watched it last night after you fell asleep. It's so sad. I heard on the radio on the way home that there are still no leads on Emma's abduction. I feel so horrible for her parents."

"I know," I say. "Listen there's something I have to show you. I should have let you see it earlier, but was afraid of what it would do to you with all that's going on."

Amy sits on the corner of the desk and waits for my revelation.

I remove from my briefcase the letter I received on Friday and hand it to her. "This is a copy of a letter that was under the door of my office."

Amy begins to read. After about two minutes she moves to the love seat and stares at me. "Who wrote this?"

"I don't know."

"When did you receive this?"

"Last Friday morning," I say sheepishly.

"Friday! That's three days ago. And why, Ron, did you wait three days to show this to me?"

"Because I didn't want you to be upset. I was hoping I could figure out who wrote it before I let you see it."

"This is not the kind of thing you keep from your wife. Did you not learn that at Grace Baptist when you waited weeks to tell me about the vote of the deacons?"

"I suppose I didn't," I admit.

"What else have you not told me?" Amy asks.

I take out the second letter and tell her I just found it an hour ago. I carefully hold it by the edges and read it to her. She slumps further in the chair, obviously very upset as I assumed she would be.

"This is awful. You've never done anything to warrant this. You may keep secrets from your wife, but you've never hurt a fly. Who else has seen these letters?"

I tell Amy about Ken Matthews, Carl Brody, and the FBI agents. Then I describe my interview with Neal Heard this morning. She's astounded by all of it.

"I can't believe that all of those people know about these accusations, and I, your wife, learn of this only now. Have we not always been able to share everything?"

"I just didn't want you to have to deal with this until I knew more about it," I say.

"But I do have to deal with it. This affects our lives, yours, mine, and Sarah's. I need some time to let this sink in," Amy says.

"I'm sorry. All I wanted to do was protect you from this as long as I could."

"And, who is going to protect you? I'm just as tough as you are, you know."

"I know."

She places the first letter on the desk and begins to walk away. She stops and turns back toward me, her eyes now filled with tears. I knew she would become emotional when made aware of the letters.

"I deal with some tough situations in my work," Amy says. "There are so many bad cases out there. I just don't want them to invade my family. These letters are an intrusion into our personal lives. This is…" She pauses to collect herself. "This is just not fair. And, I'm really hurt you did not tell me about the first letter right away."

CHAPTER TWELVE

MONDAY EVENING

After dinner we take Sarah over to Mary Grogan's house. Mary has babysat for us for years now. Sarah's begun to protest recently that she doesn't need to be looked after while we are out of the house. I get the feeling this evening that she doesn't mind a couple of hours with Mary.

On the way to the Wells' house Amy does not speak a word. I know enough to not force conversation when she chooses to be silent.

Ted and Rachel greet us at the door as I've already apprised them that Amy will be coming with me. There are only two press vehicles out front, but we're told that more were there most of the day. The Wells are alone this evening as all relatives and friends are giving them some space. Rachel's wearing a yellow sun dress which belies the sadness in her eyes. Ted's wearing a green Izod knit shirt tucked in, and it is as though the two want to appear their best for the visit of the pastor and his wife.

Amy sits on the white upholstered couch beside Rachel as Ted and I sit in the two navy barrel chairs across the room. It was Rachel who directed us to our places. "I'm so sorry about Emma," Amy says. "Ted has let me view the video of her and she's an incredible girl. I hope it's alright if I watched the DVD."

"I'm glad you can get to know our daughter," Rachel says as she touches Amy's arm. "We're trying to have hope, but every hour she's gone we find our hope slipping away. I think of her every waking minute and am sure she occupies all of my sleeping dreams. There is this dreadful void which fills our house."

Amy leans closer to Rachel. "I can only imagine what this is doing to you. I could hardly focus on my work today as every few minutes I would think about Emma."

Ted Wells speaks with a deliberate tone, obviously trying to hold back his emotion, "Mrs. Fowler, we're so thankful you have come over with the pastor. My wife has had a number of friends and co-workers visit, but she was looking forward to meeting you. You deal with families in your social work which have all kinds of problems, and you have a daughter as well. We both welcome your interest in our daughter."

"I'm embarrassed that this is the first time we've met," Rachel says, turning to Amy. "We should have come to church with Emma. She wanted us to try your church, but never pushed us. She has so much insight for an eight year old."

Amy grabs Rachel's hand and squeezes it.

"Kristen from your church came by this afternoon," Ted says. "Emma thinks of her as a friend. She's really torn up over this."

"She's very emotionally invested," I say. "I've never seen anyone who can capture the imagination of children like she can, and she cares deeply about them all."

"This is not her fault, Reverend," Rachel says. "I want you to know that Ted and I do not blame any of you at the church. We don't feel that this could have been someone from your congregation."

"I don't either," I say, hoping I'm right.

"Would you and your wife come with us, Dr. Fowler?" Ted asks. "We want to show you Emma's room. Rachel and I have tried to not spend too much time in there since last Friday, but the pull is so strong to want to in some way be near to her."

The four of us make our way down the hall and pass by what appears to be a guest room. There's luggage in one corner and personal items on the mule chest and cherry wood dresser.

"Ted's parents and sister are staying with us," Rachel says. "They've been very helpful. His mother and Emma are very close. This is so hard on her. The three of them have gone to the grocery store tonight. I think they wanted to give us some time with you."

"This must be so hard on everyone," Amy says.

"Ted's father can't even say Emma's name," Rachel admits.

Emma's room is at the end of the hall on the right, across from the master bedroom. The entire space is pink from wall to bedspread. There are a variety of dolls perched on shelves and reclining on the bed as if waiting for the return of one who will animate them. It's fairly typical of a little girl's room and reminds me of our Sarah's "princess chamber," as we call it, which she is now outgrowing.

Rachel Wells stands in one corner of the nice-sized room and points to a bookshelf. "This is what we want you to see."

On the four foot high shelf there are a variety of books from *Nancy Drew* to *Doctor Seuss*. But, on the top shelf there's an open Bible with a tasseled bookmark lying across the page.

"We found her Bible open like this when we came in here Friday after we learned she was missing. We were surprised at what we found as there is a pencil inscription beside one of the verses."

Amy and I look closely at the page and read the little girl's note: "I am not afraid to die. Rest is good." It's in the margin beside Revelation 14:13 which reads, "And I heard a voice from heaven saying, 'write this: blessed are the dead who from now on die in the Lord.' 'Yes,' says the Spirit, 'they will rest from their labors, for their deeds will follow them.'"

"What do you think this means, Dr. Fowler?" Rachel asks.

I'm caught off guard and study both the verse and the note in the margin. Being careful to not disturb the open Bible, I try and remember the passage and its place in the last book of the New Testament.

"I only remember a little about this part of the Bible from my studies," I say. "I know this is one of the seven visions the writer of the book offers. I think this section is trying to comfort the Christian martyrs. It probably means they will rest from their sufferings by means of death."

"And what about Emma's note?" asks Ted.

"I think Emma is saying that she's tired of the cancer and that if she were to die she would have the consolation of no more pain. That is, of course, a big assumption on my part."

"That's what I thought it meant," Rachel adds.

"I don't think that Emma is studying the book of Revelation at our church," I say. "She probably came upon this by herself."

"She asked me to help her with a concordance," Ted adds. "She was surprised that I had one on the bookshelves in the den. I kept it from my college religion courses."

"Did you take many religion courses in college?" Amy asks, diverting the conversation from the morbid discussion.

"Yes, several. Rachel and I met in a world religions class at school. She sat in front of me, and I got up the nerve to ask her to have lunch with me in the cafeteria."

"He used the old copy my notes routine to get my attention," Rachel says.

This is the first time I've seen her smile, and Amy casts a glance my way as to say this is a nice little refrain from the sadness that permeates this house.

"Dr. Fowler, I actually majored in religion in college," Ted confesses. "I was interested in knowing about how religions impacted world history. I knew that I would join my dad's real estate firm, and that it really didn't matter what my major was. Now, I wish I had concentrated on how religion helps people face life."

"I know I should have asked this before, but what is the doctor's prognosis of Emma's battle with the cancer?" I ask.

Rachel and Ted look at each other. "Ewing's Sarcoma is in the bones," Ted volunteers. "Emma's disease is not too far along, but the doctors are not sure about surgery because it's located near the spinal cord. The chemotherapy is to be tried first. Until those treatments are given a chance, the verdict is not clear."

"They can't promise us she will survive this," Rachel says. She walks over and picks up a stuffed tiger, holding it to her chest. She then turns away from us and faces the wall.

Ted moves over to her and places his arms around his wife. Amy moves closer to me and takes my hand. The brief moment of smiles is past, and the four of us stand in the bedroom of a little girl who has a life threatening illness which may not even matter if her adductor has harmed her. The silence is pervasive, and the room seems to have swallowed all resonance.

Ted is the first to speak. "Emma told the doctor on her last visit that God will help him plan his treatments. He smiled and agreed that such help would be welcomed."

"Most doctors I've met welcome the possibility of divine intervention but are aware that God has already contributed much in the way of knowledge provided to medical science," I add.

A few minutes later the four of us stand on the front porch and engage in typical parting conversation as though this was some social engagement which was so pleasant that each participant wishes it would not end. Amy and I finally leave this couple to their mounting concerns over the plight of their daughter.

I can't help but remember the words in Matthew's gospel where it speaks of the Old Testament Rachel weeping for her children. This ancient woman who died at the birth of her second son refused to be consoled. What consolation will there be for Rachel Wells if she loses her daughter?

In the car Amy speaks first, "What would we do if our daughter had cancer?"

"I suppose we would find a way to deal with it like Ted and Rachel are doing," I say.

"Are they really dealing with all of this?" Amy wonders out loud. "How can anyone have enough strength to face what they are facing?"

I know these are not questions she expects me to answer this evening. She's imagining herself in their place. I do the same on the quiet ride through town.

* * *

We pick up Sarah and return home to find a message from Ken on the answering machine. He will come by at eight-thirty. It's late in a long day, but Amy and I need to hear from our friend as to what he knows about my accuser.

When Ken arrives a few minutes later he's warmly greeted by Amy who thanks him for pushing me to share the letters with her. The three of us settle in the den with cups of coffee and Krispy Kreme doughnuts brought by Ken. Sarah's in her room.

After some discussion of our visit to the Wells, Ken looks over my latest letter and then proceeds to tell us what he thinks. "Well, from this one line it looks even more like this is a female. It's also clear this person was in church on Sunday. My gut feeling is that the letter writer is likely the one who took Emma Wells."

Amy gasps, "Oh, no. You really think the letters are from the abductor?"

"They certainly could be," Ken says as he nods his head up and down several times.

"This is awful," Amy says. "You think that a woman from our church took Emma Wells. If that's so we must narrow this down as quickly as possible."

"If we assume the correspondent is a woman," Ken says, "then there are about a hundred and seventy possible ones in worship Sunday. I have reduced that down by about thirty through brainstorming those who would have fingerprints on file, government employees and such. Now I have to find out which ones are left-handed. I've spent some time on that this afternoon and already ruled out another thirty or forty whom I'm sure are right-handed."

"So, there are almost a hundred women still to consider, one of which may have this grudge against me?"

"That's the way I see it," says Ken.

"So, what do we do now?" Amy asks.

"We try and refine the list further. I'll find a way to see which of the remaining women write with their left hand. Not sure exactly how to do that without going to see each one. Actually, I will ask around some more and be able to cull the list tomorrow. The FBI team is going to want to be a part of this even though they don't agree with my suspicion the letters and the abduction are likely related."

"What about James Turner?" Amy asks. "I thought he was the main suspect."

"He has still not been found," Ken answers. "There's a lot to make him look like one who could have done this. I have my doubts though. For one thing he doesn't have a car. I want to hold my opinions about him until after he's found."

"What if he's not found?" Amy asks. "Do you think he could have taken this child and left the area with her?"

"That kind of thing does happen," Ken admits.

"So, the letter writer is, in your mind, just as likely the person who took Emma as is James Turner?" I ask.

"Yes, since your letters coincided with the girl being taken, but it's only circumstantial at this time. I'm going to work more in the morning on who could have sent these letters."

Ken leaves, and Amy and I sit for a few minutes recapping the evening. She has met the Wells, learned of my letters, and seen some of the DVD made by Emma. I know how disturbing all of this is to her. She decides to go upstairs and check in on Sarah. It's nine-thirty in the evening now and no word on Emma.

* * *

The phone call is from Sam Haverty.

"I hear you may need a lawyer," Sam says.

"I hope not," I answer.

"Well, one of my partners in our firm was at the police station this morning and tells me the police and FBI questioned you for almost an hour," Sam reports. "You should never let them do that without an attorney present."

"I thought bringing an attorney along meant you were guilty of something," I say.

"Having an attorney with you means you're smart. Did they call you a suspect in the Wells case?" Sam asks.

"Not exactly, but I was on a list of those they refer to as possible suspects."

"Was, meaning you are not now?"

"Well, a neighbor has vouched for my presence at the critical time, or some of the time."

"Is there something I should know that I don't?"

"Just one thing, and it's a pretty big thing."

I tell Sam about the letters, and he sounds shocked. He asks several questions about the content. I also tell him that Ken is helping me. Sam acts hurt that he was not consulted. I never really thought I would need his services.

"Ron, I'm your friend as well as a church member. I want to help. We have a lot of resources at our firm. Keep me posted on everything that happens. One other thing – there is no one who knows you that is going to believe you would hurt a child."

After we hang up, I think of all that Sam said. I feel bad, but I've never thought of Sam as a friend. He and I have never socialized, and he's always so professional acting that it's hard to imagine sharing a casual friendship with him.

One of the advantages of being a pastor is that through the church there are ready-made friends. They show up on the day you move in with cakes and pies, eager to be of help when needed. There are so many wonderful things that church people do for a pastor and family. In my first pastorate in the rural setting there were two families in the church who owned businesses that produced and sold eggs. Each of them would bring to the parsonage once a week a dozen fresh eggs and leave them on the back porch. We could not eat all of those eggs, but it was just one of those perks of being a pastor.

There is, of course, the downside in that the attention is sometimes smothering. There are so many eyes upon the pastor's family that it can become uncomfortable. One morning in that country church parsonage I left my car lights on as I went into the house to retrieve something before going out on a visit. Within three minutes there were four phone calls apprising me of the fact my lights were on. The homes of several church members had clear sight lines to our house.

"The lack of privacy can become an impediment to normal family living," as Edward Bratcher once wrote his book titled, *The Walk on Water Syndrome*. Bratcher also points out that "members of the congregation consider their pastor to be a professional and as such to be endowed with certain gifts and skills." This means the pastor is to be the expert in certain areas such as theology and counseling. The pastor is seen as the one with all the answers. Evidently, Sam thinks my expertise doesn't include legal matters. He's right on this. I will need to be more aware of Sam Haverty's consideration that he and I are friends and of his desire to be helpful.

I find myself full of doubts this evening, not very confident in my pastoral abilities. I doubt my ability to handle what may come tomorrow. I'm not sure I have what it takes to help Ted and Rachel Wells. I reflect on my reasons for leaving Grace Baptist Church years ago when the going got rough. I also have doubts this evening about my faith. Events like these of the last few days have the power to turn a person into a skeptic that there is a god who has any involvement in the lives of human beings. There are so many things I don't know, so many pulls to agnosticism.

The Jews have a word "apikoros". It comes from rabbinical literature, and the word can be traced to the Greek philosopher, Epicurus. It means skeptic, agnostic, unbeliever. I remember a story about a young Hebrew student who went to an old learned rabbi and exclaimed, "I must tell you the truth! I have become an apikoros. I no longer believe in God."

"And how long have you been studying the Talmud?" the rabbi asked.

"Five years," said the student.

"Only five years," sighed the rabbi, "and you have the nerve to call yourself an apikoros? Come back in fifty years when you have had more experience and tell me then about your beliefs and doubts."

I remember hearing that story when I was in seminary studying to be a minister. I realized then that I had so much to learn. Now after serving as a chaplain and then pastor for these years, I still do not have the wisdom to question God. I just wish that God would give to me some sign that I'm headed in the right direction in how I'm handling my latest challenges. But that is probably not how it works. I have a profound faith, and my agnosticism is actually what I believe to be a healthy lack of presumption that I know all there is to know.

CHAPTER THIRTEEN

TUESDAY MORNING

I have less than two days left before my secret accuser is going to expose my alleged sins. I woke up this morning thinking about how I can best use these two days. There's actually little I can do. I don't know who my adversary is and have no idea why they have decided to accuse me. I have admired the writings of Texas pastor, Gerald Mann, for a while now. He has said, "It's what happens to what happens to you that matters." Most of the time we have little control over what happens to us, but we do have control as to how we respond. There's a deep seeded need to be proactive that rises from within me this morning.

Emma Wells hasn't been found. She has been gone four nights, and the likelihood of her safe return is becoming more and more negative. Every forty seconds in this country a child goes missing. Only a small portion of them are physically harmed, but seventy-four percent of those killed are dead within three hours of their abduction. This is what Ken told me yesterday. And, I'm supposed to defend a god who lets this happen? What a crappy job it is at times being a clergy person.

One of my favorite novels is John Updike's *Rabbit Run*. In it a husband comes home and finds his wife in a drunken stupor. She has accidentally allowed their infant daughter to drown in the bathtub. The father removes the dead child and lays her on the bed. He goes back into the bathroom, the water still in the tub. Updike writes, "Stillness makes a dread skin on the water's unstirred surface." The sad man rolls back his sleeve, reaches in and pulls the plug. As the last water is sucked down the father thinks how easy it was to let the water out, "Yet in all His strength God did nothing. Just that little stopper to lift."

I have often thought of that scene and wondered what defense of God is available for a minister to employ when an innocent child dies through carelessness or meanness.

Is God periodically absent, occasionally uncaring, or just oblivious to our human suffering? There'll be those who will look to me today for answers and for insights into faith. I will need to meet with staff, some of whom have had their homes searched and time analyzed. I will face the press again and be asked why this has happened, some in an attempt to cast more doubts on the relevancy of religious beliefs. I'll look into the eyes of Ted and Rachel Wells who are using up their hope. I feel like a magician who must go on stage without a bag of tricks and still be forced to perform.

On the way to work I call Janice Moore. I'm sure the police search of her house was difficult on her.

"Janice, I wanted to catch you before we get to church where it'll be harder to talk. I know the police searched your house yesterday. I'm so sorry that happened. I told them they were wasting their time."

"It wasn't so bad, Ron," Janice says. "They were very careful. My cats did not take it so well, but I'm okay. I told the police that I didn't know the Wells child, but want to help in any way possible."

"I'm sure they'll take you off the list today," I venture.

"Is there any news on the girl?" Janice asks.

"No, not that I've heard. Listen, Amy and I are concerned that you have to face this alone. Please let us help if we can."

"I'm handling this pretty well, and my son called last night to check on me. He's coming down this weekend. Thank you for your concern, Ron. I'll see you at church later."

Janice is very much a private person. She comes to work and goes home. I wish she had more of a social life, but it's not my place to interfere. She's the most organized person I've ever known. The choir room looks like a Montessori classroom. It must have bothered her more than she lets on when the FBI came to her place and disturbed her things. I wonder why she told the police she didn't know the girl since Emma had come to her and asked about joining the children's choir. I suppose that brief encounter did not qualify in her mind as knowing Emma.

A couple of months ago I experienced one of the most awkward moments in my life. I had gone over to the choir room to ask Janice a question about the music selection for the coming Sunday. When I entered her office I could tell she had been crying. This was a surprise since she always seems to be so poised and in control. I sat in a chair a few feet away from where she was seated and asked her what was wrong. She waved her hand at me to say she could not speak. We both sat for what must have been a minute when she got up from her chair and came over to me. I stood up as she drew closer, and Janice put her arms around my neck and hugged me. As lightly as possible, I touched her on her back and again asked why she was upset. Her arms tightened their embrace and she put her head against mine with her ear pressing against my cheek. We stood this way for what seemed like fifteen minutes though it was probably only two.

There are those times in life when there is no move which seems appropriate. Of all the choices available to us none seems to offer a way to extricate us from the quandary we find ourselves in. Continuing to stay in the embrace was not wise in that we were alone together in her office which was both too private and too public. Wrenching myself from her clinch felt too unsympathetic. Speaking to her with our heads together did not present a comfortable means of communicating. My only choice was to do nothing until she decided to release her hold on me.

Finally, there was a sudden shudder, and Janice withdrew her arms, walked back over to her chair, and sat back down as though the past few minutes had been some time anomaly that had never really taken place. She offered only the words "I'm sorry."

I stood frozen in the middle of the floor trying to decipher what just happened. After a minute passed, Janice handed to me a piece of paper – a note from her son. It was only a few sentences and was his announcement to his mother he was planning to get married. Janice told me that she had just opened the note when I came in and was overwhelmed with two conflicting emotions, joy and fear. The fear was that her son might experience the pain she had in her marriage. Since that day neither of us has spoken of the few minutes in her office.

* * *

Alice Stevens is our church secretary and my protector. She screens all my calls and visitors when she can with a special sensitivity to my preferences and moods. I sometimes feel that she knows my wishes better than I do myself. It's nine when I arrive at the office, and she greets me with her usual morning calm demeanor.

"The staff will gather at ten, if you want to keep your routine today," Alice says. "Ken Matthews will be here in fifteen minutes to see you. I've told all other callers that you will be tied up until noon."

Her glasses have slid down on her nose and she looks over them at me. A notepad in hand, she checks off the agenda she has prepared for me. Her black and gray permed hair frames a pleasant face which portrays her genuine interest in the well being of others, even if her mannerisms seem stern at times.

"I could not function without you, Alice. Besides my wife and daughter, and possibly a few dozen others, you're my best supporter," I tease.

"None of them can do for you what I can," Alice comes back as she often does to my jostling. She is perhaps a little too feisty and irreverent for a church secretary, but her attitude is refreshing to me.

"How many years have you been at First Baptist now?" I ask.

"Almost as long as you've been alive," she comes back.

"If that is the case then you sure look young for your age."

"I get plenty of sleep. It looks like you could use more."

"Is there any news I haven't yet heard?" I ask, knowing that her sources are widespread.

"The police picked up James Turner this morning."

"How do you know that? I listened to the radio on the way over and did not hear anything about it."

"It just happened a few minutes ago," Alice informs me. "My policeman cousin just called. It seems that Turner was hiding out in an old trailer a friend of his owns outside of town. He was alone when the sheriff's men busted in the door. They're bringing him in now to the police station where the FBI team is waiting to interrogate him. They're also questioning his friend."

"Do they think Turner took Emma?"

"Don't know yet. I'll brief you when I learn more. You better get to your office before this place fills up with reporters and who knows who else."

Ken Matthews comes in a few minutes after I sit down at my desk.

"I guess you heard about the Turner fellow," Ken says even before he sits down.

"Yes, just learned of it," I say.

"I know what I said last night about him being a long shot, but the guy does fit the bill in some ways," Ken says. "He has a record of molestation, lives near the church, probably has been to the church before, and has been hiding out. Someone must have driven him out to that trailer, so he could have a partner in his actions."

"What happens now?" I ask.

"Oh, they will question him and search every place he's been. They can hold him on probation violations but will need some physical evidence to charge him with abduction."

"How long before we'll know something?"

"Today, we may know if he had anything to do with it," Ken says. "Let's talk about your letter writer. I've been over the group of possibles in the congregation and there are eighteen women who were here Sunday that remain on my list. The best I can find out they're all left-handed. Here's the print out for you to look at."

I take the single sheet of paper with two columns of names. Most of them I know well. "Do any of these seem more likely to you?" I ask Ken.

"Those who live alone must be at the top of the list. You will see that I have put asterisks beside them."

I count twelve names with the designation. They include Janice Moore as well as Arlene Jones, a divorced teacher, Karen Sylvester, a recent widow, and Sandra Hutchens, a lawyer. Each of these three I know very well, as they are active in our church and close friends. I can't imagine any of them accusing me of doing these horrible things. Several of the women I do not know so well. A few others are long time church members such as Joan Riebert in our choir and Dot Marshall who teaches an adult Sunday school class. Both of these women are well thought of in our church.

"You will see that it's not an easy task," Ken suggests. "I know

155

many of these women well myself. There are two on this list I don't know as they are fairly new here. If it's okay with you, I'm going to see what I can learn about them today."

"I hate that you have to do this kind of thing, Ken."

"Me too," he agrees. "But, this is the kind of work I did for years with the bureau. A little different when it is church friends you're investigating."

After Ken goes, I sit with the copy of the list. He and I both know that the author of my accusatory letters may be someone whose name is not on this page, but we must go with what is most likely. I stare at the list to try and remember if I've ever done anything that might offend any of them. It just doesn't seem possible that someone on this list would accuse me of child molestation. If it was one of these, then the problem lies in their past not mine.

* * *

It's ten now, and I sit down with the church staff in the conference room. Usually this is one of the highlights of my week as these sessions are often productive and enjoyable. Those present are: Kristen Davis, Deanna Crowder, Janice Moore, Steve Ayers, Karen Gravitt, Alice Stevens, and Becky Royston, our financial secretary. This is our full time staff except for the custodian, Joel Weaver. I open the meeting with prayer as usual, including a petition for the Wells family.

"Before we get to church business," I open, "I want us to spend some time on what is on all of our minds. This is a difficult period for our church family and for those of us on the staff. We are all very concerned for the Wells and can concentrate on little else. Everything we do or plan to do is under this cloud today. So, let's talk about this."

"I can't focus on anything else," Kristen says.

"But, we owe it to our congregation to do our regular jobs," Deanna adds.

I can see this could turn into a debate as to how we handle the stress and decide to set us on another course. "We all have deep feelings about what has happened, and we all have jobs to do. I want us to try and handle the routine matters we must, but still keep Emma Wells foremost on our minds. I know that will not be easy."

Steve picks up on my suggestion. "Listen, I've not slept much since Friday and am having trouble with my guilt in our letting this happen. Still, I have a whole bunch of kids who are touched by this. Sunday night our youth group spent the entire time together debriefing this whole thing. There's a real opportunity to minister here."

"Our senior adult group is holding an around the clock prayer vigil with over a hundred people taking turns at thirty minute periods," Deanna informs us.

I realize that I'm so preoccupied with my own situation that I was not aware of this. "This is a caring church family. Did you organize the prayer chain?" I ask Deanna.

"No, this was their doing. A strong church is one where the staff does not have to orchestrate everything that happens."

"That's true," I respond. "A really strong church is where a fine staff like ours facilitates the lay people to do their own ministry. Let me clear the air about the investigation. Janice and I have been scrutinized by the authorities more than others since we were not in public on Friday when Emma disappeared. She and I talked earlier this morning and want the rest of you to know that we have come through this without too much harm done to our privacy."

"The FBI and police searched my home," Janice says. "It was a less than pleasurable experience, but they were very professional. It only took about thirty minutes."

"I can't imagine having strangers go through my house," Alice says.

Steve jumps in. "My wife gets nervous when anyone comes over, mainly because I'm such a slob. She would have asked the police to wait outside for thirty minutes so she could straighten the house first."

"I talked to Rachel Wells this morning," Kristen says. "Her doctor has prescribed medication to calm her, but she's determined to not stay in a daze while they are looking for her daughter. She is amazingly calm today; I'm not sure what to make of that."

"I can imagine the anguish she must feel," Karen says.

"Can you believe this Turner man lives so close to the church?" Becky asks.

"One of the kids in the youth group told me Sunday night that James Turner shops in the grocery store where he works," Steve says. "He's bagged the guy's purchases on several occasions and says the man is creepy. One of the other clerks told him Turner had been in prison."

"Can you believe that he cashes his disability checks at the bank where Rachel Wells works?" Alice asks. "They have probably seen each other there."

The meeting goes on for an hour with the discussion concentrating on the missing child and our response to this. Each of us is in the middle of this terrible situation, and we all need to vent our feelings. I'm worried for Kristen – she's so young and naturally very emotional. Janice has to be more upset than she seems over the search of her house, and Steve is carrying a lot of weight on his shoulders because he was responsible for the children getting on the vans Friday. A terrible thing has happened, and we are all grieving over it.

As I sit in my office alone after the meeting, I wonder what's going on with James Turner. Did he come into the church Friday and take this little girl? I can't help but think of the time a few months ago when someone broke into our church and forced the door to the office for the community helping agency, The Good Samaritan. The intruder found the agency's check book and tried to pay for three hundred dollars worth of video equipment at a nearby Walmart. A suspicious clerk summoned the manager, and the thief fled before being apprehended. The checking account had to be closed and a new one opened.

We live in an evil world, and that becomes even more evident when someone tries to steal from a helping agency. The Apostle Paul in the biblical book of Romans advises, "Do not be overcome by evil." I think Paul was talking about our responses to evil. Paul goes on to advise that we should overcome evil with good. That's easier said than done.

Child molestation is likely at the top of my list of evils. Some years ago the Los Angeles Times took a nationwide poll and found that ninety-eight percent of those who had been sexually molested as children felt the harm done to them was permanent. The feelings stirred up last a lifetime and include: anger, fear, guilt, confusion, and worthlessness. They try to live life as best they can, but life for them will always be lived in the shadow of this past experience.

I've learned from counseling books that many who suffer from abuse have trouble ever trusting God. Why did God allow this to happen to them, they wonder. Shouldn't a caring God protect children from the evil of abuse, they reason. There is often theological confusion, and struggle with doubt.

The phone call is from Carl Brody. "Pastor, I guess you heard that we have James Turner here."

"Yes, how's it going with his questioning?" I ask.

"He's in there with Heard and his team. They are good, and the guy is scared. So far, no breakthroughs. Have you seen his picture in the paper?"

I answer, "I've seen it."

"Do remember ever seeing him at the church?" Carl asks.

"No, I don't think so."

"Well, he has been there several times to get food. He claims he's never been anywhere in the church but in the Good Samaritan area. I'm going to email over a photo of him and would like to know if anyone else on the staff has seen him."

"I'll check with my staff."

"Thanks, Reverend," Carl says. "I want you to know that we have removed the scout kid and the maintenance guy from our list of possible suspects. They were both seen by someone at noon on Friday where they said they were."

"That's good to hear," I say.

The photo of Turner is passed around in the offices, but no one remembers seeing him. I seek out Joel Weaver to show it to him. He's in the sanctuary polishing the pulpit furniture.

"Good morning, Joel. How's it going with you?"

"Doing alright, Padre," is his response.

Showing him the picture of Turner, I ask, "Have you seen this guy around here?"

Joel studies the face and shakes his head no. "Is he a suspect in the abduction?"

"The police and FBI are questioning him," I say. "I heard they came to your apartment. How did that go?"

"It wasn't too bad. The Heard fellow is a real hard ass, like many officers I dealt with in the military."

"Yeah, he can be tough on people."

Joel nods in agreement. "He's not through with me yet, wants to go over my entire past. I think he has a thing about Catholics. He keeps asking me about my religion and throws in comments that are aimed at provoking me. The man doesn't understand that such stuff does not work with someone with my experiences."

"You mean your military training?" I ask.

"That and my years spent in Catholic schools with the nuns. I'm not sure who worked me over the most, the hardnosed army types or the no nonsense women in black habits. And then there was my dad. He was a career army enlisted man and a believer in discipline at home."

"Sounds like you have had your share of disciplinarians," I say.

"That's one reason I like working here. I do my job and nobody bothers me."

"We're glad you're with us."

"Don't worry about me, Padre. I had nothing to do with the missing kid and I can take anything the MP types throw at me."

As I head back to the office I'm intrigued by this man who cleans our church. I want to ask him about his interest in philosophy, but am reluctant to pry into his life further. In my view Joel is a good person who would never hurt someone except in self defense. I also can't imagine any of the people I know who are on Ken's list as capable of abducting a child. But, I realize that we humans are not really very adept in making judgments of others, and we pastors often lack the cynicism of those who deal with crime every day.

I read a tongue-in-cheek story recently of a church that was going to purge its rolls of people who were not virtuous enough to be a part of the congregation. Those with certain known vices were removed as well as those who were seen as the cause of family problems. The church clerk was doing the purging based on information relayed to her from the pastor and other leaders. She even had reason to be suspicious of the pastor and deacons. Finally, it came down to the clerk and her husband as the only ones left who did not have some known flaws, and she was considering removing him. The point of the story was that there are no perfect people, and making moral judgments is a very subjective experience.

Before lunch I place a call to the Wells home. Ted Well's mother answers the phone. She tells me that Rachel is resting and that Ted is out in the garage doing some repair work. I ask if there is anything I can do today to help, and Mrs. Wells says, "Just keep us in your prayers."

I tell her I plan to drop by this evening, and she says that would be nice. Mrs. Wells is very poised and must be extremely helpful to Ted and Rachel. Grandparents often find themselves in supportive roles in the most critical times. Over my years as a minister, I've observed many parents of adult children who were the providers of calm and reassurance when things fell apart with the marriages of their sons or daughters. How many grandparents have helped raise the children of divorce and have been on call when stability was needed for the innocent young victims of family turbulence?

* * *

Amy and I have an early lunch date at the local Pizza Hut. We try to once a week arrange for this time together. Sarah's at a friend's house. After being seated we see several people we know, some from our church. Teresa Simmons comes over to our table. She's one of those people you try to avoid when you can, for she likes to hear herself talk; she's both outgoing and loud. Standing over our table like a fox over a cornered rabbit, we know there's no escape from her.

"Pastor, this is the most awful thing that has ever happened to our church," Teresa says. "I just know this little girl has been murdered. This is dreadful, dreadful."

"Teresa, we don't know what happened to her yet, so we should keep hoping she's alright," I say.

"I knew when that Turner man moved in he was trouble," Teresa goes on. "You know he lives above the Neely's garage, right down the street from us. I can't imagine why they let someone on the pervert list rent from them. They should have checked him out and refused to have a deviant on their property."

"I didn't know about him until this week," I reply.

"I've seen him walking in the neighborhood," Teresa says. "He's only a little over five and a half feet tall, and stops to watch children playing in their yards even though he's not supposed to go near them. Reverend, you wouldn't believe just how weird this guy is."

Teresa's husband, Warren, takes her by the arm and pulls her away. "Reverend, you and your wife have a nice lunch. Come on, Teresa, these folks want to be alone."

"That man's a saint," Amy says.

"We husbands have such burdens to bear," I say with a smile.

"Ron, have you thought in the last few days how this all has taken over the lives of so many people?" Amy asks. "Last week at this time we were all going about our routines with no idea any of this would come about."

"Yes, we expect each day to be the continuation of the one before. We expect that any new challenges will be manageable. We expect everyone to stay in character and fit the molds we have made for them."

"I can't help but wonder how all of this will change us," Amy says. "How will it change you, me, and Sarah? How will it change our future?"

"I suppose that depends on the outcome of this temporary drama," I offer. "I also suppose it depends on what we learn from it."

"This life is a real mystery," Amy says. "You never know whether you are headed for good times or for trouble." She looks out the window for a moment and then continues. "How can you tell whether the changes that occur bring something you need or whether they are something that destroys?"

We both pause the conversation for a minute, each thinking this is probably too heavy a discussion for a lunch at Pizza Hut. I change the subject, and we talk of more mundane things like what do we need from the grocery store.

After lunch we both head our separate ways; Amy to social services and me to my new job as a criminal investigator. I decide to drive past James Turner's place. The garage apartment has a set of side steps and is very similar to the place our custodian, Joel, lives only a few blocks away. Perhaps Teresa Simmons was right that people like James Turner should not live among the respectable. That thought immediately bothers me. It's always problematic when we resort to the term, "people like that." So many of the world's problems result from such a designation.

CHAPTER FOURTEEN

TUESDAY AFTERNOON

Julia Wagner is the most respected person in our church, by far. For forty-seven years she served as the church's education director and worked with six different pastors. When I arrived at First Baptist six years ago she had announced her retirement at age seventy-five and stayed on one year as I got my feet on the ground. For all those years she was the glue that held the programs together and was the confidant for the many ministers. Now, at eighty-two years, she's home recuperating from a hip replacement, but her mind is as sharp as ever.

Palmer Street is only four blocks from the church and is lined with modest homes, most of which are sixty or more years old. Julia's house is on a hill with abundant concrete steps rising up from the street which makes for a nice ascent. The driveway also climbs the hill and ends with a garage in the back on the same level as the house. As I reach the top of the steps, slightly winded, I notice that the flowers on the porch are in need of attention. In my previous trips here the plants were thriving. The hip injury has certainly set her back in giving them her care.

Every pastor before me has made the pilgrimage to her door on occasion to seek her advice and draw upon her wisdom. On at least three occasions before I have made the trek up this hill to ask guidance of Julia. Two were when I was indeed in a quandary as to how to cope with a delicate matter, another was simply to allow her to assure me I had made the right decision.

She's expecting me and told me on the phone to let myself in. I find the tiny woman dressed in a robe seated on her couch with her walker nearby. The small living room is as tidy as ever. The space has a rich array of photos of Mrs. Wagner's family, her two sons and one daughter plus nine grandchildren, and three great ones as well.

Mr. Wagner died some twenty years ago from a heart attack, and she's lived alone for the two decades. Her gray hair in a bun on top of her head almost looks like a crown of shimmering silver – she's the epitome of a grandmother or great grandmother, wise and gentle.

My purpose here today is to share with her my letters and ask her if she has any idea who my accuser might be. It came to me early this morning that she would be the one to help narrow my list. Ken has done an excellent job in his investigation, but Mrs. Wagner knows things about people that Ken and I will never know. For three generations she watched the children of the church grow up and undoubtedly was privy to the most private of details about life in our fellowship. Julia is not a gossip by any means but understands that pastors must sometimes know the intimacies of their congregants.

"Don't get up," I say as I enter the room.

"Never intended to," Julia replies.

I take a seat in a chair across from her and try not to muss the doilies that protect the arms of the flowered rocker. I wonder how many times pastors have sat here awaiting the insights of her stored up memories. I have often called her the church's computer as I have marveled at the facts she retains. There are many seniors her age with Alzheimer's. I say that she has reverse dementia in that her recollections of the past are as keen as can be.

"I hope your hip is healing properly," I say.

"At my age healing is a drawn out process," she says. "But, I can't complain since this is my first time to need crutches or a walker."

"You are remarkable," I say then realizing that she does not welcome such praise.

"I'm not remarkable, just as brittle as any other person my age."

We spend a few minutes with updates on her medical progress and about the awful situation of the missing child.

Eventually, I pull from a folder the copies of my two letters, "Julia, I have something I need your help with. Would you look at these and tell me if you have any idea who might have written them? I'm very concerned over who is accusing me of things I've not done, and the anger is disconcerting."

I pass the two pages to her and watch as she studies them. After she has read them thoroughly she places the two letters beside her on the couch and then motions with her hand to a cabinet across the room. "Ron, would you mind going over there and opening that wheat chest?"

I move to the chest, undo the wooden hasp, and then turn to her for further instruction, confused as to what this is all about.

"You'll find an accordion file on the top shelf. Please bring it to me."

I take the thick paper file and hand it to her on the sofa. She opens it with practiced effort and removes several pieces of paper. Then she hands them to me and motions for me to sit down. I go back to my chair holding the somewhat aged pages carefully as I rest back on the upholstered rocker. To my amazement I hold in my hands letters that are remarkably similar to the pages I just handed her, only faded with time, all addressed to "Reverend". The language is vehement, and the accusations are so approximate to the ones leveled at me that I make a guttural sound of disbelief. There is the charge of child abuse and the demand for resignation.

"I don't understand, Julia, where did you get these?"

"I've been expecting this visit from you for a couple of years now. The letters usually come after the pastor has been here awhile. You are now the fourth pastor of First Baptist to endure this same attack. Each of your last three predecessors was the recipient of the same charges. These are copies of the letters they each received."

"Do you know who wrote the letters?" I ask.

Julia shakes her head sideways, "We were never able to tell, except that it's someone in our church as you can see."

"When did the first letter come?"

"Let me see. It would now be about thirty-six years ago. Reverend Snyder was the first to get one. Tom Carlton was the second and Ray Gardner the third. Just like you, they were at first confused about them and troubled over the anger expressed."

"What did they do?"

Julia looks down at my letters on the couch beside her, then back up at me. "Tom took it the hardest. Within a few months he resigned. He was already under some strain in that his wife was ill. I think the accusatory letter pushed him into leaving our church sooner than he would have otherwise. He went on to teach at a community college. Tom was a very sensitive man who was so cautious in his dealings with others. He told me once that he thought himself not cut out for the ministry because he was not thick skinned enough."

"I can understand his being upset over the letter. There are not many people thick skinned enough to fend off such a personal attack without letting it affect them deeply."

"I've worked closely with several pastors and well know the pressures you're under," Julia says. "Tom was different, however. He was such a gentle man; any criticism wounded him to the point where he would brood for days."

"And Fred Snyder, was he this sensitive to criticism?"

"No, I don't think so. Fred decided to ignore his secret correspondence, and never received another. We thought at the time the person may have gotten counseling and progressed past their anger. As far as I know he only told me and the deacon chairman at the time, Luther Wilson, who passed away a few years ago. Fred kept his feelings to himself most of the time, so I never could tell how much the letter affected him."

"Your memory is amazing, Julia. You are a walking historian."

"It's not so amazing. I often call one of my grandchildren by the name of another."

I smile at this woman who is considered by many in the church to be a saint. "I've had the chance to get to know Ray pretty well through the few times we have been together or talked on the phone. We had a few hours to chat when he was here for homecoming a couple of years ago. I don't picture him the type to let a letter like this threaten him."

"Oh, Ray was angry and tried his best to determine who the author was without letting many in the church know about it. He did share it with the staff at the time which included Alice and Karen. He was not successful in his search. His last four years were without incident, however. We sat down on a couple of occasions to brainstorm who the accuser might be. Not knowing really bothered him."

"So, obviously none of them resigned as they were commanded

to do?" I ask.

"No, unless you count Tom's leaving soon after."

"And this has been going on for thirty or more years?"

"That's so," Julia says. "I know my reputation for having a great memory is legendary, but in the past few years I've slipped some. As far as I know Stephen Riebert did not get letters, or at least he did not share them with me. He was pastor before Fred."

"But, my first letter came the day Emma Wells disappeared. Did the others come during any unusual event?"

Julia ponders the question for a moment. "I can't recall any special circumstances around them in the past. Ray believed that the writer must have had some personal trauma that periodically triggered the attacks. He was sure the person had some grudge against all pastors. Fred assumed the person was mentally ill and had some kind of bi-polar episodes."

"And you have no idea who the person is?" I ask.

"I wish I did, Ron. I've been puzzled all of these years by this and was waiting to see if it would happen to you."

"Why did you not warn me when I first came?"

"I was hoping it would be over and did not want to add to the stress you pastors already endure. As far as I know, I'm the only person in the church other than the letter writer who knows each of the pastors received these."

I put the letters in Julia's file and return it to her cabinet. She asks me if I could have copies of mine, and I agree. We talk for a few minutes about Emma Wells. Julia does not know Ted and Rachel Wells who moved to town only a few years ago. She's up on the latest news, however. I assume Alice keeps her informed of most that happens at the church as they worked together for many years.

As I make my way down the steps to my car, I wonder what other secrets this now fragile woman holds in her active mind and what else might be in her wheat cabinet of memories. I leave her house with more questions than when I arrived.

Julia is a living history of First Baptist. There are so many rich stories in church life. A few years ago in my rural pastorate I found the old minutes to church business meetings that dated back to the early twentieth century. They were fascinating reading for one interested in history as I am. The most intriguing entries were ones where certain deacons of the church were dispatched to deliver "church discipline" to people in the congregation who had been accused of certain moral transgressions. The term used in the old ledgers was "waited upon." The minutes would say that Deacon Smith waited upon Brother Jones because he had a problem with drink. Brother Jones was then given a period of time to clean up his act, or he was excommunicated from the church.

These were public records at the time and entered for all to see. On occasion the result was a remorseful plea for forgiveness while other sinners had their names removed from the church roll. This was serious business in that having your name on the church roll meant you had a place in the church cemetery reserved for you and your family. A cemetery plot was a very important matter.

* * *

On the way back to the church I call Ken and tell him what I learned from Julia. He's as surprised as I was to learn of the previous letters. We agree to meet later to take another look at who the sender of the letters might be. As I pull up to the side of the church and park, I sit in the car for a minute and try to figure out what it is that still bothers me about the assumption that last Friday Emma was taken out the back door. I can see the corner of the church down the hill closest to that door. The scenario that has been supposed is that the abductor took her from the restroom, down the stairs, and out that back exit. Her name tag was in the ditch about fifty yards from that end of the building. From where I sit I can't see the door, but there must have been some parents arriving at noon on Friday to pick up their children who drove past that end of the building. And yet, no one saw Emma leave the church. How's that possible? Something about that is not right.

A newspaper reporter is posted in the church foyer as I enter. He asks me if there is any news on the missing girl. I tell him he probably knows more than I do. He then asks me if the police suspect the church custodian, Joel Weaver. I tell him that I don't know who all the police suspect. He says that an FBI agent just entered the church and told him she had no comment on Weaver's involvement when asked, and such a response usually means that the person is under suspicion. I shake my head and express my ignorance as to what the agent meant. The reporter says that he knows they have searched Weaver's residence.

Agent Chevalier is waiting to see me when I get inside. She's dressed in jeans and a dark blue shirt with an FBI identification printed on it in white letters. She doesn't appear to be armed. Her short black hair is parted in the middle, and she's wearing a musk perfume or cologne which dominates the air as she enters my office.

"Reverend, did you know that I'm a Baptist?" she asks.

"No," I respond as I motion for her to sit opposite my desk.

"I go to a small Baptist church where I live."

"That's good to hear," I say with some enthusiasm.

"It's nothing like your church here. We probably have only about seventy-five people in worship each Sunday."

"There are some advantages to smaller churches. It's much easier to know everybody."

"Wouldn't take long to know who a letter writer is in my church."

I decide not to tell her about Julia's letters until Ken arrives. "What's the news from the Turner interrogation?" I ask.

"Neal and Carl Brody are still in there with him. They took a lunch break and started back as I was leaving a few minutes ago. The guy says he doesn't know anything about Emma Wells, but he can't account for his whereabouts on Friday except to say he just hung around that trailer most of the day."

"Do you think he's telling the truth?" I ask.

"I haven't been in there much, so it's hard to say. Neal's good at this, and if anyone can get something out of him, he will. I wanted to ask you about Joel Weaver."

"I don't think Joel should be your focus," I say.

"Pastor, I've only been with this team a year now and still have much to learn, but I know enough to recognize that your custodian fits the profile for this kind of thing. He also had the best opportunity to snatch the child in that he was near the restroom where she is thought to have visited."

"Just how does he fit the profile?"

"Well, he's a loner for starts. On top of that he has certain skills that would allow him to be stealthy and violent. Sometimes those who have experienced combat never get over it."

"Certainly, you're not going to hold his military career against him," I say with some agitation. The young agent shrugs her shoulders.

"And, the man is strange," she says pulling a small notebook from her pocket. "He has quotes from the philosopher, Kierkegaard, on his refrigerator door. I wrote this one down, 'But the moment I speak of being in the ideal sense I no longer speak of being, but of essence.' What do you make of that?"

"I know Kierkegaard was opposed to what is called the ontological argument for God's existence, and I suppose Joel likes what he wrote about this view."

Agent Chevalier looks at me with a frown and asks, "So this is not a strange thing for a janitor to have on his refrigerator?"

"Unusual, but not strange," I say.

"This Kierkegaard fellow was a cult leader?" Chevalier asks.

"No, he wasn't a cult leader," I explain. "He was actually against any rigid system of beliefs like most cult leaders teach. He was an existential philosopher."

"I'm afraid I don't remember much about existentialism from college."

"Well, existentialism has to do with finding oneself through personal experience."

"I think I will need some time to process that. So what about these words we found highlighted in one of this philosopher's books on the bedside table in Weaver's apartment: 'dread, despair, death, and hope?'"

"They were themes that Kierkegaard emphasized in his writings."

"And you don't think this morbid stuff makes your custodian look like a person with some psychological problems?" Chevalier asks.

"No, I think it makes him look like a deep thinker."

"So, Reverend, you know a lot about this philosopher?"

"Some, I studied him in seminary."

"Then you know, Dr. Fowler that he had five brothers and sisters die," Chevalier offers with a bit of pride showing in her knowledge. "I did some research on the web last night and learned a few interesting things about Kierkegaard."

"That is probably not the typical investigation for FBI personnel," I say smiling.

Referring to her notebook again the young agent says, "What about these words that your janitor also highlighted? 'I am in the profoundest sense an unhappy individuality which from its earliest years has been nailed fast to some suffering or other, bordering upon madness…'"

I become curious as to why Joel has chosen to highlight such a quote from Kierkegaard's journals. "It looks like Joel Weaver has some interest in the sadness which drove the man," I guess.

"Did you know, Reverend, that Weaver lost a child himself? While he was in Vietnam on one of his tours his ten year old daughter died in a car accident. Weaver's wife was driving and survived. Shortly after he returned from the war, he and his wife separated and divorced."

"No, I was not aware of that."

I'm embarrassed that I didn't know this about the man who has worked with us these last few years. I knew he had experienced a hard life, but not about the death of his daughter. It was enough that he endured two tours in the war, but to face such a loss when he got home is terrible.

"We often find there are secrets kept from co-workers."

"I guess there are," I admit. "Just because a person has experienced such a loss as Joel doesn't mean they should be a suspect in a crime," I argue.

"Come on, pastor, you can recognize how all of this causes us to take a closer look at him. I may not be up on philosophy and theology like you, but I do have a few deductive skills. I came over here to see if you could help me with this guy's motivations. We've questioned him three times and searched his place. Nobody remembers seeing him last Friday at the time the child was abducted. He had enough time to take her somewhere and harm her. We're just trying to find out what happened to Emma Wells.

We now have Turner in custody, Weaver looking suspicious, and then the letters to you. In my opinion, any one of these three could be the key to finding this child."

I tell Chevalier that I understand the need to follow all of these leads and promise to share anything I learn. "Could you wait here a few minutes until Ken Matthews gets here?" I ask. "I have something I want you both to hear. It concerns my letters."

The agent agrees and asks me what else I know about Kierkegaard. I tell her that he was a great storyteller and that he has been criticized from some conservative Christians for his existentialist views and from some humanists for his keen interest in the teachings of Jesus which was more emotional than rational.

Ken arrives as Denise Chevalier is looking at a couple of books on the Danish thinker I have in my personal library. I ask her to fill my friend in on what we just discussed about Joel. It's my turn then to tell both of them what I learned from Julia Wagner.

"Damn, Ron, this is getting weirder," Ken says. "This changes everything. Your accuser has been around here a long time. This person must be at least fifty years old if the first letter came thirty-five years ago, assuming that they must have been fifteen or older to write such a letter. This rules out several on our list."

"So, how many people are left on your list?" Denise Chevalier asks.

Ken thinks for a minute and says, "If we confine the list to women and to those who are over fifty years old, left-handed, and still young enough to have such a steady hand... this would leave maybe six. I found out less than ten percent of all people are left-handed which greatly reduced the possibilities. I had to make a number of calls in order to determine which people in our church write with their left hand."

"Do you two think, now that we have learned of the former letters, that this person is more likely responsible for the disappearance of Emma?" I ask.

Ken speaks first, "Could go either way. It could be that something else prompted the person to write you, or it could be that this person decided this time to do more than just put their feelings into words."

"I agree," says Chevalier. "We need to know who this is and
173

fast."

"We should go back and see Julia Wagner," Ken proposes. "She may know things about those on our list."

I call Julia and ask if we can come over. She agrees, and now there will be a trio to climb the hill to the home of our wise sage.

* * *

Julia comes to the door with the aid of her walker this time and apologizes for not offering us refreshments as we enter her living room. Agent Chevalier tells her there is no need to apologize. "Very few of my home visits involve such social graces as tea and cookies. We are just appreciative that you are willing to spend a few minutes with us."

"So, Ken, I finally get you to my house," Julia says. "We've worked on a few things together over the years at the church, but you've never sat in my living room."

"Yes Ma'am, I guess I haven't. I've had the opportunity to be around her at church often," he says to Chevalier. "We've been at the table together at many church socials. My wife always wanted to sit next to Julia."

"She was one of my favorites," Julia says with a wink. "I guess you have come to see my letters, Ken."

"Actually, Julia, we have come to ask your help in a very serious process," Ken says. "We think we may have narrowed the letter writer down to a few people. We need your assistance in refining our list."

"For all of these years I've tried to figure out who sent these to our pastors. Now, I may find out. I'm not sure I am ready to know."

"In my experience," Denise says, "it's better to know. There's a release which comes with knowing."

"I will accept your wisdom, Miss Chevalier," Julia says. "I am still open to the insights of those younger."

"And I'm very much willing to defer to the wisdom of my seniors," Denise says.

Ken shares the names of six people with Julia and explains that he's pretty sure this writer is one of the six. "These are the only women in the church who were in the worship service last Sunday, who are between fifty and eighty years of age, left-handed, and who have never been fingerprinted before."

Julia looks at the note card with the six names and tears come to her eyes. She reaches into a pocket and pulls out a tissue. The three of us watch as she dries her eyes and places the card on her lap. Adjusting herself on the couch with what appears to be some discomfort from the healing hip, she looks over at me. "Ron, these are all close friends of mine who have been in our church for ages. It's hard to believe that any of them could have written these letters."

"I know this is a difficult thing to ask of you Mrs. Wagner," Denise says with empathy. "Any little bit of information could be crucial. We're not sure the writer of these letters had anything to do with what happened on Friday to Emma Wells, but we must explore all of the possibilities."

Julia shakes her head in agreement, looks again at the note card, and says, "You can take Marian Brown off the list. I think she could have only been nine or ten when the first letter came. She is younger than she looks. Joyce Richard's family and Polly White's did not move here until after Fred Snyder left, so they can be removed. This would mean that Dot Marshall, Joan Riebert, or Alexia Thompson wrote those letters, if your list is exhaustive. I just can't imagine any one of them doing this."

I can see that the FBI agent has no idea who these three ladies are, so I proceed to fill her in on them. "Dot Marshall is from one of the most prominent families in our city, and, besides Julia here, may be the most respected woman in our congregation. Joan Riebert is the head librarian at our local branch and is the daughter of one of our former pastors. She grew up in the church and remained here after her parents retired. Alexia Thompson is called the flower lady because she has delivered the sanctuary flowers to shut-ins after the services for many years now."

"What will you do now?" Julia asks.

Ken, who is sitting on the couch beside her, volunteers an answer. "I need to get their fingerprints to match them with Ron's letter. In doing so the one who's the author of the accusatory messages may admit to sending them. If we do not get an admission then the fingerprints will do the trick."

"Please be gentle with them, Ken," Julia says.

"Mrs. Wagner, I will go with Mr. Matthews to see them," Denise says. "I promise we will handle this carefully. It's very possible that the letter writer didn't take Emma, and we just have a confused person who has needed help for years. The two who did not send the letters will appreciate our effort in light of the circumstances. We're going to have to ask that you not call them before we have the chance to talk with them."

It's agreed that Ken and Denise will visit the three this afternoon. We thank Julia for her help.

* * *

Back at the church Ken makes the calls to see if the ladies are home, or at work in Joan Riebert's case. Alice helps him with the numbers in the church office. I must leave to pick up my daughter at the library.

As I get in my car, it dawns on me that Sarah is at the library where Joan Riebert works. I'm not alarmed, just slightly concerned. Joan's one of the pillars of our community as well as our church. There's no way she could write such angry words. But, the other two women are also unlikely authors of such attacks. Four pastors have been the recipients of this same bitterness. But, I'm the only one whom has received a letter the same day a child has gone missing from our church. Of course, I can't say anything to Sarah about this.

My daughter is not on the steps of the building when I pull up. Usually she's ready and waiting when I arrive, and I'm about ten minutes late. Probably went back in when I didn't show up on schedule. Five minutes pass and no Sarah, so I park in a metered space and go inside. There's no sign of my offspring as I search the main lobby so I decide to ask the young lady at the service counter. I don't recognize her and she doesn't seem to know who I am.

"I'm looking for Sarah Fowler," I announce leaning over the counter.

The twenty-something librarian looks me over for a few seconds and says with a note of disdain in her voice, "I'm sorry, but I cannot know every person who's here today."

"She works here, one of the summer volunteers," I say emphatically.

"Oh, sorry. Sure I've seen that Sarah. She may be in the work room, but you can't go back there. Only staff are allowed in there."

"I'm Sarah's father. I've come to pick her up."

Again the plump attendant looks me over with her head cocked to the right. "You're the preacher, the one on the television talking about the missing kid."

"Yes, that's me. Could you see if my daughter is in the back?"

The girl turns slowly and makes her way deliberately to the open door behind her. In a minute she comes back out. "She's not back there. Why don't you just look around; the place is not that big. Just don't call out. We have a quiet policy here."

There are a number of tables in the reading area, most empty on this nice summer day. At one far table is an elderly gentleman, head resting on the oak top, likely asleep.

Two ten year old boys are seated at another with a stack of books between them, both clearly absorbed in some youth adventure tale. These three make up the contingent of book lovers in this static respite from the outside world. There is no Sarah to be seen.

My search has only lasted five minutes or so to this point; certainly not enough time to be alarmed on most days. But this is not most days. Where is my child? That very unspoken question strikes an uncomfortable chord within me. I rein in any sense of panic and proceed to look further. Another woman wearing a name tag emerges from the women's restroom. Upon seeing me across the room she straightens her hair and inadvertently checks to see if her blouse is properly secured in her skirt. I approach her as she prepares for my advance.

"Dr. Fowler," the tall thin woman says with a whisper. She's obviously been well doctrinated to her chosen surroundings of low decibel conversation. "We don't often see you in here."

I work hard to process who she is and just in the nick of time recognize Ginny Locario on her badge, one of our less than frequent attendees at First Baptist. "Hi, Ginny, I'm looking for my daughter, Sarah. Have you seen her?"

"Oh, she is such a sweet child. We love having her here this summer. What a dedicated reader you have there, Reverend."

"Yes, she's certainly one of those. Do you know where she is?"

"She was at the door a few minutes ago when I went to the ladies' room. She's not in there. Did you look outside?"

"Yes. Thanks, I'll keep looking."

I have only been in this building a couple of times, but the place is not all that big. It's basically a rectangular box; one end is the book stacks, the other the reading area. Along the back of the building are the offices and work rooms. I remember the computer room which is on my far left and move in that direction to see if Sarah's in there. A middle aged man is seated at one of the work stations doing a search on the Internet. No Sarah to be seen.

The head librarian's office is ahead, so I move in that direction, uncomfortable as to what I might do if Joan is in there. I never intended to come into the library, certainly not to speak with Joan at this time. But, Sarah may be in there. The door is closed, and the young woman from the desk is right behind me when I turn.

"Ms. Riebert is not in her office," the girl says. "Are you looking for her?"

"No, I'm still looking for my daughter."

She continues to stand only two feet in front of me now. Her hands are on her hips which means I must make a wide step or two to pass her. As I proceed to go around her on the right she takes a lateral trajectory which forces me to sidestep even more. We seem to be moving in some kind of stilted choreography that will cause us to travel the full width of the open area if we continue this way. I make an abrupt stop, feign to my left, and then slip back right, breaking free from her.

"It is so sad about the Wells child," she says as I'm walking away.

I'm not interested in a conversation at this time but turn to face her, now with my back to the front door. I take the time to read her name tag: Sylvia Nelson, Library Assistant. "Sylvia, we are all concerned about Emma Wells."

"She likes to read," the young woman says as I walk away.

"Emma Wells is a regular here, or was."

"Oh, I didn't know that," I say surprised to learn of this. I make note of the fact, but am now focused on finding my daughter. Back to the front door, still no sign of my Sarah. It's then that I think of my cell phone. In the car I hit speed dial and the entry for "No. 1 daughter" which is what my only offspring likes as her identification. Her voice answers, "Where are you, Dad?"

"I'm out front of the library where I'm supposed to be," I say with some frustration in my voice.

"Well, I'm down the street at the drug store. Did you not get my text message?"

"What text message?"

"The one on your phone, low tech dad."

It's then that I see the text message icon blinking. Two minutes later I'm in front of the pharmacy where my daughter is waiting as her message said she would be. Today she doesn't carry any books and walks to the car with her long gait and distinctive bounce of the head. Sarah is lovely, bright, and witty. She's our special joy in life, a gift my wife and I cherish every day. I'm sure that Ted and Rachel Wells must have similar feelings about Emma. It's such a relief to simply watch Sarah walk to the car.

"You're not supposed to leave the library until I pick you up," I say, trying to hold back my emotions.

"Dad, it's just one block, and Mom said I could come down here to get some eye shadow. You were late."

I want to tell her that things have changed, and a walk of even this short distance is too dangerous. I discard that inclination in favor of reaching over and hugging her momentarily. She just shakes her head sideways and frowns.

"Dad, you won't believe what I found at the library today," Sarah says excitedly. "I was processing books that were due in, and there was the name of Emma Wells. She had checked out three of the *Chronicles of Narnia*. I couldn't believe it."

Putting together what Sylvia Nelson just told me and Sarah's news it dawns on me that Emma has frequented the library where Joan Riebert works. Could they know each other?

"Sarah, was Miss Riebert at the library today?"

"No, she wasn't there yesterday either. Why do you want to

know that?"

"I was just wondering if she was aware of the books checked out by Emma," I say.

"I think she's too busy to know every book checked out by every person. It just kinda freaked me out to see Emma Wells on the list. I looked it up, and she's checked out a lot of books. Have you heard any news about her today? Everybody at the library has been talking about it. They're saying that this scary Turner guy took her."

"We don't know that, but he's still being questioned," I tell Sarah.

* * *

It's now five o'clock and Amy gets home from work. I tell her that I must go back to the church for a few minutes and may be late for supper. This is not unusual, so she understands and makes me promise to fill her in when I get home on the latest news.

Ken reaches me by phone as soon as I get in the car. "Ron, we've visited with Alexia Thompson, the flower lady. She's a bit eccentric but was volunteering at hospice on Friday from ten until about noon. She allowed us to fingerprint her and seemed not at all upset we would ask such of her. Denise is in the car with me, and she says no way this woman wrote those letters. I think she's right. We are on the way to see Dot Marshall now. Joan Riebert isn't at work or home. At the library they said she was taking petty leave and had not heard from her all day."

"I'm going to the church, Ken. Let me know as soon as you finish with Dot."

The church office closes at five-thirty. Alice and Becky are getting ready to leave when I step into the reception area.

"Ron, I just heard from my cousin at the police station," Alice says. "Someone has called in and reported that they think they saw Turner hanging around the school where Emma Wells was a student back in May. Evidently, they saw his picture in the paper and remembered him. This is being followed up on right now."

"Alice, I was just with an FBI agent this afternoon, and still have to get my most current updates from you."

"She needs a police scanner in the office," Becky says.

"What else do I not know?" I ask Alice.

"They uncovered some children's underclothes in the woods about a hundred yards from the trailer where Turner was hiding. They were buried in a hole. They found girls panties probably taken from homes here in town. Do you remember the reported break-ins a few months ago?"

"You mean the ones on Lexington Street behind the church?" I ask.

"Yes. Three people reported that someone took clothing and toys from the rooms of their children. One of the homes belonged to Terri Mills in our church. Her daughter, Casey, was missing a yellow top with ladybugs on it. They found a top like that in the hole."

"If you ask me," Becky says, "Turner is the one who took Emma, and I shudder to think what has happened to her."

"My cousin on the force tells me that the FBI is calling for a wider search of the area near that trailer," Alice informs us. "They're also bringing in Frank Allen, the guy who owns the trailer. Allen works at a garage in town and usually sleeps in the back of the garage, only going to the trailer on weekends. He and Turner used to work together at a tire service center before Turner went to prison. Allen lets Turner use the place when he's not there and gives Turner rides when he needs them."

This is one more huge check on the suspect board for James Turner, I think. Perhaps he did take Emma, and my letter writer is not involved in her disappearance.

The two secretaries leave for the day, and I return to my office. A few minutes later Ken calls again.

"Ron, you will not believe what happened with Dot Marshall. She refused to be fingerprinted, saying that we would have to have a court order requiring her to do so. She said we are not allowed to trample on her rights."

"Did you ask her about the letters?" I ask.

"Yes," Ken says. "She said she has not written any letters to any pastor. Specifically, she said that if she has a beef with a pastor she would go to them in person. The woman is very strong willed. Even though she's seventy-five, she's almost six feet tall and physically imposing."

"Sounds like you had your hands full with Dot," I lament.

"We did find out she was at home alone at noon on Friday, and she was irate at the idea we were considering her a suspect in the little girl's abduction. She was especially upset with me and said I should know better."

"So, what do you think?" I ask.

"I think we wait on getting a warrant for Dot until we can find Joan Riebert. I don't want to mess with Dot unless I have to. I just called Joan's cell phone and left a message for her to return my call. Not much else we can do right now. By the way, you and this Danish fellow have really piqued the interest of Chevalier. I will talk to you later."

It sounds like Dot really gave Ken and Denise a hard time.

Could Dot be the one with so much anger in her?

I still haven't had much time to think about Joel Weaver and his interest in Kierkegaard who was certainly an intriguing character. He was not well known in the middle eighteen hundreds when he lived, but has many followers now. He's often referred to as the "Gloomy Dane". Truth, for Kierkegaard, is learned through suffering and despair. Joel Weaver has evidently encountered his measure of suffering and despair through his military career and family tragedies, so the attraction to this philosopher is natural for our custodian.

Soren Kierkegaard's most fascinating writings were the many parables he formulated to make his philosophical points. I remember one story where he imagines the pilot of a boat who has passed every examination with distinction to begin his career on the seas but who has never been on the ocean in a storm. The man has never known what it's like when the skies are so dark that the stars are not visible or the sense of impotence when the wheel in his hand is hard to manage, when the waves are overwhelming. He simply has no concept of the change that takes place inside a person when one has to apply his knowledge to an actual challenging situation at sea.

I understand this parable well. My twelve years of higher education, theology classes, counseling training, and seminars on how to handle church crises did not prepare me for what I'm facing now. Life's most valuable lessons must be learned in the crucible of struggle.

CHAPTER FIFTEEN

TUESDAY EVENING

Dinner tonight is at Ruby Tuesday's which is my daughter's choice. Amy, Sarah, and I sit at a table in the restaurant where a television mounted on the wall is visible in the corner of the dining room. The sound is off, but the images on the news program are easily identifiable. The face of James Turner appears with a caption at the bottom which reads, "James Turner, still in custody." Soon after, a picture of Emma Wells appears, and the caption under her image reads, "Day four and still missing." There are pictures of the school Emma attends and of our church with another caption that says, "Turner has been seen at both of these places in the past." Finally, there is a shot of the police standing over a hole in the woods followed by an array of clothing items and toys laying on a tarp beside the hole.

Amy has her back to the screen, but Sarah's intent on the story. "Dad," she says, "Turner is an evil person, isn't he?"

"It looks like he may have some real personal problems, but we still don't know if he took Emma," I respond.

I tell Amy about the report on the television as she turns to see what we're watching.

Sarah asks me, "Do you think that Emma was afraid when she was taken on Friday? I mean she's read some books about brave kids. Maybe she has more courage than most kids her age."

Amy asks, "How do you know what she reads?"

"I found her name in the files at the library," Sarah responds.

"Did she tell you this, Ron?" Amy asks.

I nod yes.

"So, when am I going to be let in on all that's happening?" Amy says with frustration.

"I just haven't had a chance to tell you all I've learned today."

"So tell us now," Sarah says.

"First of all, this is not the place," I say. "And secondly, there are some things I don't talk about in front of my daughter."

Sarah crosses her arms over her chest. "Your daughter is the one who told you about Emma's reading habits. Your daughter is old enough to hear everything."

"Our daughter will have to accept that she's not yet an adult," Amy says.

The ride home is without conversation as we are all likely thinking of our places in this unfolding drama. Sarah's trying to deal with her age keeping her from being included in adult conversations. Amy's upset that she has been left out of the loop again, and I'm trying to figure out how I handle all of my roles in this situation. I feel I must spend a few minutes with Ted and Rachel before it gets too late, I tell Amy. She agrees that I should check on them.

* * *

It's seven-thirty when I arrive at the Wells home. Ted greets me at the door and invites me into the living room, then leaves to find Rachel. I hear voices in the kitchen and assume they belong to other family members. Ted returns in a couple of minutes with his wife, and the couple sits on the couch across from where I'm seated. Rachel looks rested and offers a pleasant smile. Ted sits on the other end of the couch as though there's some needed divide between them.

"I guess you have heard about the Turner fellow having been seen at Emma's school a month ago," Ted says.

"Yes, the FBI agents and police have been questioning him all day," I state. "We might have some word on his involvement by tomorrow morning."

"This means our daughter must spend another night away from us," Ted says while holding his wife's hand across the empty space between them on the couch.

"I know that Emma has not been hurt," Rachel says in a resolute way. "It came to me last night that she's alive."

Ted looks at his wife for a long moment. "Rachel woke up this morning feeling more positive. She's been saying all day that our daughter has not been harmed."

"Rachel, it's good to not lose hope," I say.

"No, Reverend Fowler, this is not hope. I'm sure she will be brought back to us soon, alive. It was not a dream, but a feeling of assurance that came over me during the night as I lay awake thinking of her. Ted's been trying to caution me on being prepared for this to go either way. I was trying to do that until last night, but then an impression of Emma alive and speaking to me changed everything. I went into her room after the experience, and it became even stronger. I fell asleep on her bed for a few hours and woke up with this great positive consciousness of her safety."

I don't know what to say in response to this and look to Ted for a cue as to how he's accepting what his wife's saying.

"I don't doubt my wife's intuition," he says sincerely. "I only wish what came to her had come to me also." He looks at his wife, and she looks at him sympathetically.

"I understand that neither of you can share my impression," Rachel says. "I'm not a psychic and I'm not going crazy. This is unexplainable, but it's real for me. My daughter is alive and will come home soon. Reverend Fowler, you know the story of Jairus in the Bible, right?"

"Yes, I know the story," I respond, wondering where this is going.

"I know that it's far different from our situation, but I found it while reading in Emma's Bible yesterday. There's a verse there where Jesus tells Jairus, 'Do not be afraid, just believe and your daughter will be well'. I think this verse is what was on my mind when this feeling came over me last night. I just know she's alive."

It strikes me that Rachel may have chosen only the part of the Bible story she wanted to focus on. I don't venture into the part of the story where it seems that the girl in this old healing tale was declared dead before Jesus found her.

Ted's mother comes into the room from the kitchen and asks if I would like some refreshments. I tell her that I must leave in a few minutes to go home since I've been away most of the day.

Mrs. Wells appears to want to say something else to me, but I notice Ted nodding for her to refrain from doing so. I assume she is also concerned about Rachel's newfound assurance of the well being of Emma. Ted's mother returns to the kitchen.

"Your wife will probably understand how I know about my daughter's safety," Rachel announces. "Many mothers have special connections with their daughters."

I agree to ask Amy about this. "There is something I would like to ask the two of you. My daughter is helping out at the library this summer, and she tells me that Emma has a library card. Do you happen to know Ms. Riebert who works there?"

Rachel answers, "Yes, she has helped us a couple of times. She goes to your church, doesn't she?"

"Yes," I answer. "She sings in our choir."

"She's been very helpful and knows a lot about children's books," Rachel says. "It was Ms. Riebert who introduced Emma to the poems of Shel Silverstein and to the *Chronicles of Narnia*. Why do you ask about her?"

"Ms. Riebert has not been seen for a couple of days and we are concerned about her."

"Is this concern related to Emma?" Ted asks. "Agent Chevalier called this afternoon and asked us if Emma knew any of three ladies in the church she named. Joan Riebert was one of the three. I told her about Emma's frequenting the library."

"Did Miss Chevalier tell you why she asked about them?"

"She just said they were following new leads. Do they now think someone from the church took Emma?" Ted asks.

I do not tell him about the letters but say, "They have not closed the door on that possibility."

In a few minutes I stand to leave, and Ted walks me to the door. On the front porch this distraught father says, "Reverend, I don't know what to do with Rachel. I haven't seen her like this before. She has not cried one time today and has this calmness about her that scares me. I try to agree with her vision of Emma's well being, but can't shake my fear that I will not see my daughter again."

"My guess is that this is a coping mechanism Rachel has found to help her get through this," I suggest.

"You know, Reverend, I hope she does have this special connection to Emma. I want to believe what Rachel says she knows is true."

On the way home I can't get the image of this positive and assured mother out of my head. My gut feeling is that she's creating this sensation of her daughter's well being in order to be able to handle the pain she feels inside. Her confidence in her perception is shocking, however, and makes me wonder if there is some level of human awareness beyond what most of us know. I'm also disturbed that Emma knows Joan Riebert. Could this connection have anything to do with her abduction?

* * *

I tell Amy about the conversation with Rachel when I get home. She doesn't agree that this is a natural vibe that mothers inherently have. Amy is even more concerned for Rachel Wells now. I also tell her about Ken's attempts to find out if any of these three women is the author of my letters. My wife is astounded that one of these three could hold such anger in them.

The phone interrupts our discussion. It's Ken, and he sounds like one who has had much of his energy drained. "Ron, we can't reach Joan Riebert. As you know she does not have any relatives in town and not really any close friends. The people at the library are worried about her since she left them with no idea of where she was going."

"Has anyone been back to her house?" I ask.

"Chevalier and I went back there thirty minutes ago. There are no lights on and no one answered the door."

"Can you enter the house with some kind of warrant?" I ask.

"We would have to get a judge to sign one, and we are working without much cause here," Ken explains. "All we can tell a judge is that we think this lady wrote some terrible letters to you. That's not much reason to break down the door of a respected person in our community."

"So, what can you do?"

"I'm trying to convince Heard that this is a serious lead and we should follow up on it. He's now focused on James Turner as the most likely suspect, and Chevalier is pushing him to keep after Joel Weaver."

"I found out today that Emma frequented the library where Joan Riebert works and knows her," I tell Ken. "We need for Heard to know that."

"Wow, that does change things, but it's still not enough to go to a judge."

"Is this all we can do tonight?" I ask with deep concern for Emma Wells.

Ken replies, "My hands are tied. Heard is in charge of this thing. Chevalier wants to find out who the letter writer is, but she must follow Heard's orders. I have no official standing so, for now, we let it go and try again in the morning."

* * *

Dot Marshall and Joan Riebert are all I can think of this evening. One is defiant, the other not to be found. Who would believe that either of these women could be the author of such slanderous diatribes? I can't imagine such, but then, who else? Dot and I are not close, but we have had numerous conversations over the years. I can't remember our ever having a disagreement even though she's very opinionated. There was the time the Sunday school director tried to relocate her classroom which went over like he was suggesting we relocate the entire church. The proposed new room was nicer and in a better location, but the opposition from Dot and her ladies, all of whom are in their seventies, was fierce. The idea was abandoned, and the director ended up resigning. I wasn't involved in the decision but may have caught some of the blame for the try.

Joan Riebert has been over to our house a couple of times, and I went to her to ask if Sarah could volunteer at the library. She was very helpful in seeing that Sarah became one of the summer staff at the branch, a semi-coveted position. Joan literally grew up in this church. She was only five when her father became pastor here, an only child who was given the favored position of pastor's child just as our Sarah is. Pks are always given much attention by those in a congregation, and when an only child of a pastor they are lavished with it all. Joan's father moved on to another pastorate when Joan was in college, but she came back here to work as this city was what she knew as home. Her dad died a few years ago, and her mother is now in a nursing home about two hours away. Joan goes to see her every Saturday. Like her mother before her, Joan Riebert is a much appreciated member of the choir.

I think of Rachel Wells who is so sure this evening that her daughter's alive. Is she delusional or does she indeed have a connection to her daughter that defies reason?

There's a part of Walt Whitman's *Leaves of Grass* which has always enticed me to believe there are those things beyond what we commonly experience. Whitman, in a section called "assurance" wrote, "I do not doubt interiors have their interiors, and exteriors have their exteriors, and that the eyesight has another eyesight, and the hearing another hearing, and the voice another voice." This poetic musing speculates on things that may be. Are there ways of communication that I've not yet experienced? Does Rachel Wells enjoy a connection to her daughter that's beyond logic?

Lost in thought, I don't at first realize that Sarah is standing in the doorway to my office. She is in her Tweety Bird pajamas; it's evident she's been crying.

"Can I come in for a few minutes, Dad?" she asks.

"Sure!"

Sarah crosses the room and kneels beside my chair as I instinctively place my hand on the top of her head. She leans against the side of my leg. For a solemn minute no words are spoken by either of us.

"I wish Emma was with her dad tonight," Sarah says.

"Me too," I reply, still stroking her hair.

"I don't even know her but she's all I can think of. What do you think she's like?"

I begin to answer her but stop before any words come out. Standing up and helping Sarah to her feet, I place her in my desk chair as she looks puzzled.

"I want you to see something," I say to Sarah as she frowns in confusion.

Placing a disc in the computer on my desk and hitting the play button I start the Emma DVD from the beginning. Sarah places her elbows on the desk and her head two feet from the monitor. I sit in a chair across the room and look at these two girls, the cancer stricken abductee, and my healthy and safe at home only child. Sarah sits back in the chair and swivels from side to side as the other child tells her story.

Finally, the program comes to the place where I stopped watching earlier, and both of us take in the conclusion of the recorded testimony of Emma Wells.

> The doctor told you today, Mom and Dad, that my chances of recovery from the cancer depends on how the chemotherapy works. I heard him, even though he did not think I could. It's my body, so I think he should tell me what's going on.
>
> I don't think that doctors should tell people they are going to die soon. I don't think they know. I just read a poem in my favorite book called "*Where the Sidewalk Ends.*" It goes like this: "Listen to the mustn'ts, child, listen to the don'ts, listen to the shouldn'ts, the impossibles, the won'ts. Listen to the never haves, then listen close to me-Anything can happen, child, anything can be."
>
> I believe that anything can happen. I may die from Ewing's Sarcoma, or I may live to be very old, like fifty even. I just want you to know, Mom and Dad, that I will be okay, whatever happens to me. If you are seeing this, then I must be very sick or dead. But, maybe you will not see this, and I will grow up to be a very good person. If I do grow up, then I know you will be proud of me.
>
> I know you love me, and that you always will. If I do go to heaven before you, I hope I can see how you are doing now and then. I don't know how that works. I guess nobody does.
>
> Today the pain was pretty bad until I took the pill you gave me, Mom. The last few minutes before I'm supposed to take another is rough. Mom, you told me that you wished you could take

away the pain and that you wish it was you who had cancer, not me. I don't think that would be very good. You have dad to take care of. I don't have anyone counting on me right now. If I get well, I promise I will take care of both of you when you are old.

It is so hard to make choices now. I mean – since I learned that I might not live much longer. Like when I have to choose which book I want to read next. I think it was easier when you just asked me questions that yes or no was the answer. You know – like do you want to go to the park? But, when you have to make a choice then you have to give up something. For most kids that's not so hard, but for sick ones the thing you choose not to do may never be there again. There is so much I want to do. I know it makes you two sad, Mom and Dad, to think of what I may not be able to do. Please do not be too sad. We have done a lot of great things together.

This is truly a remarkable little girl; she has so much to offer. We must find her. With the computer turned off I sit for few minutes trying to hold back an eruption of sadness from gushing out of my innards. I find that I'm trembling, my body reacting to the overwhelming sense of grief inside.

Emma's words cause me to remember a passage of scripture from Jeremiah. "For I know the plans I have for you, says the Lord, plans for welfare and not for evil, to give you a future and a hope." Does Emma have a future? Is there hope that she will survive her abduction and her cancer? I'm counting on tomorrow being a breakthrough day, a day when we will find this child alive.

Sarah is now sitting on the arm of my chair and pats me on the back. I realize she has picked up on my grief and now seeks to comfort me. It's as if the adult-child relationship has been flipped.

"Thank you, Dad, for letting me see that," Sarah says with a calmness that would be the envy of any pastoral counselor. "I know you thought it might make me sad. It does, but I'm so happy that I can know more of what she's like."

Sarah stands up and begins to leave as I finally collect myself. "I'm so very proud you are my daughter," I say as she reaches the door.

"Can't imagine not being," she says as she looks over her shoulder and winks.

* * *

There's a text message on my phone. It's from Denise Chevalier: "Reverend, I've been reading the books you loaned me on Kierkegaard. Do you remember the parable of the dangerous instrument? This is amazing! I've never read anything so profound."

I do recall this particular writing from Kierkegaard. He asks if a person handing someone a sharp two-edged knife would present it in the same way he would present a bouquet of flowers. No, one presenting such a two-edged instrument would tell of its excellence but would also warn against how to handle it, of its danger. Kierkegaard says that the Christian faith should be presented the same way as the knife – its value extolled, yes, but sermons should be preached warning against Christianity. He meant that Christianity, specifically the love of Christ, is dangerous in that it can change life in a radical way. Denise has been introduced to the thought provoking world of this existentialist religious genius.

I must admit that today has been the most confusing day of my life. I learn of the letters to other pastors and find out about Joel's fascination with Kierkegaard. The visit to the Wells' house and the calm assurance of Rachel was outside of my realm of experience. And there is the possibility that one of these respected women in the church may have written the accusatory letters. James Turner is in jail and may very well have taken Emma which means she is likely dead by now, this child whose wisdom I've seen in the recordings she made.

I'm reminded of a book I used to read to my daughter when she was younger, *Alexander and the Terrible, Horrible, No Good, Very Bad Day*. The point of the book is to remind us that other people have bad days too, and that we can get through them. My question this evening is what will tomorrow bring? Surely, there is a better day ahead.

CHAPTER SIXTEEN

WEDNESDAY MORNING

Today's the day I've been asked to resign by my accuser. This evening the church will hold its quarterly business meeting where reports are given and decisions are made. There are no major decisions on the agenda this evening, and I'm always allotted a few minutes to share my thoughts as pastor. Sam Haverty and Suellen Grayson are scheduled to report on the church's liability coverage in light of the abduction. I'll not be resigning this evening which makes me wonder what my letter writer will do.

Stan Brantley is waiting for me when I arrive at the church office at eight-thirty. My Presbyterian friend is here to check on the progress of the search for Emma Wells who is still missing this morning. I usher him into my office and proceed to tell him about my letters.

"I'm sure you will keep all of this to yourself," I say. "I invoke clergy-client rules of privacy. Reverend, you are the closest thing I have to a pastoral counselor."

"Boy, the river has run over its banks and you are in it neck deep," Stan says, using a fitting analogy as there are times when our city is threatened with flooding after major storms.

"I haven't thought of it that way, but the symbolism works," I say.

"I never thought you, the model pastor, would face any accusations from a church member. Across the street at my parish I can name several who want me replaced, but I thought you were immune from such pressure here."

I know Stan has endured some opposition from a few because of his ministry style which is brasher than mine. He's really a very caring person, but sometimes his brusque tone causes others to see him as having little concern for the feelings or opinions of others.

So much of being accepted as a pastor is based on personality. Theological beliefs and even preaching ability are not as crucial in being well received as is temperament.

"As far as I know my nemesis is a sick person who hates all pastors," I say.

"Well," Stan says, "I can tell you from experience that the mean but sane church members are the most dangerous. So, do you think your sick person took the child, or was it this Turner guy the police have in custody?"

"My best guess is my letter writer is the most likely suspect."

"That's unbelievable – one of your church members actually took her."

"I know. It is beginning to seem possible."

"Just want you to know that we'll be having a special prayer session at our church tonight for Emma Wells. Let me know if there is more that we can do."

I thank Stan.

"Oh, by the way, we Church Street pastors have met and decided that you will lead our monthly discussion in a couple of weeks. The subject is role conflict among the clergy. We think you are now an expert on this."

"Thanks for the opportunity," I say. "I certainly know a lot more on the matter than I did a few days ago."

"Seriously, Ron, the three of us want to help you if we can. We will sit down with you anytime to serve as sounding boards for you. There's no group who knows more about the pressures you face than your colleagues in ministry."

Stan leaves, and I think of how good it is to have a friend in the ministry such as him. He's right, of course, that I have a valuable resource in my fellow pastors.

Jim Wallis has written that "every new direction in one's life journey begins with some new questions." This morning I'm filled with new questions. Where's Joan Riebert? This one question presses upon me as I try and imagine her sitting down and writing the letters to me and to other pastors before me. The image is baffling. How can a person hide for so many years this kind of inner turmoil that erupts periodically like a smoldering volcano? How in the world can someone sit in the choir Sunday after Sunday and feign support, all the while hiding their vengeful animosity?

* * *

I make my second visit to the law enforcement center. This time I haven't been summoned for questioning, but am here to talk to Neal Heard about my letter writer. I find the agent in the FBI's command center with Denise Chevalier. Heard sits on the corner of a table and is chewing gum with a smack that must certainly irritate those who work with him. Chevalier is seated in a chair with a laptop open in front of her.

"Well, Dr. Fowler," Heard says, "you've been doing some of my work for me. It seems that you and Matthews have narrowed down who it might be that sent you those threats."

"Yes, and I want to talk to you about that," I say.

"Reverend," Heard interrupts, "before you take the time to make your case, I want you to know that we are going for a search warrant on the house of Joan Riebert and for a warrant to fingerprint the Marshall woman. One of our agents and Carl Brody are before the judge as we speak."

"Reverend," Chevalier says, "We've made no progress with James Turner. He sticks to his denial that he was not at the church last Friday. We've found no physical evidence at the trailer where he was holing up to implicate him in any way in this case. The report that he was at Emma's school turned out to be false. Right now we're holding him on suspicion that he did break into houses and steal items since we found his fingerprints on them. The man is a pervert, but that does not prove he took this child."

"This doesn't mean," Heard warns, "that Turner's in the clear, and I still want to talk more with your janitor. The fact that this Riebert woman can't be found is bothering me in light of all you and Denise found out yesterday. We also learned that Ms. Riebert took an extended lunch break Friday from ten until two. This means she could have been at the church during that period."

Denise Chevalier looks pleased that her boss is taking steps to find Joan Riebert and informs me that Ken Matthews left early this morning to visit Joan's mother over in another city.

"Matthews is a valuable aide in this investigation," Heard says. "I know you think I'm an ass for the way I questioned you the other day, Reverend, but I'm smart enough to use all the tools available to me in finding this girl. This is about finding her, and I'll do all that's legal to accomplish that."

"We hope to be able to go to the Riebert house within the hour, and will keep you informed of anything we find," Chevalier promises.

As I leave the police station it occurs to me that I may have misjudged Neal Heard. His obnoxious manner has clouded my opinion of his professionalism.

On the way back to the church Ken calls. "Ron, I just spent some time with Joan Riebert's mother in the nursing home over here. The lady is not very mobile, but her mind is pretty clear."

"Does she know where her daughter is?" I ask.

"She saw her Saturday but hasn't heard from her since. Ron, when I told her about the letters she started to cry. She wouldn't tell me why she was so upset, and I'm sure there's something about Joan that she's keeping from us."

"Did you learn anything else from her?" I ask.

"Only that Joan has been very faithful in visiting her over the years since her husband died. The two seem to be close, but the distance and Joan's work schedule have prevented more frequent visits."

"Does she think that Joan has changed in any way recently?"

"I asked her that question, and she told me that Joan was no different Saturday than on any other visit."

'Were you able to get anything out of her about the years they lived here?"

"I learned that when her husband was pastor at First Baptist they lived in the church's parsonage. The church sold the parsonage when the next pastor was called. Mrs. Riebert has fond memories of living in the house. She also told me that Joan was a little girl when the new sanctuary was being built and liked to go with her father to check on the progress of the construction."

"What about Joan's father?"

"She said that her husband was very strict with his daughter, but that Joan loved him very much. I picked up on some hesitancy to talk further about Reverend Riebert, and when she told me that Joan loved her father my instincts told me she was not being totally honest."

"Do you have any guesses as to why she cried when you mentioned the letters?" I ask.

"It could be that as a pastor's wife she felt for you in your situation, but I think it had something to do with her daughter. Ron, I'm even more suspicious of Joan after my visit with her mother. We need to find her as soon as possible. I'm pretty sure she's the letter writer, and possibly these feelings about pastors goes back to her father."

I tell Ken about the warrants. He plans to be back in town by one.

* * *

Deanna Crowder's waiting to see me when I get back to the church. In my office she takes a seat in front of my desk and asks, "Ron, what's going on? Dot Marshall called and said that you have accused her of writing threatening letters to you."

"I haven't accused her of anything," I say. "The authorities are exploring several possibilities related to the Emma Wells case."

"And one of those involves one of our most respected church members?" Deanna asks.

"The FBI has questioned a number of our church people in the last few days including myself. They are doing everything possible to find this little girl."

Deanna looks at me across the four feet that separates us. "You don't think that your staff can be trusted to help with this, do you?"

"I'm sorry," I say, "but there are a few aspects of the case which must be kept in a tight group right now."

"But, Dot is very upset," Deanna says. "She's seventy-five years old and they are treating her like a criminal. She wasn't even at church last Friday."

"I know how you feel. When her name came up in the investigation I was astounded. Today, this should be cleared up. I can see that perhaps I should let the staff in on what is happening.

199

It's a part of your job to counsel church members and you can't do your job without knowing the whole situation."

"What letters are they talking about?" Deanna asks.

"I can only tell you that someone has written letters to me accusing me of some awful things which I haven't done. It appears that this same person has written similar letters to pastors here before me."

Deanna is obviously surprised over this revelation. "And you think that Dot wrote them?"

"We only know that whoever wrote them has probably been a member here for a long time, and that it's likely a woman who is left-handed. There are only a few who fit that bill. I think it would be good for you to go over to Dot's house now."

"Why? What are they going to do to her?"

"Just go over there and be with her. The police have a warrant to search her place."

Deanna looks at me with what I assume is great concern. As this tall and strong woman stands up to leave, I surmise a force has been unleashed which could present some problems for Neal Heard and his team when they arrive at Dot Marshall's house.

I feel so helpless sitting here this morning waiting for things to unfold. There must be something I can do to speed the search for Emma Wells. Like a person lost, I walk out into the hall and stand here for a minute or two trying to imagine the scene last Friday. There were all of those people in the sanctuary, and in the last few minutes before they were released this one little girl skips toward the restroom, like many children who wait until the last minute. Her pony tail swishes from side to side, and her smile displays her innocent joy. She's experiencing her last few moments of freedom. Someone is waiting for her, someone intent on a deed of drastic proportions.

Back to the present, I can hear someone moving about and realize that the noise is not coming from the other offices. The sound is coming from the end of the hall, so I proceed to investigate the origin of the clamor. There is an open door to a closet on the left side of the hall, and the disturbance is definitely emanating from this closet. Before I reach the opening, from within it a large shape emerges in the hall that at first startles me. After a time of revamped perception, I can see that the object before me is one of those life size figures of a biblical character, and behind it is Joel Weaver. As he stops to readjust his hold on the awkward shape of Jonah, I notice, Joel sees me standing there.

"Hello, Padre," Joel says. "It's time for these fellows to find a more suitable resting place. Miss Kristen says we should keep them, but they need to be stored somewhere out of the way."

"Sounds like a good idea," I say. "I sorta took a liking to them and wouldn't want to see them trashed."

"Would be almost sacrilegious to toss them in the dumpster," Joel says. "I'll find a spot for them."

"Let me know where you put them," I announce. "I might want to seek their counsel at some later date."

"Pastor, you can always seek their wisdom in the scriptures," Joel says with a smile.

It's somewhat disconcerting to consider that the church custodian may be wiser than the pastor. But, I remind myself that Joel Weaver is a philosopher masquerading as a janitor.

Peter, Paul, Ruth, Jeremiah, David, and Jonah will now spend their days and nights in hibernation until their services are called upon again. The words of Jonah come to mind: "And what does the Lord require of you but to do justice, and to love kindness, and to walk humbly with your God?" What a remarkable challenge that is.

Alice steps out into the hall and informs me that Carl Brody's on the phone. I hurry back to my office and pick up the receiver.

"Reverend, we are at the home of Joan Riebert. She's not here, but we have searched her house," Carl reports. "Neal Heard has found typing paper in her office which may be the same brand as in your letters and a pen they will test to see if she wrote them. Her fingerprints are on the way to the crime lab."

"Is there any clue as to where she is or any sign that Emma Wells was there?" I ask.

"No sign of the girl being here and no suggestion as to where Ms. Riebert is. It looks like she's not been here for days."

"So, we have to wait for the lab tests to know any more?"

"That's about it, Dr. Fowler," Carl says. "There's one strange thing here. There are pictures of Ms. Riebert's mother all over the house but not one of her father. Heard and I both found that to be unusual."

I'm reminded of what Ken told me earlier about Joan's mother's reluctance to talk more about her husband. Ken thinks there was something wrong in that relationship.

"Reverend," Carl says, "We'll let you know as soon as the lab reports come back. It could be as early as this afternoon. We're going to the Marshall house now to get fingerprints from that feisty old woman. I told Neal that we might want to call in for backup."

When I get off the phone with Brody, Alice tells me that she has reached Ray Gardner, and he's expecting my call. Ray was pastor here before me and is now serving a church in another state. He was very well respected at our church and a hard act for me to follow. I have often wondered which is best: to follow a beloved pastor or one who left the church in a mess. Perhaps the best position to be in is to follow a pastor who was moderately liked but didn't leave behind any lingering animosities. I was briefed ably by Julia Wagner when I first came on board here as to the work of the pastors before me, and learned that I was entering into special company in that in all her years at First Baptist the church was served by capable and hard-working ministers who experienced relatively conflict free pastorates.

It's not an easy task being a pastor even in the routine times in a church. The pastor must every week prepare sermons and lessons, plan for worship services, guide outreach programs, see that bulletin information is turned in, delegate building maintenance, keep an eye on church finances, be on call for emergencies, visit the sick and shut-ins, attend endless committee meetings, promote fellowship, guide the staff, and find time for family and personal development. Then there are the special circumstances which arise like building programs, major anniversaries, baptisms, weddings and funerals.

I reach Ray Gardner at his church office. It's been almost two years since I've talked with him. He did send an email expressing his concern when he heard of the story of Emma Wells. We spend a couple of minutes catching up on our families and then I turn to the reason for my call. "Ray, Julia Wagner tells me that you received an accusatory letter from someone in the congregation when you were here that implied that you had abused children."

"So, you have gotten one too," Ray says. "I was wondering when and if that time would come."

"Mine came the morning before the girl went missing," I tell Ray.

"Wow, that's not a good time to receive such an attack. What do you think the timing means?" Ray asks.

"I'm not sure, but the FBI thinks that the child abduction and the letter may be connected. It's possible that either Dot Marshall or Joan Riebert sent the letters. I called to ask if you had any suspicions as to who wrote to you."

"No, I never figured it out. I never considered Joan Riebert to be the letter writer, and Dot Marshall was a close friend of mine," Ray says. "I was not close to Joan, but she was always supportive of my ministry."

"Do you remember any special circumstances around the time when your letter came?" I ask.

"At the time it seemed to come out of the blue, and there was never another letter. Dot and I worked closely together; she could not have written those letters."

"Did you do any counseling with Joan Riebert?"

There's a moment of silence and then Ray responds. "She never came to me for counseling, but there was one strange incident I recall. Joan was asked to sing at a funeral, agreed to help, met with the organist to practice, but just didn't show up at the time of the service. Later I called to check on her, and she said she had forgotten. The phone conversation was very weird, and I wondered at the time if she was on some kind of medication."

"Did you know of any substance abuse on her part?" I ask.

"No, not that I knew of back then."

"Was this funeral close to the time of your letter?"

Ray says he doesn't think so but will try to recall when this happened. He remembers the funeral was for Martin Joyner who had been one of pastor Riebert's best friends. "This is why the whole thing was so unusual," Ray remembers. "Martin's wife made a big deal of how Joan and her daughter, Pamela, had grown up in the church together. Joan had even visited the family after the death. Mrs. Martin and Pamela were both surprised when she was absent from the funeral."

I thank Ray for the information and promise to keep him informed as to what happens with all of this. That is a bizarre story of the missed funeral. I'm sure that Joan has sung at three or four of the funerals I've conducted.

Where is Joan Riebert? She has not been seen by anyone for two days. On Saturday she visited her mother and on Sunday she sang the moving solo in the worship service. The woman sat behind me while I preached. I can't remember turning even once to look back at the choir. All the while I scanned the congregation; was my accuser seated only a few feet behind me? Does Joan have a key to the church? Probably. Has she harbored ill feelings towards all pastors because of something her father did to her? I have so many questions.

I try to imagine what it must have been like all those years ago when a young Joan sat here and listened to her father preach. There's no way for me to understand what her life was like then. I'm reminded of a poem that has haunted me for years written by Annette Wynne:

> **Where we walk to school each day**
> **Indian children used to play,**
> **All about our native land,**
> **Where the shops and houses stand.**
>
> **And the trees were very tall,**
> **And there were no streets at all,**
> **Not a church and not a steeple –**
> **Only woods and Indian people.**
>
> **Only wigwams on the ground**
> **And at night bears prowling round –**
> **What a different place today**
> **Where we live and work and play!**

I do know this – the present is dependent on the past. It could very well be that Emma Wells, the last three pastors here, and myself are all the victims of events that took place many years ago when this was a different place for Joan Riebert.

CHAPTER SEVENTEEN

WEDNESDAY AFTERNOON

Pamela Joyner Evans is a school teacher and longtime member of our church. She's open to my visit as I tell her I need to talk to her about Joan Riebert. Pamela's house is in a nice subdivision on the outskirts of our small city. I've never been here before, but did visit her husband in the hospital a couple of years ago, and got to know Pamela better during that period. She and John are not very active in the church, but are very committed to Habitat for Humanity and give much of their time there. She invites me in to their living room where we sit facing each other across a coffee table covered with magazines. Probably about sixty years old, she is young looking for her age, and wearing a tie dye dress.

"Sorry about the clutter, Pastor," Pamela says. "I'm doing some reading in preparation of my new teaching assignment in the fall when I will become a literacy coach for other teachers."

"That sounds like a challenge," I say.

"Yes, after all of these years in the classroom with children, this will be a big change for me. It will be less pressure once I get up to speed on the job, but I'm sure I'll miss the children. You said you wanted to talk about Joan."

"Pamela, have you and Joan been close over the years?" I ask.

"We grew up together, and went to the same schools. Over the past twenty years or so we've not seen each other that much other than occasionally at church. Until we went off to college we were like sisters. Is there something wrong with Joan?"

"There could be," I answer. "She has not been seen for a couple of days, and no one seems to know where she is."

"That's not good," Pamela says. "I'm sorry, but I haven't talked to Joan in months. I pray she's okay. How are you dealing, Pastor, with the stress on you over the missing child?"

"I'm okay. It has been rough on a lot of people."

"John and I joined the searchers on Saturday. Her poor mother and father."

"They are coping as well as can be expected. I was hoping you could share some insights about Joan when she was younger. This might help us understand why she has taken off now."

"She was maybe four or five years old when the Rieberts moved here. Their backyard was adjacent to my family's yard. The Rieberts lived in the parsonage on Church Street. We lived around the corner on Blake Street. You know which house was the parsonage, don't you Pastor?"

I nod yes. "The house is only five doors down from the church. You and Joan are the same age?"

"Yes, we were in the same grade from kindergarten until our senior year in high school. All but two of those years we were in the same class. Her bedroom was upstairs in the parsonage on the corner across from my house and mine was upstairs, also on the corner. We could look out our windows and see each other. Joan would often sleep over at my house. She loved my parents."

"Did you ever spend the night at the parsonage?" I ask.

"Not very often, maybe a couple of times. Joan's father was very strict and did not like for her friends to come over. Mrs. Riebert was very nice and would have let me stay there more if Pastor Riebert had allowed it. I was never comfortable around him."

With trepidation I venture into a more sensitive area. "Pamela, do you know of any psychological problems Joan had when she was young?"

The veteran school teacher takes a moment to reflect on my question. She takes her glasses off and rubs her eyes with her free hand. The sun streaming in from a window illumines the top of her head and the loose strands of hair are silhouetted against the chocolate painted wall behind her.

"No, not really," Pamela replies. "When we were in elementary school, she and I were, what you might call, the terrors of Church Street. We would cut across the backyards to the church playground or to the church itself. We often played hide and seek in the sanctuary and education buildings. Joan knew every possible place to hide in the buildings because she had watched as the new sanctuary was built. She even had a key we would use to slip into the church through the door over beside the Robinson house. It was a good time to grow up. Joan seemed pretty normal to me back then. Later, there were times when she would become quiet and less sociable, especially in high school. She didn't date much, actually hardly ever. Once I got a steady boyfriend, we were not as close. As she grew older she did become more moody, but what teenager is easy to understand? I have raised three and would say that personality changes are typical."

"Do you have any idea where Joan could be now?" I ask.

Pamela's look changes from smiles of pleasant remembrances to obvious concern for her childhood friend. "I don't. I feel bad that I haven't been a better friend these past few years. With family and career some relationships change. I hope she's okay. Joan was my best friend during those childhood years."

I thank Pamela and leave her house to head back to the church. On the way back to the First Baptist I take a detour down Blake Street and turn onto Church Street. The two-story frame house which was the parsonage stands much as it probably did fifty years ago when Joan Riebert lived there. I notice there's a "For Rent" sign in the yard. The house has been a rental for years now. I lived in a parsonage in my first pastorate and am glad that I don't live in one now. You never truly feel like it's your own home.

Emma Wells has been gone five full days now. Joan Riebert hasn't been seen since Sunday afternoon. I can't help but think that the two are connected.

* * *

There's a host of people waiting for me when I get back to the church, Deanna, Denise Chevalier, and Ken Matthews. I ask Denise and Ken to go into my office while I spend a minute with Deanna in hers.

"Ron, Dot Marshall was very upset when the FBI arrived at her house today with a warrant for her fingerprints," Deanna says. "It was a humiliating experience for her. I think you're going to have to pay her a visit when this is all over."

"I will do that," I promise. "The problem is that someone has written angry letters to me and also to former pastors here in the past. We need to find out who this is because the letters have to do with child abuse. In light of the abduction from our church the authorities need to find out if the letters are related to Emma having been taken."

"Ron, Dot did not write the letters to you or the former pastors, but she has an idea who did write them. She told me a story I think you should hear. It involves Joan Riebert."

"Why did Dot tell you a story about Joan?"

"Because she put together that Joan is also left-handed and has been here a long time as well."

"Did she tell the police or FBI any of this?"

"No. It just dawned on her after they left. When Dot was in her twenties, and her daughter was about two, she volunteered to help with Vacation Bible School here at First Baptist. She was asked to teach the nine and ten year old class. Joan Riebert was one of her students that summer. Joan was excited like the other children over attending the school and was very eager to take part the first two days. But, on Wednesday of the week Joan's demeanor changed. She became quiet and sullen. Dot pulled her aside to ask her if anything was wrong. Ten year old Joan began to cry. She would not tell Dot why she was so upset. The next morning Joan seemed awfully withdrawn and would not take part in any of the activities."

"What did Dot do?" I ask with mounting concern over this event which happened over fifty years ago.

"She decided to talk to Joan's mother, Mary Riebert. After the school day was over, she took Mrs. Riebert aside and told her that she was worried about Joan. At first Mary Riebert brushed it off as being one of Joan's moods, but Dot persisted since the change in the child had been so dramatic from one day to the next. Joan's mother then confided with Dot that Reverend Riebert was being especially strict with Joan because he had noticed her misbehaving in the opening programs before the students went to their classes."

"That does not seem to be all that unusual. Many pastors are uptight about the way their children behave at church," I say, having had some experience with this when our Sarah was younger.

"That's not the end of the story," Deanna continues. "The next morning, Friday, Joan came to VBS even more withdrawn. Again Dot asked her at the refreshment break time if there was something she wanted to talk about. Joan only shook her head no."

"As they were talking, Dot noticed bruises on Joan's leg and asked her about them. The child told her she fell out of a tree the afternoon before. Dot let it go and the school ended. The next week Mary Riebert called Dot and asked her if she could come over for a visit."

"Was Dot close to Mrs. Riebert?" I ask.

"She says they had spoken on only a few occasions before. The purpose of Mary Riebert's visit was to ask Dot to not tell anyone else about the way Joan acted that week and the bruises."

"Dot agreed to let it drop, but remained concerned over the deep sadness she saw in the child's eyes those few days. From then on Dot took a special interest in young Joan and made it a point to speak to her at church when she could."

"So that was the end of the matter?"

"Not exactly. About a year later Dot heard that Joan was sick and had not attended her public school for over two weeks."

"She called the Riebert house and pastor Riebert answered the phone. When Dot asked about Joan he told her that she was doing better. Then in a very strange exchange he asked Dot why she was taking such an interest in his daughter and suggested that it was not really her business. I guess Dot was just as feisty back then as she is now, so she told her pastor that she was making it her business to take a special interest in Joan."

"I guess that did not go over well."

"Let's just say that from then on Dot Marshall was given the cold shoulder by her pastor. She did, however, continue to speak to Joan whenever she could. This went on until Joan graduated from high school. Over the years Dot sensed that things were not right in the Riebert household but never had enough information to make a public fuss about it."

"Thank you Deanna," I say. "That's a very revealing story. I will speak with Dot as soon as I can. I'm so sorry that she's been so upset over the FBI visit."

"Ron, you need to trust your staff more. We all want to help.

You may find that when you pool all of our knowledge about people in the church we have some very valuable information."

I thank Deanna again and reflect on what she's said. When I was an associate pastor years ago I found out that different people in the church would become close to certain staff members and share with them more freely. On several occasions I was able to enlighten the senior pastor on personal needs which helped him minister to people. There was the time I stumbled into a situation which was very uncomfortable for me. Making a visit to a family after their son had died, I found out they were very upset with the pastor over his lack of attention to them in their grief. He had called but not yet visited. I sat in their living room and listened to them share their sorrow, and tried to make excuses for the senior minister. When I shared with him the family's disappointment, he was shocked at the degree of their frustration with him and quickly went to their house. It was a very humbling experience for him.

I wonder if Julia knew of any problems in the Riebert home. If she had she probably would've told us when Joan's name came up yesterday.

* * *

Denise and Ken are seated in the two wing chairs in my office and are discussing the case when I enter. I sit at my desk and can tell immediately that what they are discussing is not sitting well with Ken.

"Ron, Agent Chevalier has just told me that Joel Weaver has been taken back to the criminal justice center for more questioning," Ken reports.

"What?" I exclaim. "The man has been hounded enough!"

"Calm down, Reverend, we've learned of some new information about your custodian that does not look good for him," Chevalier says.

"What new information?" I ask.

"Neal has found out that Weaver was dismissed from a maintenance position a few years ago because he was accused of taking indecent liberties by two young women. He was employed at a college, and two of the female students filed charges against him."

211

"But we ran a security check on him when he was hired here and his record was clean," I argue.

"That's because the charges were dropped and never entered into the official records," Denise says. "We did a more thorough check and this came to the surface."

"But, what about Joan Riebert?" I ask. "We've learned things today which raise questions about her. I just learned that her father may have abused her when she was young."

Denise shakes her head up and down and looks over at Ken who is listening to all of this. "We just got the fingerprint report back," the young agent declares. "It looks like Ms. Riebert did write your letters, but we are not sure she took the little girl. We have no evidence she was at the church last Friday. We do know that Weaver was here, and this new information makes him a more likely suspect."

The news about Joel does not really register with me as I now learn that it was definitely Joan who wrote the letters. What happened to her those many years ago? What kind of pain did she endure at the hands of her father? No wonder she has these feelings toward ministers. The tenor of her letters makes sense now.

Ken breaks the silence, "Ron, I tried to impress upon the agents that Joan is an emotionally disturbed person and she did know Emma."

"I've learned even more about her in the last hour which concerns me greatly," I say. "Denise, you and Heard need to hear what I have to say."

"We will, but right now we're going to follow through on Weaver as a person of interest in the abduction of Emma Wells. We will still have the police look for Joan Riebert. I'm going back down to our command center and assist in the interview with Weaver."

Denise leaves, and Ken and I sit in silence for a minute or two. Then I tell Ken about my conversation with Pamela Evans.

"Ron, you and I are going to have to proceed on our own in finding Joan Riebert," Ken says. "I think I should go down to the library and ask some questions of the staff there. There may be something the police and FBI missed."

I agree that this sounds like a valuable next step. After Ken leaves I walk down to the drink machine on the hall, stand with a Diet Coke in hand in front of the restroom where Emma may have been abducted, and again retrace my steps of last Friday afternoon. I'm still bothered by the assumption that the little girl was taken out of the church to the back parking lot. The police surmised that this exit was the quickest way to take someone to a waiting car. I descend the stairwell and at the bottom stand in front of the door to the exit in question. This time, however, I don't go out that door, but instead turn down the hall on this ground floor. It's possible that Emma may have been taken or led this way, even though this means winding through the entire bottom floor.

Around the corner of this hall I approach the rooms allotted to the Good Samaritan, the helping agency. From what I was told there was no one down here last Friday as the agency was closed. Past the door of the Good Samaritan the hall continues to a stairwell on the far side of the building. These little used stairs arrive at a landing and an exit that opens to the side of the building facing the house next door. It would have been so easy for someone to take the little girl out this way without a soul seeing them. The door can be opened from the inside by pushing on the panic bar.

Outside the church now, I face the two-story white house with mildewed boards owned by Lucy Robinson. Walking a few yards down the incline between our church and the neighbor home, I come to a path that leads up a slight hill just before the kudzu bank begins. It was only about twenty yards further along the overgrown hill that Emma Wells' name badge was found in the ditch. It's this path that beckons me, and I climb up to the small backyard of the Robinson house. Now Pamela Evans' words come back to me: she and Joan Riebert would cut across the backyards from the parsonage to the church when they were young.

Two massive oak trees shade the Robinson yard. Very little sun is able to penetrate this plot of ground, and hanging from a large limb is a pair of ropes that must have at one time held a board and served as a swing. Perhaps Joan and Pamela made brief stops here for a few undulations on the swing beneath the large oaks; two young girls who were at home in these parts. The supporting branch high above protrudes from the trunk like a policeman's arm extended to stop all traffic at a school crossing; its reach extends some twenty feet out parallel to the ground and is abruptly amputated to display a knob-like a fist.

On the other side of the Robinson yard, I find an opening in a six foot high wooden fence which leads to the next backyard like a portal leading to a well traveled pathway. I don't know who lives here, but the grounds have obviously not seen much care for years. The weeds are tall and there are the remains of what once must have been a small greenhouse. The sun finds ample openings so as to reflect off the remnants of the glass and metal structure. Forty years ago this may have been a place full of life and growth, a garden full of thriving plants and blooms. Today it's the home of dried brown weeds and distorted vines with threatening thorns.

I'm now just two houses from the backyard of the old parsonage. The next home is a one level structure which seems to have been remodeled in recent years. The courtyard is well landscaped with a koi pond to one side, and I'm aware that this is the home of Ed and Marge Downey, two of our church members who are in their seventies. They're away on a trip to Alaska which they have been planning for over a year with two other couples from our congregation. Marge is a master gardener who prides herself in her knowledge of southern fauna. It must pain her to live beside the untamed jungle next door.

Only a row of shrubs separates the Downey yard from that of a large patio behind a well-kept Tudor styled home. As I cross the patio, I hear the rattle of a chain and turn to see a large dog staring at me from beside one of those gray plastic animal abodes sold at pet supply stores. For a moment the bulldog and I face each other in a silent standoff, neither sure of the next move. Thankfully, the black and brown canine makes no effort to approach me as I take a few steps to cross to the other side of the yard and out of the reach of his tether. He's likely a veteran of chasing intruders who are just out of the reach of his bind and has decided I'm not worth the effort. The only barrier to crossing this next boundary is a line of cedar trees. Moving between two of the closely planted evergreens, I keep my eye on the animal who watches me in turn with silent curiosity.

Finally, I emerge behind the parsonage where Joan Riebert grew up. The house is empty and the property is devoid of anything personal. I've never been here before and wonder what it must have been like growing up in this church owned house. There's a screened porch running across the full width of the rear of the home. Trying the door to the porch; I find it locked. There's a strong desire to see inside this house, so I decide to go around to the front and look more closely at the rental sign. The agency is Foster and Lee. I call the number on the sign and ask for Don Lee. Don is one of our deacons. The receptionist informs me that Mr. Lee is out of the office, but she volunteers his cell phone number. I reach Don at the YMCA where he is getting ready for a board meeting.

"Hello, Reverend," Don says. "What can I do for you? Don't tell me you've decided to sell your house."

I've talked with Don recently about an appraisal on our house. Amy and I have given some thought to moving a little closer to the church, perhaps in one of the older homes which we could remodel.

"Don, I'm standing in front of the old First Baptist parsonage which is now for rent. I was wondering if someone from your office could bring a key over so I can see inside."

"Pastor," says Don, "why are you interested in a rental?"

"I would just like to see where our former pastors lived out of curiosity," I tell Don, which is mostly the truth.

"OK, I can have someone let you in," he says. "The place needs some repairs as the last renters didn't treat it well."

"Who owns the house now?" I ask.

"Oh, I thought you knew," Don declares. "Joan Riebert bought the house some years ago. You know she grew up in that parsonage. She bought it for an investment she said. She seems to be in no hurry to rent it again. I'm sure Joan would not mind if we let you inside."

I'm stunned. This house belongs to Joan Riebert. After I end the call to Don, I stand by Church Street on the sidewalk looking at the two-story home which has white columns supporting a deep front porch. I see down the street the church sign in the distance. After a brief time contemplating what to do next, I call Ken Matthews who's at the library.

"Ken, did you know that Joan Riebert owns the rental house

down the street from the church, the one that used to be the parsonage?"

"She does!" Ken says with great surprise.

"Well, I'm standing in front now and the place is vacant. A key is being brought to me in a few minutes."

"I'll be there in fifteen minutes," Ken announces.

The street is lined with large oaks, but the heat is still stifling even in the shade. Moving to the front steps, I sit for a few minutes wondering why Joan Riebert bought this old house. Perhaps it was simply for investment, but there are many other houses in this city with better investment potential. A more likely motive might be to hold onto a part of her heritage. That would make sense if the memories here were good but why hold on to a place where you may have suffered pain?

In about ten minutes a young woman drives up and rolls down her window. "Reverend Fowler, here's a key to the house. Mr. Lee said I should give it to you and ask you to return it to our office when you are finished."

I take the key, and the agent drives away. I decide not to wait for Ken and move up to the front porch. The concrete slab is chipped and cracked from years of weathering. The black painted wood door isn't very inviting. To the left there's a window light which affords a way to both look into the house and out to see who might be on the porch. Peering through the glass little is visible of the darkened interior. My imagination conjures images of the young Joan looking out through this vertical portal to see who is at the door. For a moment this startles me, and I stand back realizing that anyone inside can easily see my figure with the backlight of the outdoors. The key turns the lock, and the door opens with a creak giving away the age of the house. A home inspector would write this up before ever going inside.

I stand in a foyer with rooms on each side. The wide planked hardwood floor is dark and dusty. There's the usual musty odor of a house that's been closed up for some time. The room to the left has a red brick fireplace with a thick oak mantle. The curtains on the front double windows are made from a heavy material and let in little light. The room to the right is square, a dining room I assume in a house of this style of architecture, common in this section of town. I hesitate to move further into the home, but my curiosity is such that I'm compelled to explore more before Ken arrives. My suspicion that Joan Riebert may have been here in the last few days causes me to pause and consider my next move.

"Joan!" I call out. There's no response. "Joan, this is Ron Fowler." Listening closely I hear no movement in the house. It's broad daylight outside, but inside the light is as sparse as are the rooms which contain only a few empty moving boxes. To my surprise the power is still on, and I switch on a small glass chandelier which hangs in the entry hall. It appears that this central passage must run all the way to the back porch. A set of stairs rises on my right to the second floor.

Moving down the hall I listen for any signs there is someone present, but the place is completely quiet except for my measured breathing. On the right, behind the stairwell, is the kitchen. It's as bare as one would expect in an empty house. Yellow café curtains hang above the window over the sink. Another window looks out onto the screened porch. A relatively new Whirlpool refrigerator stands in one corner, looking out of place in this hundred year old house. The counter tops are green formica and the single sink is large and deep, farmhouse style. There have been few remodeling changes which make me wonder if this was the way the house looked when the Riebert's lived here years ago, except for the refrigerator.

I'm startled by a noise behind me and hear footsteps on the bare wood floor of the hall.

"Ron, you in here?" Ken calls out.

I step out to greet him. "Just doing some exploring," I say.

"Don't touch anything," Ken advises. "We don't know who may have been here. We may need fingerprint evidence. Here, I brought some latex gloves. Put these on."

With the gloves on, I feel as if I am truly a part of the fraternity of crime fighters.

For the next five or so minutes we inspect the downstairs and find nothing but the empty boxes and broken glass from light bulbs. A bathroom and bedroom are on the opposite side of the hall from the kitchen. We conclude this is likely the master bedroom of the house, or could be used as a den. Between the kitchen and dining room a door stands closed. Opening it and switching on a light, it's obvious this leads to a basement. Ken tells me that he'll go downstairs and check it out while I go upstairs.

The stairwell up is bordered by a wall on one side and a light stained maple banister on the other with a darker stained rail on top; both curve slightly as they reach the bottom landing. Perhaps children have used the rail as an expressway from the top floor, I think. I know my daughter would be tempted to try such a ride. The third step moans as I put my weight on it announcing the presence of someone ascending. At the top there's a small landing which looks down to the hall below. The house has a half story on this level with a roof that slopes toward the front, and four doors open onto this corridor. I remember Pamela telling me that Joan could look out her window and they could see each other, so I assume the door to the left must open into the bedroom where this preacher's daughter likely spent much of her time.

This room's about twelve feet square and completely empty except for a quilt over to one side folded double and a single covered pillow resting on it. Someone may have slept here recently. One of the curtain rods on the window is broken, and the faded pink fabric hangs lop sided from the dangling dowel. Don had said the last renters were not very considerate of the property. From the window on the back corner of the room it's possible to see all the way down the backyards of the houses on Blake Street. I spot what must have been Pamela's window those many years ago where she and Joan could look out at each other. This was Joan's bedroom from her preschool years until she went off to college, I surmise. For thirteen years this was her corner of the house while her father served our congregation. It was about forty years ago that she left this place to go off to college, and now she owns it. Again I wonder why would she want to own the house where she may have experienced so much hurt? Are the quilt and pillow signs that she has spent the night here in what was once her room?

As I turn from the window, Ken calls out from below, "Ron, there's nothing in the basement. Find anything up there?"

"Yes, Come on up. There's some bedding in a room up here."

Just as Ken reaches the top landing, I notice that there's a door on the hallway with a padlock on it. Many rental homes have an owner's closet, so I assume this is why the door has been secured. Ken arrives on the landing as I stand before the locked door. He quickly appraises what I'm thinking.

"We need to find out what's in there," he says.

"How do we do that, call the realtor?"

"Can't wait for that," Ken says. "We're going to have to remove the lock."

He pulls out a Swiss army pocket knife, folds out a small screw driver, and begins to work with his right hand while his left hand holds the padlock. The screws on the hasp are on the outside which means they can be removed and the lock itself not a factor. After about three minutes the entire mechanism is detached.

Ken pulls open the door, and we see that it's a large closet or small room, perhaps ten feet wide by maybe twenty feet deep. The single light is operated by a pull chain, and Ken yanks on it, but the bulb arcs, then pops, and all we see are spots where the light flickered so briefly. It takes my eyes half a minute to begin to adjust to the darkness of the closet as limited light penetrates from the bedroom windows across the hall.

The windowless room is not full, but there are enough obstacles to warrant caution before going further. The ceiling of the room slants down toward the front of the house, and we have to stoop as we move forward. Our bodies block some of the little light there is, but I can make out a large dresser of some type and a bookshelf that reaches to the full height of the tapered ceiling. On another wall there's what appears to be a dollhouse, perhaps three feet tall. In the limited light, barely visible, is the corner of what looks to be a low bed on the floor behind the bookshelf. I'm beside Ken on my knees now as he peers around the shelving. We can just barely see the full form of a single mattress. Separating from my partner in order to let more light in, I see a shape on the bed.

Ken drops to his knees and then crawls over to the mattress in order to get a better view. "It's a child!" he says. "We need more light!"

I stand up and exit the closet to search for a good bulb to replace the burned out one. When I return with one from another closet fixture Ken is sitting on the floor beside the figure on the bed. He looks up at me from the darkened space, his eyes barely visible in the faint illumination from the open door. He has not moved for the two minutes it took me to search for a light bulb, evidently wary of any action in the semi-darkness.

I insert the sixty watt bulb into the porcelain socket in the area where the ceiling is only about seven feet high. It gives off ample light for us to see the full scope of the small room. Down on my knees again I crawl back over to Ken where the ceiling slopes to only four feet. On the mattress before us is indeed a little blond headed girl. I move over to her and can make out the tee shirt that says "Life is Good". The child's face is partially covered by an arm, but I can see enough to know that we have indeed found Emma Wells. A whole town has searched for days, and here she is, just a few hundred yards from where her name tag was discovered in the ditch, and only a block from the church where she was abducted. She's motionless on the thin mattress. I sit beside Ken and lightly touch the arm of this curled up child. Ken removes his latex glove and checks her pulse. He looks at me with an expression I can't decipher.

"Ron, she's alive but seems to be asleep," Ken says softly. He calls her name, "Emma, Emma." She doesn't stir. He prods her gently. The child does not respond. "I think she's been drugged. You'd better call 911."

I hurriedly punch in the three numbers and hit send.

On the other end a female voice answers, "911. What is your emergency?"

"We need an ambulance! We have found a little girl in an abandoned house, and she may be in critical condition. It's the missing Wells child."

"From your id I can't tell your location."

"We're at a rental house on Church Street, five doors down from First Baptist. There's a Foster and Lee sign in the yard and a Jeep Cherokee out front."

"Is the girl breathing?"

"Yes."

"Stay on the line, Sir." There's a long pause. In a moment the dispatcher comes back on, "The responders are five minutes away. Don't hang up. Let me know when they're at the house. Now, what is your name?"

"My name is Ron Fowler. Do I need to do anything else?"

"No. If you're sure she's breathing, don't move her until the EMS gets there. Remain calm."

Ken says to me as he stands up, "I'm going to see if I can find anything else on this floor."

Carefully I put my now ungloved hand on the head of the little girl who has been missing for five days. She's alive just as her mother said she was. Her hair is disheveled and her clothes dirty, but this is definitely the child I watched share her hopes and fears in the video made for her parents. This is the cancer-stricken eight year old whose pictures adorn the mantle in the Wells home. Her breathing is calm, and it's as if I were sitting beside my own daughter after she has fallen asleep on the couch. What has this slumbering little girl been through these last few days, I wonder? My eyes move to the words on Emma's pink shirt, and I think, yes, today life is good.

I feel the faint movement of her lungs and can detect even the rhythm of her heartbeat as my hand rests gently on her back now. Her skin's warm. Somewhere in this small child there's the dreaded cancer. One ordeal possibly is about to be over yet another awaits. Will she survive this threat to only succumb to that other one? This is not the time for those thoughts. Right now I'm so relieved to have found this beautiful girl still alive. Days of fear that she's dead now pass as she so peacefully sleeps. My thoughts jump to Ted and Rachel who will be so happy to see her.

In the stillness of this waiting for what comes next, I look around this chamber at the array of stored heirlooms. My guess is that these are items from Joan's childhood, ones she could not accommodate in her other house or ones that brought memories too painful to manage. The dollhouse sits empty which must have once been the residence of a pretend family, a happy family perhaps. There are a few books on the shelf: several volumes of *Nancy Drew*, *Alice in Wonderland*, and *The Diary of Anne Frank*. What did Joan go through during her years in this house? Was she locked in this same closet when she was Emma's age?

On the floor in another corner of the room, only about six feet away from where I'm sitting, there's something we did not spot as we came in. Hesitant to leave the child, my curiosity still dictates I check out what it is. There are several objects in a pile, and I carefully separate them. One is clearly a well worn black leather Bible. Beside it is a photograph of a family. I recognize the man in the picture from ones I've seen in the church. It's former pastor Stephen Riebert, posing with a woman and a child, his wife and daughter I assume. After a moment, I see the resemblance and am sure this is Joan at about the age of Emma now. The other object is another picture frame face down on the floor. Turning it over I'm shocked to see that it's a picture of my family, Amy, Sarah, and me. It's one I keep on a bookshelf in my church office. I hadn't noticed that it was missing. Two pictures, each of a minister and his family, a mother, father and daughter.

Ken returns in a minute and reports, "There are two bottles of Ambien and one of Tylenol PM in the bathroom. It looks like Emma has been given a strong dose of both to keep her sedated. There are also water bottles, individual containers of apple sauce, and some pop tarts. What have you found there?"

I point to the Bible and then show him the two pictures still on the floor beside me. "She had a picture of my family here," I say. "She must have taken it from my office, probably in the past few days. What do you make of this?"

Ken stands for a moment looking at my collection and then speaks with his usual calmness, "I guess we now know that Joan Riebert is both your letter writer and the person who abducted this child. It appears that she has become fixated on you and your family."

We hear the sirens approaching. Two men get out of the ambulance, and a young woman arrives in her car. Ken meets them at the door and leads them upstairs to the closet. "This is the missing girl who has been in the news," he tells them.

The female medic gets down on her knees beside the sleeping Emma and checks her vitals. In a minute she expresses her concern as to what the heavy doses of sleeping medicine might have done to the small girl, but basically Emma is breathing well and her blood pressure is only slightly depressed, the EMT says. The female medic asks us to leave the room while she examines the child more thoroughly in order to determine if there are any reasons to make other preparations in her transfer. After a couple of minutes, the thirty-something medical technician calls us back over. "I couldn't find any obvious breaks or lacerations," she says. "We need to get her to Community Hospital in order to let her wake up under close supervision."

They prepare to take her out of the house to the ambulance.

"We better call Neal Heard and Carl Brody," I suggest.

Ken agrees. "They will want to give the house a thorough going over."

Ken dials Heard.

While Ken is calling Heard, I place a call to Ted and Rachel Wells. Ted answers the phone.

"Ted this is Ron Fowler," I say with as much composure as I can muster. "We have found Emma. She's alive."

There's no response on the other end. I can imagine that Ted is in shock. My emotions are so overwhelming; it's hard to imagine what the news is doing to him.

"She is on her way to Community Hospital in an ambulance," I continue. "She has been given sleeping pills, probably for days, and is sound asleep. We're not sure of any other medical issues."

Finally, Ted speaks, "Thank God! Oh, thank God, Pastor! Do you think she's going to be okay? Where was she? No, that doesn't matter. The only thing that matters is that my Emma is alive."

"She does not appear to have any external injuries," I say.

"Oh, that is great to hear! This is such good news, great news. Please hang on for a minute, while I get Rachel!"

After a brief period, Ted's back on the line. "Rachel's on the extension, Ron."

"You were right, Rachel. She's alive," I say with joy.

"I knew it! I knew it! My little girl is not dead," Rachel says with obvious tearful emotion. "I told you, Ted. I told you. My Emma is alive. I knew it!"

"She's probably at the hospital by now," I say. "I'm so happy for you. Go see your little girl."

Ken's listening as I conclude the call. The big former FBI agent has tears in his eyes. We both stand in the downstairs hall trying to collect ourselves.

Neal Heard, Denise Chevalier, and Carl Brody arrive in a few minutes. Ken and I fill them in with the details of what we found. We tell them about Emma's condition and of our call to the Wells' home.

"How'd you know to look here?" Carl Brody asks.

"I was led here by a little girl," I say.

"What little girl?" Heard asks.

I tell them all about my talk with Pamela Evans and explain that I followed the path of the young Joan Riebert. "She led me here," I state. "You will find some of Joan's childhood possessions in the house."

Ken decides to go to the hospital. Neal and Denise begin their examination of the house. Carl goes back to the police station to initiate a more thorough search for Joan Riebert. I walk down Church Street back to First Baptist. The trees are still as there is no wind. The steeples of the four churches reach above the oaks proclaiming from their perch that places of worship occupy this street. The Lord is in His heaven and all is well below, I think. Never before have I appreciated this scene any more than today.

In the church office I ask Alice to summon the other staff members. Kristen, Janice, Steve, and Deanna all are present and within a few minutes the associates are standing in my office, curious as to the nature of the meeting.

"A few minutes ago Emma Wells was found alive," I announce. "She's on the way to the hospital to be checked out, but she may not suffer much if any physical damage from her ordeal."

"Where was she found?" Kristen asks what they all want to know.

"In a house down the street from the church," I report. "Years ago this was the church parsonage. Joan Riebert owns the house now and likely has been there in the last few days."

"Joan Riebert?" Alice asks.

"That's impossible," Janice says. "Joan sang in church Sunday. She couldn't be responsible for this."

"As of now she's a prime suspect," I say. "This will all be made known today by the police and the FBI. She hasn't been seen since the end of the service on Sunday. The police are trying to find her and have reason to believe she's somewhere in town. When Emma wakes up we will know more."

"So, Joan did write the letters?" Deanna asks.

"Yes," I say.

Steve speaks up, "What letters?"

"It's a complicated story," I tell the staff members. "For now let's just rejoice that Emma is safe, and thank God for her return to her parents."

"I need to go to the hospital," Kristen says. "I want to be there with Ted and Rachel."

"We all have some calls to make," Deanna says. "I will call Dot Marshall first."

I nod my head in agreement.

As she leaves my office, Alice speaks a parting word as she goes out the door, "Looks like you beat me to the scoop on this one."

I smile.

It hits me that I've not let Amy know what has happened this afternoon. She doesn't answer either of her phones. I send her a text message: "Emma was found a few minutes ago. She's alive. They have taken her to Community Hospital. Love you." I send the same message to Sarah's phone.

It then dawns on me that Joan is out there somewhere, and she had that picture of our family in that closet. Could Amy and Sarah be in danger? Where are they? A new set of fears take over. For the last few hours I've been so intent on my search for Emma that I've not thought of my own family.

My thoughts are interrupted as Alice comes on the intercom, "Ron, your wife is on the church phone."

"Hi, where are you?" I ask.

From Amy's wonderful voice I hear, "Hello, my hero. I'm at the dentist with Sarah, braces appointment, remember? I got your text message. Alice just told me you found Emma, yourself. I'm so proud of you and so relieved for the Wells. Sarah is still in the dental chair and doesn't know yet. I can't wait to hear all of the details. Is Emma going to be alright?"

"Yes, I think so. It was Joan Riebert who took her."

"That's hard to believe. Are you sure?"

"I'm afraid so. We haven't found her yet."

"Sarah's coming out now. See you at home later."

I call Carl Brody and express my concern for my family's safety. He tells me to not worry, that he will get a car over to see they get home safely. I decide to go home and meet my wife and daughter when they arrive. I need to hold them both.

There are two white wicker rockers on our front porch. Sitting there, waiting for my family, and rocking gently, the serenity of the moment is only broken by the sounds of some neighborhood children playing down the block. It's a welcome sound. Amy pulls in the drive, and Sarah bolts from the car. She runs up on the porch and launches herself into my arms as I stand up. Amy takes her time coming up the walk savoring the scene, I assume. For several minutes I'm peppered with questions from Sarah as to the details of the events this afternoon. In the street a police car parks at the curb, two officers taking in the scene.

After a full recap of the last few hours Amy speaks, "Ron, I want you to go to the hospital and see the Wells. We are well protected here. Sarah and I need to know how Emma is. For this mission we will gladly share you."

I agree and promise to return soon.

* * *

The news media is waiting outside the hospital and eager for my story. I had hoped they would wait until tomorrow, but that's too much to ask. Carl Brody has already briefed them on some of the details of the rescue.

"Reverend, you realize that you're a national hero, don't you?" a newspaper reporter asks.

"Tell us, Dr. Fowler, what led you to search the old parsonage?" A TV feature reporter shouts over the dozen or so people gathered in the hospital foyer.

"I'm just thankful that Emma Wells was found and is with her parents," I say.

"We hear that the house belongs to Joan Riebert from your

church. Do you think she took the child, and why did she do it?" one young woman with a press badge asks.

"I don't know for sure who took Emma, and I cannot guess at motivations," I respond.

"What led you to look in the old parsonage?" another reporter asks.

"I had a hunch, but that is all I can say now."

As I get on the elevator I hear one last question, "Pastor, are you sure it was a hunch, or did you receive a sign from God as to where the girl was?"

As the door closes, I ponder that last question. I'm not sure if God directs people with signs. But, there have been some surprising insights which have come my way, ones which make me wonder about the nature of serendipitous events.

As I exit the elevator on the pediatrics ward I see Ken standing in the hall along with Kristen. "What's the word on Emma's condition?" I ask.

"She's somewhat awake," Ken answers. "It seems that she was given enough medication to keep her from experiencing much pain from her cancer, but not enough to do any permanent brain damage. They're running tests on her liver and kidneys now and will know tonight if there is any need for treatments to repair them."

"Did Joan hurt her in any other way?" I ask.

"Emma is still very groggy, and they have not yet been able to ask her much," Kristen volunteers.

"There's no sign of physical abuse," Ken adds.

"That's good to hear," I say.

Ted Wells opens the door to Emma's room and without a word comes over and hugs me. After what must be thirty seconds, he says, "Pastor, I would like for you to formally meet my daughter, Emma."

Inside the room, Rachel is seated in a chair beside her only child. She looks at me and smiles, then stands up and speaks to her daughter, whose eyes are closed. "Emma, Reverend Fowler is here from the church."

Emma opens her eyes a little and lifts her right hand in a weak waving motion. She then gives me a sign with one finger that appears to be a gesture for me to come closer. I move to a position beside her bed opposite of her mother and bend over. Emma whispers, "It was you who found me up in the closet, wasn't it?"

"Yes," I respond. "I was so happy to find you, Emma."

"I knew God would send help," the child in the bed says with a weak smile on her face.

"I'm sure He was with you these last few days," I say.

She touches my hand and then drifts back off into her half sleep.

"We will never be able to thank you enough," Rachel says to me.

Ted Wells comes over and shakes my hand, "Ron, you have..." He becomes choked up and can't finish his statement. He just shakes his head as he shakes my hand.

I nod that I understand and leave this family to go home to mine.

In the hall Kristen hugs me and says, "I'm so happy to be a part of First Baptist and to be on the staff with you. I promise you I will not mess up again."

"Kristen, none of this was your fault," I say, holding her shoulders by my outstretched hands. "You have done an excellent job in helping the Wells through this. We are fortunate to have you on our staff."

Ken is looking on as Kristen and I talk.

"We make a pretty good team don't we, Dr. Fowler?" Ken asks as he leans against a wall.

"Yes, and not just on the golf course," I answer.

* * *

On the way home a red light causes me to stop, and I remember something I read recently in a book called *Living with Cancer* by Mary Beth Moster. In it the author cites a friend of hers named Nell Collins, a nurse, who herself had cancer. Nell Collins compares life to traffic lights. There are those times she says when we do not consider death, when the light is green and we go our way with little thought of anything preventing us from our normal routines. Death is like the red light that signals life must stop. But when cancer is diagnosed the light turns to yellow which jolts us into the reality that death is coming.

For the last few months the Wells family has been living under the warning that life may end soon for Emma. The past few days another yellow light flashed to bring them to a second cautious stop, again not knowing when the end might come. Today, that light bypassed red to cycle back to green, but the journey for Emma has many more intersections ahead. The events of the past few days have made me aware of how easy it is for the light to change colors as we navigate the journey of life. I don't think I will ever again take for granted the times when the lights seem to all turn green in the positive sequences of life.

CHAPTER EIGHTEEN

WEDNESDAY EVENING

It is half past five and Emma Wells is no longer missing. Joan Riebert is still missing, however, and I'm afraid of what may have happened to her. Yes, she sent to me those awful letters. Yes, she abducted this child and put her parents and this community through days of anguish. But, who knows the anguish Joan has experienced most of her life. I hope we have the chance to help her recover from her long-suffering ordeal.

As I pull into my driveway at home Kristen calls from the hospital. "Ron, Emma is more awake now. She has confirmed that it was Joan Riebert who locked her in that room. Her parents are so thankful for your finding her and so appreciative of the support from our church. I don't think I've ever seen a more moving portrait of life than witnessing the three of them embrace. I will try to make it back for the business meeting tonight."

My daughter is waiting at the door for me as I enter our home, holding a poster board sign that reads, "My Dad, Super Detective." My wife stands behind her with a look of pride on her face.

"Dad, are you going to become an FBI agent?" Sarah asks. "You may be better at this than you are at being a preacher."

"Thanks, I guess," I respond.

Amy holds our daughter by the shoulders and says to me, "Your picture's all over the TV along with ones of the old parsonage, Emma Wells, and Joan Riebert. We are both so proud of you."

"And so happy for Emma and her parents," Sarah says as she hugs me.

"It's been quite a day," I say as I sit down on the couch. "I think sitting beside Emma after we found her was second only to holding you, Sarah, for the first time at the hospital after you were born."

"Is the child going to be alright?" Amy asks.

230

"She's coming to periodically and there may not be any lasting problems from the medications she was given."

"Why did Ms. Riebert do all of this?" Sarah asks. "I always thought she was so nice. How can a nice person do such a terrible thing?"

"I think she had some terrible things done to her in the past by her father which led her to take Emma."

Sarah looks puzzled and responds, "I just don't see how something that happened so long ago can make a person do such a thing now."

"I know. It's hard to understand," I say to my twelve year old.

"Ron, Joan has sung those beautiful solos and is so involved in the church," Amy adds.

"Sometimes we never really know what a person is going through," I say. Later, when Sarah is not present., I will tell Amy about the picture taken from my office.

"When can I go see Emma?" Sarah asks.

"In a few days, I hope. Right now she and her family will need some time to deal with all that has happened."

"Do you still have to go back to church tonight?" Amy asks.

"I'm afraid so. We still have the business meeting. I have to leave in an hour."

* * *

It's now six-thirty and Joel Weaver has just returned to the church. He was released when it became evident that he did not take the child. I intercept him as he walks down the hall. People are just beginning to gather for the meeting tonight in the sanctuary.

"Joel, I'm terribly sorry about the FBI treatment of you," I say.

"I'm just glad the little girl has been found alive," Joel says calmly. "There is some mercy in this world after all."

"We are all very thankful she has been found."

Joel looks down at the floor and then slowly lifts his head. "Padre, I suppose you will want me to resign."

"Why would I want that?" I ask.

"I'm sure the FBI has told you about my problems back at the college where I worked. You can't have someone employed by the church who has had that in their past."

"Maybe, Joel, you could tell me what that was all about, and then let me decide what we should do."

"There's not much to tell. I was accused of bothering these two female students. I had to leave my job."

"I understand the charges were dropped," I say.

"Yes, but the administration still didn't think it advisable that I stay on."

"Did you do anything wrong?" I ask.

"Yes, I fell for a joke the girls were playing on me. They led me to think they wanted me to come to their room, but when I got there other girls were waiting to make fun of my stupidity in thinking these two were really interested in me."

"So, it was a college prank?"

Joel looks down the hall for five seconds and then turns back to me. "I guess I looked like one foolish enough to be the brunt of the joke. The word got out as to what happened and the girls were forced to make it look like I came to their room uninvited. The campus police came and began to question me. Eventually, one of the other girls waiting in the room felt bad that I was going to be charged with taking indecent liberties and told the truth to the dean of students."

"So you think you must now leave here because you once were accused of a wrong you did not do?" I ask. "Joel, I was recently accused of something I did not do. I know what it's like to be in this position. The power of an accusation can really mess with your well being, but we can't allow it to control our lives."

"So, you think I can keep my job?"

"If you want to."

Joel shakes my hand and says, "I want to stay here."

"Alright."

"Padre, do you have any idea what caused Ms. Riebert to take this child last week?" Joel asks.

"For some people the difficulties of the past are just too much to let go of. Evidently, this woman harbored deep pains from years ago."

"I can understand that."

I nod that I know what he means. "Do you remember, Joel, the passage from Kierkegaard's journal when he writes of his father saying, 'How terrible about the man who once as a little boy, while herding flocks on the heath of Jutland, suffering greatly, in hunger and in want, stood upon a hill and cursed God-and the man was unable to forget it even when he was eighty-two years old'?"

Joel looks surprised and then recognizes that I have been told of his interest in the Danish philosopher. "I do remember that passage," Joel says. "I guess some things are just never easy to get over."

"And some things do not have to hold us back," I say.

"I guess not," he says.

* * *

The crowd that is gathering for the business meeting is full of celebration. I've never seen so many people in attendance at one of these often tedious meetings and certainly never seen this type of joy at one. Usually these border on total boredom, unless there's some controversial issue to discuss. Tonight we will not be able to conduct business as usual. I can see that this is going to be a rousing prayer meeting filled with expressions of thanksgiving.

There are well over three hundred people present, including a number from the press. Church members are interviewed as they enter the building as to what the finding of Emma Wells alive means to them. Our church has been at the center of a storm, and now the storm has almost run its course. There's still the dreaded aftermath of what will happen to Joan Riebert, but for this moment there's the joy of a missing child found safe.

I look over the crowd as I prepare to preside over the meeting. The pastor of this church is the moderator, a long standing tradition here. Suellen Grayson is seated on the front row of the sanctuary. She's scheduled to report on how the trustees have responded to the threat of a lost child. Attorney, Sam Haverty, sits beside her as he is to share his views of church liability in such matters. I can't help but notice Dot Marshall in the third row on the right and try not to look her in the eye. It'll take some work to repair the damage done since the police issued a warrant for her fingerprints. Janice Moore is a few rows back and as music minister has had to field many questions this evening about Joan Riebert. Steve Ayers and several of the young people are on the back row. I tell those present that we will later fill everyone in on what has happened today and how Emma Wells is doing.

I ask Deanna Crowder to open the session with prayer, and she does a wonderful job of offering thanksgiving for all of our blessings. Many see Deanna as being cold, but I know she has a big heart under her business-like demeanor. The meeting is called to order and the minutes are approved. There is no old business. It's time for reports. Everything is flowing as usual in these quarterly conferences when Dan Porter stands up to interrupt the course of events.

"Pastor, most of us have not come here this evening to sit through a typical business meeting. We want to know what happened to Emma Wells. I don't think that members of our church should have to get all their news from the press about something that happened to us. Let's dispense with these boring reports and get to why we have all come." Dan sits down.

Beth Dawson then rises, "Pastor, how did you know to look in the old parsonage for the girl?"

"Are you sure that Joan Riebert is responsible for all of this?" Lavery Council asks.

I can see that we're not going to get far with our planned agenda. Suellen motions me over and whispers to me, "Ron, I think these people want a story this evening, not facts and figures on church finances or legal matters."

Looking out over the crowd, I spy Ken in the back and make my determination. "I would like for Ken Matthews to come up here and brief you on the events of today, if he will."

Ken makes his way to the podium and stands before a very appreciative group of people. "For the past few days we have all been on pins and needles worrying about Emma Wells. Your pastor, myself, the police, and the FBI have all worked together to find this missing girl. Many people in our congregation have been of valuable assistance. Today we received clues that led us to think that the vacant house down the street was a possible location where the child had been taken. Ron here deduced this from an abundance of tips he had received. We can't tell you much more of how this all happened as the investigation is ongoing."

Everyone can see that we are very fortunate to have Ken Matthews in our congregation. He's been respected for his contributions to our church, never more so than today. Kristen enters the sanctuary, and I motion for her to come to front, and ask her to brief the group on Emma's condition.

Kristen stands timidly before the eager audience, her hands behind her back, her voice with an apparent tremble. "I've just come from the hospital. Emma is fully awake now and has told her parents and the FBI what happened to her. They are still running tests on Emma, but so far there's no sign of lasting damage from the medications she was given. She told the authorities that it was Joan Riebert who took her from the church last Friday and to the old parsonage. She was asleep most of the time during her captivity there. Ms. Riebert did not hurt her, she told the police."

Kristen stops for a moment, looks out over the crowd, and seems to be overcome with emotion. After a few seconds she collects herself. "Emma's going to be okay for now. She has so much courage. Her parents are so appreciative of all that the people of this church have done. We all know that she has another ordeal to face in the near future."

I thank Kristen and inform the people that she's been very involved in the support of the Wells family during all of this.

Lavery Council stands up again. "Reverend Fowler, I have known Joan Riebert for over forty years, sat behind her in the choir, been a regular at the library where she works. I can't imagine she would ever do something this bad. My God, she's the daughter of one of our former pastors." Lavery's wife pulls on his arm and scolds him for his choice of expressions.

"Lavery," I respond, "Sometimes we are surprised by the actions of people we think we know. It's never easy to get behind actions in order to determine motivations. I'm as much at a loss over this as you are. Right now, we must pray for Joan and hope that she's found safe. We should never jump to conclusions as to the driving forces that are the foundation for certain behaviors. Human experience has so many shaping aspects. We all go through stages in life where breakthroughs or breakdowns redefine who we are. At one point a person may live life in one way and at another point see the world and themselves differently. We must always be wary of making judgments of others before we can know much about what they have undergone in life."

Lavery, who is still standing says, "Pastor, now you're preaching. Perhaps you should expand on that message Sunday. Where is Joan now?"

"The police are searching for her. As of a few minutes ago she hasn't been found," I reply.

Suellen speaks up, "Ron, all of us in this sanctuary are so thankful that you are our pastor. We know this has all been stressful for you and hope you can now get some rest."

Hands begin to come together and a contagious applause thunders through the sanctuary. It's not just for me. It is an outpouring of relief as well. I suggest that everyone here offers a prayer this evening for Joan Riebert.

I suppose my words and those of Ken and Kristen have satisfied for now the curiosity over the tumultuous events of the last five days. It's clear that there is much more healing to be done. We lost and then found a child in our charge. Members of our congregation were suspects in this dreadful abduction. Now, one of our own is out there somewhere afraid and confused as to what to do next. The meeting is adjourned, and the celebration continues as television cameras record the enthusiastic joy of the exiting members.

* * *

The police have posted officers at the home of Joan Riebert, at the library, and at the old parsonage. There's also an officer on watch over in the town where Joan's mother resides in the nursing home. Denise Chevalier has made the trip to speak with Joan's mother again, to follow up on Ken's visit. There's someone posted outside of my house since she did threaten me in the letters. Joan's car has not been spotted even though a bulletin on it has been issued to law enforcement jurisdictions in our area.

We know that Joan was at the former parsonage as late as this morning when she gave Emma the last dose of medication. According to Kristen, Emma told Neal Heard that Ms. Riebert took her to the bathroom sometime early in the morning and then made her take several pills. Without saying a word she locked Emma back in the closet and left. This had been the pattern since Joan coaxed her to go to the house Friday after Bible School.

After the business meeting Ken comes to my office for us to brainstorm where Joan might be. It's now almost nine in the evening and both of us have had a long day.

Ed Dickinson taps on the door and comes in.

"Pastor, there's something you might want to know. When Joan Riebert was a child my mother used to babysit her. I was a teenager in those days, but remember well the times my mother went over to the parsonage. When Joan came back to town my mother was living alone after my dad had died and Joan would visit her often. In recent years she's been to the nursing home each week to see Mom. This may not be of any help in finding Joan, but I thought you might want to know this."

I tell Ken and Ed about my strange conversation with Doris Dickinson on Monday at the dementia unit.

"Sounds like Joan went to the one person she trusted for help," Ken says.

"My mother has no short term memory, but she was always very fond of Joan," Ed says.

After Ed leaves, Ken and I ponder whether this information is of any help in finding Joan. We decide to pass it on to Neal Heard. I'm pretty sure that Joan went to see Doris before I was there on Monday. I imagine what it must be like for your only confidant to be someone with Alzheimer's. Joan must have been very desperate to have turned to Doris. I wonder if over the years she told Doris of the abuse she received from her father.

"Ron, is there some piece of information we gained today that we've overlooked?" Ken asks.

"I don't think there's anything else Pamela Evans shared with me that could be of help."

"Denise should be on her way back from visiting Joan's mother in the nursing home. I have her cell number here," Ken says.

Denise answers on the second ring and she and Ken talk for a couple of minutes.

"Did she learn any more?" I ask as Ken gets off the phone.

"Denise did get Mrs. Riebert to admit that her husband at times locked Joan in that closet when she was a child. She tried to get him to stop that, but he insisted that discipline was commanded by the Lord. Evidently this went on for years. Denise said that Mrs. Riebert was in tears for the entire thirty minutes they talked. She could not get the older woman to admit that her husband abused their daughter in any way other than being severe in his discipline."

"There had to be more to it than that," I say. "The writer of these letters over the years was a person who held great anger against someone. That someone must have been her father."

"That appears to be the case," Ken acknowledges. "In my years on the job I ran into several incidences where fathers physically and psychologically harmed their children. As adults these former abused children remained disturbed enough to hurt others. We can be thankful that Emma was not given any worse treatment than she was."

"I wonder if the abduction was not a cry for help from Joan who never got anywhere before with her letters."

"That's certainly a reasonable motive for her actions," Ken offers. "It must have been a frightening childhood spending time in that closet."

"And," I add, "She had to play the role of pastor's child out in public to pretend that all was well."

* * *

At home, finally, for the night, I can't help but wonder what Joan Riebert went through those many years living in that parsonage with an abusive father. Most children who go through this feel as if they are to blame, that it's a failure on their part. This wounded child, and now woman, has been forever limited in her personal growth. All through her years in school and later in her profession she's carried the internal struggle and humiliation of her years covering up what happened at her home. She sang in church, at weddings and at funerals providing comfort and hope to others through her music.

All the while she was seeking some compassion for herself.

Her letters were an attempt to reach out for help. She was begging for someone to acknowledge her pain and rally to her side in her tormented fight to purge the demons of her past. I feel so foolish now that I became angry when I first received an accusatory letter. It became all about me. The truth is that Joan Riebert needed my assistance in her interminable cry for someone to recognize her pleas for help. For five days my focus has been on finding Emma Wells safe and secure; now I pray that I have a chance to help Joan Riebert.

Many people will want to know how Joan could function as a responsible adult with the problems of her childhood still with her. She was a career woman who evidently did a good job at the library. How's this possible if she was so disturbed? Perhaps our friend Kierkegaard could help us here. He wrote that we can escape our anxieties by what he called "defiant self-creation". This means we can make something of ourselves in spite of all the fears we may have.

Joan must have had enough faith to function. She held a responsible job. She sang those wonderful solos. She cared for her mother and for Mrs. Dickinson. And yet, at times she could not forget the atrocities of her childhood. Even her cries for help were couched in religious language. I hope we can find her soon and help her find some peace. The letters now make sense as I realize that in her mind she saw all pastors being like her father. This must not have been her mental state all of the time. But, there were those periods when she was overcome with the memories of her childhood and chose to place the blame on the present pastor. All of this is speculation, of course. How can I possibly understand all that has been in the thoughts of this tortured woman?

I do know this – our past problems contend for attention in our present lives, especially those that foster recurring depression. I can't forget the words of Kierkegaard here:

> *"In addition to my other numerous acquaintances, I have one more intimate confidant. My depression is the most faithful mistress I know. No wonder, then that I return the love."*

CHAPTER NINETEEN

THURSDAY MORNING

Emma Wells is still at the hospital this morning. I stop by on the way to the church in order to check on her. Ted Wells is in the waiting area as I get off the elevator. "Ron, I'm so glad you're here," Ted says as he shakes my hand with some force. "Emma came around a few hours ago and is talking her head off. She has quite a story to tell. She was excited when you called and said you were on your way here."

"I look forward to talking with her. So, what do the doctors say?" I ask.

"She's over the effects of the sleeping pills. The pain from the cancer is steady, but they are able to keep it in check without giving her medication that makes her too drowsy. They're thinking about releasing her this afternoon."

"That's good news!" I say, patting Ted on the back.

Ted leads me into Emma's room. She's sitting up eating fruit and toast for breakfast. The wide awake little girl offers a broad smile and taps the side of the bed opposite the food tray. I make my way over to where she has directed me as Rachel nods approval.

"Pastor Ron," Emma says, "I would like to give you a hug."

I bend over and she puts her arms around my neck, a piece of toast still in her left hand.

"Are you left-handed?" I ask.

"Yes," she says now looking up at me. "Why do you ask that?"

"I've been curious lately about lefthanders."

"Did you know that four out of five of the designers of the Mac computer were left-handed?" Emma asks.

"No, I didn't know that. I guess they might be about as smart as you."

"And you. It was you who figured out where Ms. Riebert took

240

me."

"Maybe my best bit of figuring – definitely my best."

"I guess I was not so smart to go with Ms. Riebert to that house, was I? She looked so sad in that restroom. She was talking to herself when I went in, standing there all alone and saying strange things to the mirror. I asked her if she was alright. She looked at me for a minute and then said 'Emma Wells.' I said 'Yes, ma'am. You work at the library. You helped me pick out books.' Ms. Riebert stared at me and said, 'Shel Silverstein.' I thanked her for suggesting his book. She then took me by the arm and led me out into the hall. I didn't know what to do. When we got to the stairs she stopped, and said she wanted me to go with her to the library. She said a book I had ordered was in. I told her I was supposed to get on the van and go to my neighbor's house. 'I'll take you there after we pick up your book,' she said. I thought she needed a friend right then and felt she would do what she said she would."

I'm mesmerized by the account. This is a parent's nightmare – a child enticed to go off with someone she hardly knows. I look at this mother and father who have certainly heard Emma's story already. They are very fortunate people to have this child back with them.

"Did Ms. Riebert take you across those backyards to that house where we found you?" I ask out of curiosity.

"Yes, she explained that her car was parked at her house. I thought she must live near the church. When we got to that old house, I became afraid. I told her I would wait on the porch for her. She didn't say a word but took my hand and led me inside."

"It was dark in there and empty, and looked like nobody lived there. She mumbled something I couldn't understand. It sounded like it was from the Bible. In a minute we were upstairs, and she told me she wanted me to see her dollhouse. It was hers when she was my age she said. It was in that room, that room without windows, that dark room. 'Wait here,' she said. Then she left me there and closed the door. I heard her walking down the steps. I tried to open the door, but it was locked."

Emma begins to cry and her mother comes to the other side of the bed, climbs up on it and holds her daughter.

Ted continues where Emma left off, "Later that evening when

Joan Riebert came back Emma told her about the cancer and the pain. Joan left again and soon returned with the pills. Emma says Ms. Riebert talked about her father who often locked her in that closet when she was young. She also told Emma that her father would come and read the Bible aloud, passages that told of God's punishment for sins. In the days after, she would feed Emma twice a day and read to her from the Psalms, passages like her father had read. After the meals and Bible readings, the woman would give her more pills which made Emma sleep, evidently for hours."

Emma stops crying and adds, "She told me she was sorry about my cancer. I begged her to let me go home, but she said God told her I had to stay there. I don't believe God told her that."

My visit is brief, but the most memorable hospital bedside call in my ministry career. Rachel Wells hugs me out in the corridor and invites me to come by their house after Emma gets home to get to know her better. On the way to the church my joy is only abated by my concern for Joan Riebert.

Joan Riebert is about five-eight and probably weighs in the neighborhood of a hundred and fifty pounds. Her red hair is worn shoulder length with signs of gray now very evident as she recently turned sixty. She always dresses modestly and well fits the image of the stern librarian. Her demeanor is always polite and cordial, however. According to all I have learned in the last day she settled into the role of the single matron years ago. Respected in our church and community, Joan has very adeptly covered up any psychological conditions that would have forecast her behavior in the last week.

A psychologist employed by the FBI was contacted by Neal Heard last night and with the scant details of what happened has theorized that Joan may suffer from post-sexual-abuse syndrome which is characterized by anxiety, feelings of guilt or shame, low self-esteem, and anger. Often, said the psychologist, there is no outside indication of any problems. There are no visible scars, but the internal ones are never healed. Adults who were abused as children think that most people will not believe that an apparently normal adult like Stephen Riebert could be capable of such awful behavior. They assume they face an unbelieving audience so they keep it to themselves.

Why she chose to take Emma is still a mystery. Ken thinks she may have been surprised when the girl entered the restroom last Friday and improvised a plan to take the child to the old parsonage. The encounter was possibly a convergence of several improbable coincidences: a distraught woman seeking to be near the joy of children to appease her despair by observing VBS, an emerging need to punctuate her written pleas with some tangible action, and the happenstance of this eight year old girl, whom she knew, suddenly there in front of her at this time of her heightened frustration. All of this is speculation, of course. Ken calls it a perfect storm.

* * *

I arrive at the church office at nine. Joan Riebert is still missing. Alice greets me with a few notes as to who would like to see me today. Neal Heard and Denise Chevalier both want to talk with me. Several reporters have requested interviews, and we have had a death in the church family, a sister of one of our active members. I've almost forgotten my normal pastoral duties the last few days.

As I open my office door, on the floor is a piece of white paper. I pick it up and immediately recognize that it's another accusatory letter!

Reverend,

You did not resign last night as I told you to. Do you not know the consequences of disobeying the will of God? You have spared the child, but that does not spare you from judgment. I know of your evil and will not let it go unpunished. But, I have calmed and quieted my soul, like a child quieted at its mother's breast; like a child that is quieted is my soul. I am the only daughter who is harmed by your shameful transgressions. I do not wish pain upon any other child of iniquity, indeed I have taken measures to protect others from the evil men do. Some sat in darkness and in gloom, for they *had rebelled against the words of God. Some were sick through their sinful ways, then they cried to the Lord in their trouble, and He delivered them from their distress. The Lord has delivered one from her distress, but He cannot save them all. Your unwillingness to confess your sins has left me no other recourse but to seek the sanctuary of darkness and gloom.*

There's no mention of Emma Wells by name, but couched in the language of the Psalms is the reference to this child who has been spared. Like the letters before there are the scripture quotes intertwined with the pained words of accusation and warning. One thing is different in this letter; there is a finality to it. I'm afraid the discovery of the abducted child has now created a new plan of action for Joan. Her new mindset is my greatest concern today.

The entire community is looking for Joan Riebert, and yet she is able to penetrate the defenses and leave this letter. One place that was not watched last night was the church, a mistake I now realize. She must have slid it under the door during the night or early this morning. The first thing I do is call Ken. He's astonished at the ingenuity of this woman who must be fearful for her own safety. He tells me he's on the way over and that he will inform the FBI. I'm not afraid of Joan Riebert, only afraid for her.

Within fifteen minutes the four-member FBI CARD team arrives at the church along with Carl Brody and four other policemen. A search of the church is underway now. Neal and Ken sit in my office together reading the letter.

"I feel stupid for not watching the church," Heard says.

"We all missed this possibility," Ken adds.

"This is Joan Riebert's home field," I warn. "She knows this part of town and this church better than anyone. She was raised here."

"This is like the Uncle Remus story when Brer Rabbit ends up in the briar patch where he was born and bred," Ken says. "The one place where she's at home is the place she came back to."

"At least, we know she's still in town," Neal says. "We found her car this morning over at the nursing home. It has been there for two days. One of the attendants says that Joan came to see Mrs. Dickinson again on Tuesday afternoon. She must have walked from there to the parsonage, about three miles."

Denise Chevalier enters the office and announces that the search of the building is not yet complete, but she doesn't think Joan Riebert is here.

"Where else would she go?" I ask.

"We're watching her home, the parsonage, and the library," Denise offers.

"And we have someone with her mother in case Joan tries to contact her," Neal adds. "The nursing home here in town is also under surveillance, as well as your home, Ron."

Neal and Denise go to check on the search as Ken and I remain in the office. I remember what Pamela Evans told me, that Joan and her would play hide and seek in the church, and that Joan knew every place to hide.

"Ken, I think Joan Riebert may be here in the church hiding somewhere."

"If she is the searchers will find her," Ken says.

"I don't think so. We need to find Joel."

Joel Weaver keeps a church owned cell phone on him at all times so I have Alice ask him to come to the office. Ken and I wait for him in the hall. In about three minutes he arrives and tells us he has been with Carl Brody unlocking any doors needed in the search.

"Joel, I need for you try and identify any places in these buildings where the police may not have searched. Joan Riebert may know this place even better than you," I say.

Joel ponders what I ask. "The searchers have been over the old education building thoroughly in the last few minutes. They even searched the old coal bin. Two of the FBI agents are now covering this building. There are a lot of places to hide here, but these guys seem to know what they're doing. The only place left is the sanctuary. It doesn't offer many opportunities to stay out of sight."

"She doesn't have any other place to go, and we know she was here earlier this morning or last night," I add. "Somehow she knew what took place in the business meeting last night. She may have been in the building while we were meeting."

Joel then looks toward the sanctuary and says, "I know of a

245

place where someone could hide in order to hear what happens in the sanctuary. I doubt over a handful of people know about it. Follow me."

Ken and I follow Joel. We head to the sanctuary, but stop in the hallway leading to the worship center. Joel opens the door to a small butler pantry where the communion supplies are kept and the elements of the Lord's Supper are prepared. He bends down under a counter where there's a small opening covered by a hinged door about four feet tall by three feet wide. All three of us know that this door opens to a crawl space which holds the plumbing for the baptistery above.

"Last Friday a policeman crawled up in there with a flashlight to check for the missing girl," Joel says. "It's not easy to move around in the cramped space and it goes some forty feet until you reach the other wall. There is also a lower area that extends up under the choir seating and over to where the pulpit is located. The area at the entrance is about four feet high, but it gets lower the further you move up under the choir loft, only a little more than two feet clearance way up in there. Support columns are spaced every few feet which block the view as you try and see to the lowest point. One might not look way up under there because the space is so low, especially since Ms. Riebert is not a small person."

Ken looks into the opening. Joel tells him the light switch is on his right. Ken flips the switch and proceeds to crawl in a few feet on his hands and knees.

"What the hell!" Joel and I hear as Ken begins to back out of the hole in the wall. "There are faces in there staring at me," he exclaims as he stands up. "Sorry about the bad language in the sanctuary, Ron. What is that in there? What are those things?"

Joel smiles and looks at me, "Reverend, this was the most out of the way place I could think of to store the cardboard Bible characters."

Ken asks, "The what?"

"Ken, you just had an encounter with a team of Bible heroes," I explain.

"Well, you should have warned me," Ken says, still breathing hard.

"I thought you FBI types are never shocked by what you find," Joel says to the exasperated agent. "You should have seen the tunnels I crawled through in Nam. They often contained real corpses stacked like that."

"Just caught me by surprise," Ken says. "You can't see very far up in there by the one light at the door. We're gonna need a flashlight to go further."

Joel secures a flashlight just as Denise Chevalier appears in the hallway.

"What's under there?" she asks.

"It's a crawlspace access to the baptistery plumbing," Ken answers.

"Has anyone been in there yet?" she asks looking at the three of us.

"I went in a few feet, but you need a light to go any further," Ken says. "It's pretty tight in there for someone my size."

"Then give me the light. I'm smaller than any of you guys," Denise says.

"Watch out for the cardboard characters that are on your left as you go in," Ken says. "They can be a little too intimate in a crawl space."

Denise takes the light and enters the low portal. Soon she disappears, and all we can see is the faint glow of the beam. I peer into the framed cave to check on her progress.

"What do you see," I call out.

"So far, just wood and plumbing," she yells back. "I'm almost to the other side. Nothing here, but I need to make my way up under the lower section."

I see the light change direction and can tell that Denise is some twenty feet up under the choir seating area. It must be another twenty feet before she will reach the front of the massive platform that serves as the stage for worship leaders. The flashlight beam is hardly visible at all now. Ken and Joel are on their knees beside me at the opening, and Carl Brody is right behind them. Neal Heard is now standing in the doorway to the pantry. A couple of minutes pass with only the sounds of movement deep into the crawl space.

While in college I worked for my dad's electrical company in the summers. As an apprentice it was often my job to crawl up under houses when running new lines. I know how uncomfortable it can be on your hands and knees in such a confining space. There were times that summer when the crawl spaces were super tight and bare ground was damp. Once while sitting on moist red clay I drilled up into a live wire and was propelled about fifteen feet sliding on my rear until I was stopped by a cinder block pillar. I think it was then and there that I decided a ministry career was preferable to one in electrical work, a shocking divine calling perhaps.

Neal Heard asks Joel and Ken to move so he can look into the void. He calls out to Denise, "Where are you now?" There's no response. He and I both remain at the opening waiting for Chevalier to come back toward us.

"Oh, my God! Oh, no!" is the muffled shout we hear.

"What is it?" Heard calls out. "You alright, Denise?"

There's no response so he calls out again, "Denise, are you okay?"

For over a minute there are no other sounds. The four of us men all are now kneeling on the floor of the tiny pantry listening for any clue as to what the young agent has found. Then we hear movement in the darkness. I can see the light beam now coming toward me from the depths of the crawl space. In a couple of minutes Denise emerges from the opening, and is obviously shaken.

"She's in there," Denise says. "I think she's dead. I could not detect any signs of life. She's way over to the right corner, curled up in a ball."

"The Riebert woman?" Carl asks.

"I'm pretty sure it's Joan Riebert from the pictures I've seen of her. It's so tight up under the stage where she is. I'm not really comfortable in such confined spaces."

Pieces of spider web are pasted to the side of Denise's head, and the flashlight is shaking a little in her right hand while her left attempts to brush away the mesh strands in her hair. Her eyes plead for some consoling, but her professional pride does not let her ask for any sympathy over the experience she has just encountered.

"We need to get her out," Heard exclaims.

Carl Brody calls the paramedics and describes the situation.

"She's on her side with her head tucked into her body," Denise says with a choked voice. "I couldn't detect a pulse. She's still warm, as there is little air movement under there. I didn't see any blood, but the smell is bad. She likely threw up something, maybe from an overdose of sleeping pills. She may have choked on her vomit. I've seen this before. You think you will just pass away quietly after ingesting an abundance of medications, but your body won't let go that easily."

It must have been shocking, even for a trained agent to come upon what she did in such a tight space. We all stand silent as we await the rescue workers.

Finally Ken speaks, "What a shame. Just a few days ago she stood above the spot where she now lies and sang that beautiful solo hymn about God watching over each one of us. I suppose the only one who understands what she was feeling at the time was God."

The wait for the paramedics seems like an hour. It's hard to imagine that Joan Riebert's life ends this way. I can't help but remember the words I read recently from a sermon by Helmut Thielecke, the great German theologian and pastor. Thielecke wrote something like:

> *We sometimes envision how our life should turn out, or how God should make it turn out if he is really God. But something completely different happens. In the process we had secretly set up a chance for God to prove that he was the director of our life. But he didn't take advantage of the opportunity. Moreover, we not only entertain quite definite expectations as far as God is concerned, but also in respect to persons whom we come in contact with each day. That is why we are surprised again and again when they don't fit into such a scheme and when they do something shocking for which we are not prepared.*

I don't think anyone in our congregation or community is prepared for what Joan has done or how her life has ended. Her solos have touched the lives of many people who assumed that she was a normal daughter of a pastor and an upstanding member of our church and community who had her life together. There will be shock and disbelief. There will be many who will question God and his care for his children and why God did not take advantage of opportunities to help Joan. How could Joan Riebert go all of these years without someone sensing her inner conflict? Somehow I must address these questions in the coming weeks. Today, I stand here waiting for the rescue workers wondering if there can be a way to rescue faith. I believe there is, but that belief is certainly being tested today.

Two thin paramedics squeeze into the opening. In five minutes they emerge with the body of Joan Riebert pushed out through the small doorway. Laying her on a stretcher in the vestibule they report that she likely did indeed choke from the regurgitated pills she ingested, but that must be confirmed by the coroner. Around her neck is a silver cross. She's dressed in a rumpled black pant suit, and she's barefoot. Her red hair is flat on the white sheet under her, and her hands lie beside her, both closed as one who has been through a terrible struggle. She lies in this church foyer where she has come and gone much of her life without anyone knowing of the turmoil brewing inside of her.

A young female paramedic hands a key to me. "We found this protruding from one of her closed hands. Thought it might be a key to the church."

I thank the girl and examine the key, comparing it to the one in my pocket. It is indeed one of the keys to our exterior doors.

"Did you know her well?" the paramedic asks me.

"She was one of our church members, but I did not know her as well as I should have."

By now several members of the staff have gathered in the area where people often greet each other before and after worship. Alice, Kristen, and Janice all look at the librarian and soloist as she lies still on the white covered stretcher. Janice is the most visibly shaken as she has worked closely with Joan in the choir. Denise Chevalier stands beside Janice and holds her hand. Both women have just experienced deeply the trauma of finding this poor woman's body. There is silence among those gathered as the paramedics secure her for the trip to the morgue.

CHAPTER TWENTY

THURSDAY AFTERNOON

It is now eleven-fifteen. Joan Riebert is dead. It's been confirmed that she overdosed on the same kind of pills she fed to Emma Wells. Her body has been removed and our church and community is left to wonder what brought her to this tragic end. The speculation will be endless, but the only two people who may truly know what triggered her actions are now dead, Joan and her father. Her mother cannot be counted on to share all of what she knows, and Doris Dickerson has any knowledge locked in her dementia.

I now know that the accusations addressed to me were in reality addressed to Stephen Riebert. That doesn't make it any easier for me to forget them, however, as I see myself as an accomplice in the suffering of Joan Riebert. I and the other pastors before me all took offense at the letters we received. We so readily became concerned for what such accusatory words might do to us. As it turns out the accusations were merely calls for help from a child who was abused and locked in a closet for hours at a time by a man of God. We men of God have much to atone for.

Henri Nouwen wrote in *The Dance of Life* these words: "Death indeed simplifies; death does not tolerate endless shadings and nuances. Death lays bare what really matters, and in this way becomes your judge."

* * *

"Life is good." The image of Emma Wells on that mattress in the parsonage wearing the shirt with that message is very present in my mind. She's still weak from the heavy doses of drugs she was given during her captivity but now home with her family. Rachel Wells greets me at the door and escorts me to Emma's room. She's sitting on her bed surrounded by books.

"Pastor Ron, thank you for coming by," Emma exclaims as I enter her room.

I'm guided to a chair beside Emma's bed, and she extends her hand as I sit beside her. "I like your room," I say. Her hair is in pigtails and she's wearing a purple top with a butterfly design on the front.

"There's something I want to talk to you about," Emma says with an animated spirit. "When can I get baptized?"

"Very soon, I hope. In a couple of weeks there will be a class for young people like yourself who have expressed interest. Miss Kristen and I will lead it."

"Have you ever baptized anyone with cancer before?" Emma asks.

"Actually, I have. I baptized a man named Herb one time at another church."

"Was he really sick when you did it?"

"Yes, he was very sick." I can't tell Emma that Herb died only a few weeks later. When he was baptized he used an oxygen tank and had it at the top of the steps going down into the baptistery before he descended and inhaled deeply from it when he came out. His lung cancer was very advanced.

"Was he happy when he came up out of the water?" Emma asks.

"Yes, I believe he was."

"I promise you I will have a big smile on my face. Even if I'm in pain at the time, I will smile."

"You are a very brave girl," I say.

"Not brave, Pastor Ron, just blessed." Her smile changes to that concentrated seriousness I remember seeing in some of the pictures of her on the mantle in the living room.

"You are blessed with great parents who love you very much," I say.

"Ms. Riebert did not have very good parents, did she?" Emma asks.

"I guess they were not as good to her as they should have been," I answer.

"She told me that her father locked her in that closet. Why

would a father do that?"

"He may have been mixed up in how to be a father," I answer.

Emma puts her hand over her mouth with a pensive expression on her face. "I think I know why she took me to that old house. She told me that I reminded her of herself when she was eight. She said she liked to read when she was my age just like I do and told me that she was an only child like me."

"I have seen a picture of her when she was young. She did look very much like you do now," I say, recalling the photo of her family I found in the closet.

"Will Ms. Riebert go to heaven?" Emma asks looking into my eyes.

"I think God understands why she did what she did, and God will take care of her."

"That's good," Emma says. "I don't think she meant to hurt me."

"How are you feeling?" I ask.

"I start my chemotherapy in two days. My doctor says it's time. I won't have to stay in the hospital overnight. That's good because I love my home."

"You have a nice home," I say. "It's a safe and comfortable place."

"Yes, it is. I'm lucky that way. I'm also lucky to have a preacher who found me when I was lost. But, as Miss Kristen tells me, that is the main job of preachers."

"That is a part of what we do. I'm looking forward to getting to know you better, so is my daughter, Sarah."

"I've seen Sarah at the church. I would like to be friends with her. Ms. Riebert told me that she was a preacher's daughter like Sarah is. She told me that Sarah was her friend. I think she needed more friends."

I leave Emma to her books and her rest. What a smart and precious child.

On the porch of the Wells house, Rachel grabs my hand. "Ron, Ted and I will be in church this Sunday. It will not be out of obligation, but because we feel we need to be there. We also want to be in a fellowship of caring people such as yours."

"I look forward to having the three of you with us on Sunday," I say.

"Can you tell me one thing?" Rachel asks. "Can you tell me why Joan Riebert waited all of these years to do what she did, to take a child?"

"I'm not sure. My guess is that years of inner turmoil led her to finally do something extreme as a plea for help."

"So why hurt herself?"

"It must have been time for her ordeal to be over," I offer.

Rachel nods in agreement and hugs me. "I'm glad this is over for us all."

* * *

In my office now, I hold the three letters in my hands. "We have sinned with our fathers, we have committed iniquity, and we have done wickedly." I now know why these words were chosen by Joan.

I turn to another Psalm, "Hear my prayer, O Lord; let my cry come to you. Do not hide your face from me in the day of my distress. Incline your ear to me; answer me speedily in the day when I call." If only I or one of the pastors before me had heard her cry and answered her promptly; this tortured child in the body of a woman might have found the help she needed.

Rachel's question about why Joan endured all of those years without crying out in a bolder way for help now resurfaces. Only a person who has had experiences like Joan can ever understand what it's like be a child of abuse. As tortured as her life was, it was the only one she knew. One of Kierkegaard's parables comes to mind. It's about a typographical or clerical error which becomes personified. The error is then given the chance to be changed into the form it was intended to be, but it protests because such a change would cause it to cease to be itself. It's possible that's why Joan did not reach out for help earlier; she was afraid of losing her identity, the obliteration of her personhood as she knew it. There's one quote from the Danish philosopher which has been on my mind all day: "Since my earliest childhood a barb of sorrow has lodged in my heart. As long as it stays I am ironic – if it is pulled out I shall die."

* * *

It's four in the afternoon, and I have three visitors: Ken, Neal, and Denise. The FBI agents are ready to leave town as their work is done. Carl and his police department can wrap up the case of Emma Wells.

"Reverend, we want to thank you for all of your help on this case," Neal says. "We made a pretty good team, the four of us. You and Ken need to come up to Quantico and help train our new agents. They could learn from you both."

"Thanks," I reply. "I'm content to leave all of the detective work to you guys."

"Been there and done that," Ken adds.

"Pastor, I want you to know that I will continue my study of Kierkegaard," Denise says. "I may even become the agency's expert on existentialism."

"Just don't let his sadness dampen your spirits," I warn.

"Ron, we found something in Joan Riebert's house we want you to have," Neal says. "It was mixed in with some other writings. It may help you better understand what happened."

"So, we are now on a first name basis," I say to Neal Heard.

"I guess so," the gruff agent replies. "That is if you don't hold it against me for treating you so roughly in the beginning."

"Just doing your job, Neal," I say.

I thank Neal and say goodbye to he and Denise. It's hard to imagine doing what they do fulltime. But, not many people aspire to my job either. We all deal with lives that are turned upside down. Ken lingers for a few minutes to recap the events of the last few days. He's a good friend, and we will have better times to share in the future.

"Well, Pastor," Ken says, "These last few days have reminded me of the many years I spent with the bureau. Only this case was different in that it involved friends."

"I can't imagine how this would have turned out if you had not helped," I say to my good friend. "Not many pastors have someone like you to count on, a friend and one knowledgeable in such matters."

"As you have often said, Ron, the Lord works in mysterious

ways."

"Yes, and now I think I believe that even more than before."

* * *

This day has been one of deep sadness and great joy. These two emotions compete within me as I sit alone in my office now. I look forward to being home with my wife and daughter, but first I must read what Neal found at Joan's house. This time the words are not from Joan the adult but Joan the young person:

> The house is quiet now and my prison cell is dark except for my flashlight. He will come in the morning, unlock the door, and beg me to forgive him. He will cry and sit beside me on the floor of the closet with his Bible open. He will read to me from the Psalms and tell me that God is upset with both of us for what we have done. He will ask me to not tell my mother what happened last night. I will agree to not tell. We both know that she does not want to hear the truth. We both guess that she knows the truth.
>
> How many other children are there like me tonight? What have we done to deserve the parents we have? Every child should have parents who love them not hurt them. No child should be afraid of their parents. I will never have children because I am afraid I will treat them poorly. I will never be able to marry because I could never share my secret with another person, and a wife should be honest with her husband.
>
> Who would ever believe that a man of God would do such things to his daughter? Are there any true men of God? He stands up there on Sunday mornings and talks about how God loves us. God does not love

him because of the things he does. God does not love me or He would not let my father do those things to me. I wonder if all preachers are like him and cover their sins with words they know are false.

My fourteenth birthday is tomorrow. This is the sixth year of my misery. I think of the little girl who sat in this closet six years ago after her father did those awful things to her. I wonder now how she felt then, how afraid she was. I cannot remember a time when I was not ashamed. I would run away, but I am not yet old enough. Someday I will leave and never see him again, and he will not be able to touch me again.

He will drive me to school in the morning and pat me on the head as I get out of the car. I will not speak to him in the car, and he will not speak to me. This is our daily routine. Some of the other kids at my school go to my church. They see me as I arrive and have no idea that their minister is really a monster. Someday, I hope to be able to expose him for what he is.

I carefully fold this letter and withdraw a shoe box from a cabinet behind my desk. Removing the lid to the box exposes the contents inside. I place this letter there with the three from Joan that were secretly delivered over the past week and the DVD from Emma. There's one other object in the box, the padlock that secured the door to the closet in the former parsonage. I plan to keep all of these as reminders of how I and others failed Joan Riebert over the years.

Finally, Joan has exposed her father. Her pain is now over. I make a promise to myself and to her – I will honor the memory of Joan Riebert by vowing to use her suffering as my calling to help protect other children from abuse. I hold the lock in my hands and reflect on how it imprisoned two little girls in a room of fear. I shall keep it as a symbol of how the fortunes of every child depend on someone opening up doors to freedom and closing doors that provide security.

* * *

My daughter greets me with a hug when I arrive home. My wife stands behind her. At my wife's suggestion we do not speak of Emma Wells or Joan Riebert at the dinner table. There will be plenty of time to discuss the events of the last few days. Tonight we shall be a normal family doing what normal families do.

EPILOGUE

SATURDAY MORNING

The word "bereavement" comes from the root word "reave" which means to be dispossessed. Many of us feel today that we have been robbed of something; we feel Joan Riebert has been taken from us before it was her time. We are here in this sanctuary this morning to honor her memory, to find healing for our grief, and to seek some measure of understanding as to what has brought us here today for this service.

We come with a range of emotions and questions. We ask – why Joan was not able to better handle her despair? We ask – what could we have done to better support her? We ask – who was she really? I can only say that no single act of desperation can characterize a life. Joan was more than the person who abducted a child and took her own life. She was a capable and talented individual. Her work, her music, and her faith were well appreciated gifts she donated to this community.

Death by suicide is not a rejection of life; it is a cry of anguish for a better life. Joan was engaged for much of her time on earth in a struggle within herself to come to terms with a difficult childhood, one of abuse and loneliness. She must have longed for an existence free of all of that and sought to live a more abundant life. She did not take her life out of some moral weakness. She took her life because of a pain which could not find relief. In a sense it was not her decision. The decision to leave this hurtful world was made by the demons of her past which were not in her control.

I would guess that many here today are asking this question – where was God in all of this? Well, join the crowd, and unite with the ranks of people throughout the ages who have asked that question in the midst of despair and death. I suppose that you are awaiting some word from this pulpit that will resolve this issue once and for all. I cannot think of a better time or a better opportunity for a minister to settle this matter. I am afraid that some of you will leave here in a few minutes, however, feeling shortchanged, for my words today are no different than those which have been offered for ages.

I point you to the ancient man of faith, Job, who asked why God allowed so much suffering in his life. The response he receives is a question back from God – "Job, are you wise enough to run the world?" Job, in a rush of humility responds – "Surely, I spoke of things I did not understand, things too wonderful for me to know." Job did not receive a clear explanation as to why there is so much pain. Job is asked to simply trust that God's way is best. Every time the why question is raised in the scriptures the attention is diverted from why did this happen to what is our response to the event.

Philip Yancey in his book, *Where is God When It Hurts*, writes: 'The Bible consistently changes the questions we bring to the problem of pain. It rarely answers the backward looking question, "why?" Instead it raises the forward looking question, "To what end?"'

There are no facts today that will fully explain why this has happened. There is only faith in God who is the author of the universe. Faith becomes our teacher in the absence of fact. We must let our faith absorb the shock of not knowing all the facts. We must trust. In our confusion let us trust where we cannot understand. Let us share the faith of the Psalmist who said, 'God is our refuge.' Let us seek the comfort of God's care knowing that Joan is now in a far more comfortable place than her anguished life here on earth.

I close with a prayer by Blaise Pascal, the French mystic:

I ask you neither for health nor for sickness, for life nor for death; but that you may dispose of my health and my sickness, my life and my death, for your glory... You alone know what is expedient for me; you are the sovereign master; do with me according to your will. Give to me, or take away from me, only conform my will to yours. I know but one thing, Lord, that it is good to follow you, and bad to offend you. Apart from that, I know not what is good or bad in anything. I know not which is more profitable to me, health or sickness, wealth or poverty, nor anything else in the world. That discernment is beyond the power of men or angels, and is hidden among the secrets of your Providence, which I adore, but do not seek to fathom.